Becca wanted a chance.

That was all. No fuss, no interference. A chance to grow and flower, and maybe someday produce one perfect rose. Just like the ones she was holding in her hand.

"How could I dig those rose bushes out?" he asked. She was standing within touching range, and it seemed the most natural thing in the world to touch her. Her gaze never left his face. She seemed to be holding her breath, waiting for something to happen. He knew the feeling.

"Then they can stay?" she asked.

"I wouldn't want it any other way. Will you teach me what I have to know to take care of them?"

"Just visit them every day. That's all. They'll do the rest if you let them."

"I don't think...that will be hard."

"Thank you." She reached for his hand and squeezed it. "I hoped you'd understand."

Dear Reader,

Welcome to Silhouette **Special Edition** . . . welcome to romance. Each month, Silhouette **Special Edition** publishes six novels with you in mind—stories of love and life, tales that you can identify with— romance with that little "something special" added in.

June has some wonderful stories in bloom for you. Don't miss *Silent Sam's Salvation*—the continuation of Myrna Temte's exciting *Cowboy Country* series. Sam Dawson might not possess the gift of gab, but Dani Smith quickly discovers that still waters run deep—and that she wants to dive right in! Don't miss this tender tale.

Rounding out this month are more stories by some of your favorite authors: Tracy Sinclair, Christine Flynn, Trisha Alexander (with her second book for Silhouette **Special Edition**—remember *Cinderella Girl,* SE #640?), Lucy Gordon and Emilie Richards.

In each Silhouette **Special Edition** novel, we're dedicated to bringing you the romances that you dream about—stories that will delight as well as bring a tear to the eye. And that's what Silhouette **Special Edition** is all about—special books by special authors for special readers!

I hope you enjoy this book and all of the stories to come!

Sincerely,

Tara Gavin
Senior Editor
Silhouette Books

EMILIE RICHARDS
One Perfect Rose

Silhouette Special Edition

Published by Silhouette Books New York

America's Publisher of Contemporary Romance

SILHOUETTE BOOKS
300 East 42nd St., New York, N.Y. 10017

ONE PERFECT ROSE

Copyright © 1992 by Emilie Richards McGee

ISBN: 0-373-09750-6

First Silhouette Books printing June 1992

All the characters in this book have no existence outside the imagination of the author and have no relation whatsoever to anyone bearing the same name or names. They are not even distantly inspired by any individual known or unknown to the author, and all incidents are pure invention.

®: Trademark used under license and registered in the United States Patent and Trademark Office and in other countries.

Printed in the U.S.A.

Books by Emilie Richards

EMILIE RICHARDS

believes that opposites attract, and her marriage is vivid proof. "When we met," the author says, "the only thing my husband and I could agree on was that we were very much in love. Fortunately, we haven't changed our minds about that in all the years we've been together."

The couple live in Ohio with their four children. Emilie has put her master's degree in family development to good use—raising her own brood, working for Head Start, counseling in a mental-health clinic and serving in VISTA.

Though her first book was written in snatches with an infant on her lap, Emilie now writes five hours a day and "rejoices in the opportunity to create, to grow and to have such a good time."

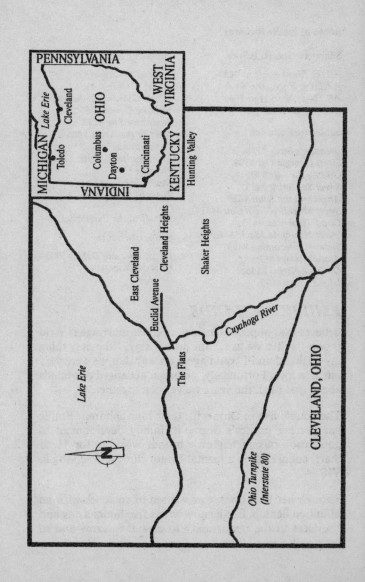

Chapter One

There were a lot of things a man couldn't do with frozen fingers. Work, for one thing. Shave or comb his hair, for another. There were a host of things he couldn't do to a woman—and a host she wouldn't allow him to do, even if he could.

Right now, the thing that Jason Millington's fingers refused to do was lift a mug off the counter of a downtown coffee shop and bring it to his lips.

"Sumpthin' wrong with the coffee, bud?"

Bleary-eyed, Jase stared at the proprietor. He was short and fat, a balding turnip of a man with the unlikely name of Red. The coffee shop was Red's Place. "Just taking my time."

"A lot of time."

Jase looked from side to side, although he already knew that he and Red were two of the six people in a room that could hold forty. "Don't exactly need the seat, do you?"

"We got laws against loitering."

"We've probably got laws against harassing paying customers, too."

"Ain't seen no money."

Jase gouged his pants pocket with his index icicle and heard the reassuring clank of change. He had recycled enough aluminum that evening to afford a sandwich, too. But he wasn't going to buy it from Red. Jase had a long night ahead and more stops to make. If he timed those stops right, he could stay out of the cold until dawn's early light.

He stood and bent his fingers just far enough to hook three quarters and slide them across the counter. Red mumbled, but he left. Jase went back to warming his hands over his cup.

Cleveland's winters were the flip side of hell. No one moved to the city because of the weather. The symphony, maybe, or the art museum. Even the lakeshore in summer or the colorful ethnic festivals. But no one made a home here—or attempted to make a home—because he liked January's wind straight off Lake Erie or February's treacherous blizzards.

The optimistic viewed March as a prelude to April. Tonight Jase wasn't optimistic. The temperature outside was thirty-eight degrees, and he had little protection. His coat had been given to him by his sister, and it had more holes than the frost-heaved city streets. What was left of the pile lining had a bad case of mange, and the sleeves were three inches too short. Pamela had never had much of an eye for size.

Jase's coat branded him, as did jeans with the knees and seat worn to a shine and cardboard-lined shoes with no shine at all. There were dozens of men on the streets tonight with the same inadequate clothing, the same minimal change in patched pockets, the same listless expression. Lack of good food and sleep made anybody listless, even the strongest and brightest.

The coffee shop door opened with a bang. Two men who made Jase look like an *Esquire* model, blew in on a gust of Lake Erie wind. One had a greasy ponytail and what looked like a brass curtain ring hanging from an ear. The other man had an angelic, toothless smile.

Red was at the door before it had banged shut. "I told you a million times, I don't want you in here. Get out."

"Ah, Red, what're we hurting?" asked the toothless one. "We got money for dinner tonight."

"Don't look good for business, you in here. Looks like a home for derelicts."

Jase listened to them argue. By the time the two men gave up and left, he figured his own minutes were numbered. He managed to wrap his hands around the cup and lift it to his lips.

Just as Red turned in Jase's direction, the door banged again. Jase followed the sound with his eyes, grateful for the reprieve. He hoped this argument would last long enough for him to finish his coffee.

A woman stood in the doorway this time. From across the room Jase could see she was shivering. She wore a coat of unattractive rat-brown wool, but no gloves, hat or scarf. Her legs looked bare, too, and he hoped to God that at least she was wearing panty hose.

"Mr. Dewayne?" She stepped forward, aiming herself at Red. "I'm Becca Hanks. I came by last night about a job, but the man behind the counter said I should come back tonight and talk to you."

She held out her hand. Jase gave an involuntary wince as Red grudgingly crunched it in his own. Shaking hands was something else at which frozen fingers did not excel.

If she was in pain, she didn't show it. She had a small chin, rounded and delicate, but she lifted it until it was the most prominent part of her face. "I'm sorry I'm here so late, but I had car trouble, and I walked the last mile." She reached inside a large plastic handbag, retrieved a piece of paper and held it out to Red.

Red looked as if she were giving him a dirty tissue. He took it as if it was one, too, his thumb and forefinger pinched at one corner as if to avoid disease. He held the paper away from his face and scanned it. Then he handed it back.

"Don't see a phone number or a real address. Just a postal box. Can't call you at the post office."

"I know. I'm sorry. But I'm new in town, and I'm—I'm staying with friends until I get a place of my own."

"Friends got a phone?"

"I couldn't bother them with my calls. But if you think you might be hiring, I can stop by as often as you say."

Jase listened to the husky twang of Appalachia in the woman's speech. She put words together as if she'd had a certain amount of education, but no one had educated the mountains out of her accent.

She wasn't pretty. From what little he could glimpse of her body, she was much too thin. Her light brown hair was long, and the ends were ragged, as if someone had chopped at them with dull scissors. The weight was pulled off her face with a rubber band, neat but unflattering, and the style exposed a face chapped with cold. There wasn't anything wrong with her features, but there was a lack of vitality, maybe even a lack of hope in her expression that canceled everything else.

She coughed, politely turning her head and covering her mouth, but the cough, deep and wrenching, seemed the final straw for Red.

"Hah. Don't bother coming back. I can't use you."

She looked as if he'd hit her, but only for a moment. Her chin lifted again. "I'd work hard. No one would work any harder or faster."

"You don't even have a real place to live. How do I know you're not passing through? I gotta train my help. I'd just get you trained and you'd be gone."

"Oh, no, I'll be staying. I—"

"How're you going to buy a uniform? Shoes? How're you going to keep them clean while you're waiting for a paycheck? Huh? Tips here don't count for nuthin', not on this shift, anyway. Less you got money to start off, you can't make it two weeks. And I don't give no advances."

Red didn't give her time to answer—although by then Jase doubted she was going to, anyway. Wiping his hands on his apron, Red went back behind the counter and disappeared through a swinging door.

Jase wanted to shift his gaze, to give the thoroughly defeated young woman the balm of privacy, but as he started to do just that, he realized she was coughing again. The cough was a racking spasm that shook her frail body until her legs no longer seemed able to hold her. As he watched, her knees began to fold.

He was off his seat and across the room before he knew he had moved. He did not want to get involved. He had his own brutal night to get through; he did not need a complication. Cold, hunger and no place to sleep were complications enough. But a stranger named Becca Hanks was collapsing in front of his eyes, and that made her problems more compelling than his.

He had his arms around her in a moment. "Lean on me," he ordered. "I won't let you fall."

She seemed to have no choice. She swayed against him. He bore the burden of her weight as wave after wave of coughing tore through her. She weighed as little as a child. In robust good health she would probably still be light, but now there was room on her small-boned frame for another twenty pounds.

"I can't—I can't—"

"Don't try to talk. Concentrate on breathing." Jase held her tighter.

Becca gasped, fueling more coughs.

"I'm going to get you to a table. Hold on. Sitting might help." He searched for the closest refuge, then, half dragging her, he encouraged her in that direction.

"What are you doing?"

Jase looked up and saw Red bearing down on them. "What's it look like?"

"Looks like you're not on your way out the door."

"You're a bright man, Red."

"I want you both out of here."

"When she's feeling better."

"Now!"

Jase succeeded in getting Becca to the table. He urged her into a chair. She doubled over and gasped. Jase watched all the color the wind had whipped into her cheeks fade away. "Get her a glass of water." He squatted beside her chair and patted her gently on the back.

"I'm not—"

His head snapped up, and his eyes narrowed. "Red," he said quietly, "you get that water now, or so help me God, your name's going to be Black and Blue."

Red started to reply. Jase got to his feet in one fluid motion, towering over the sputtering man. Red made a split second assessment and disappeared behind the counter. He returned with the water.

"You've got the milk of human kindness in your soul." Jase took the water and squatted beside Becca. "Here you go, honey. Take small sips. Don't gulp. Hold it in your mouth for a few seconds if you can and warm it before you swallow."

She reached for the glass, but her hand was trembling too hard to hold it. Jase held the glass to her lips, and she took a sip.

"Good. Great."

"I want you out of here." Red seemed to feel braver with Jase crouching beside the chair. But he backed away as he added, "You'll scare away my customers."

"Don't worry. Anybody who'd eat in this dump is too stupid to be scared."

There was noise from the chair that didn't sound like a cough. Jase wasn't sure whether it was a laugh or a stifled sob. He wondered if this woman had anything in her life to laugh about.

He held the water to her lips, and she took another sip, then another. The coughing eased until she was able to manage the water by herself. Finally she lifted her head and stared at him.

"Thank you kindly."

"I didn't do anything."

"I'd be . . . a heap on the floor."

"A very small heap."

"This place could use . . . some decorating."

"You'd be wasted here."

Becca tried to smile, but a new round of coughing ensued instead. She turned her face away from his.

Jase stood. One of the men who had been at the other end of the counter was coming toward him. He was old and obviously poor, but there was nothing about him to suggest he was homeless, probably just one of the many elderly who lived in one-room apartments in the vicinity. "I just want to warn you," he said in low tones. "Red's calling the cops. I could hear him from my seat."

Jase nodded his thanks. He and Becca had done nothing illegal, but there were an array of charges Red could threaten them with. A little intervention could actually help Becca, who, with the right kind of luck, might end up in a hospital for the night. But Jase was in no position to explain himself to the Cleveland cops.

The old man shuffled back to his seat. Jase lowered his head so Becca could hear him. "Can you walk now?"

"I think so."

He gripped her elbow and helped her to her feet. She was unsteady, but as he watched, she struggled to regain her balance.

He told her what the old man had said. "You could stay here. They'll just ask you a few questions."

"No!" She coughed again, but the spasms had lessened a little. "Let's make tracks out of here."

"It's bitter cold out there."

"I'll be okay. Thanks. Go on."

He didn't loosen his grip on her elbow. "We'll go together. No argument," he added when she tried to protest. "You collapse on the floor, I'll still be here when the cops come."

She obviously didn't have the strength to resist. She let him lead her to the door.

"Your dinner," she said as his hand went to the doorknob. "Weren't you eating when I came in?"

"No. I was just having coffee." He turned and looked longingly over his shoulder toward the counter. He thought he could see steam rising from what was still nearly a full cup.

"I'm sorry you can't finish it," she said.

"It was just coffee." He opened the door and guided her out into the cold.

Becca didn't know when the cough had begun. It had been with her for so long now that it seemed an integral part of her, like her eyelashes or her feet. She supposed it had gotten worse. The episode in the coffee shop was the most frightening she could remember. There had been seconds piled on seconds when she could not draw a breath. Breathing was one of those things she had always taken for granted, like a place to live or enough food to eat. She wondered if breathing, too, was going to become a struggle.

The wind howled past her bare ears. She reached inside her coat pocket and pulled out a scarf. Moth-eaten and faded, it had not been appropriate to wear on a job interview, but now, with trembling fingers, she wrapped it around her head and throat. As she did, she looked at the man who had rescued her.

Captain Kidd or Bluebeard had probably looked gentler. A pirate's red bandanna covered his dark hair, and half a week's growth of beard shaded his face. He was dressed much like the other homeless men she had encountered, clothes so old someone else had discarded them, shoes with soles that were marginally attached. Thankfully he was cleaner than most; even his clothes were clean.

He seemed either too young or too old to be on the streets. She guessed he was a year or two on her side of thirty, the right age to be holding down a job and earning his way. Not that age was the only requirement for finding a job. She was the right age, too, and she had been unsuccessful. Once the downward spiral began, jobs moved farther and farther out of reach.

"We probably ought to move down the block," he said. "I don't think the cops will be looking for us, but there's no point in waiting for them to show up."

"I'm Becca." She held out her hand.

He grasped it gingerly. "Jase."

"Thank you." She shoved her hands into her pockets to keep them warm. "I guess I'd better get back...to my friends' apartment. They'll wonder what happened to me."

Jase knew the truth when he heard it. He knew a lie, too. Becca didn't lie well, as if she'd had little practice, or as if it went against her basic nature. "I heard you say you were having car trouble."

"It just died." She began to cough. The change from the heated coffee shop to the cold wind seemed to compress her lungs. She leaned against a wall and forced herself to breathe through her nose.

"A mile away?"

She nodded.

Jase knew the section of town they were in. Draw a circle with a one mile radius, and there was no safe place inside it for a woman walking alone. "You can't make it a mile."

"I did once tonight. I'll do it again."

"And what if your car doesn't start?"

"It probably just needed a rest."

"Like you."

She looked up. He had clear green eyes under thick dark brows. She read concern in them. "Thanks for worrying. But I'll be fine."

"I'm walking you to your car."

"I don't need your help. You've helped enough."

"I'm walking you to your car."

She would have argued if there had been even one ounce of fight left in her. But she needed all her fight to control her cough. She didn't need another attack like the one she'd just endured. Collapsing on the street was far more dangerous than collapsing in the coffee shop.

She started walking, and Jase walked beside her. He didn't seem to think that talking was necessary, and she was glad. She had no strength for conversation. Each step was torture. A gale-force wind whipped between buildings and almost knocked her flat. Her bare legs were frozen, and she longed for the jeans packed in the trunk of her car.

They'd covered five blocks before he spoke. "Do you really have a place to stay?"

"I told you I did."

"There's a woman's shelter not too far from here, and they usually have beds for emergencies."

"I'm not an emergency."

They'd covered five more blocks before he spoke again. "I'm guessing you're from West Virginia."

"Kentucky."

"You're a long way from home."

"This is home now."

"Why Cleveland?"

She gave a bitter laugh, and for a moment she was consumed by another fit of coughing. She stopped until she had recovered. "Because there are jobs here," she said as she continued walking. "I'd heard ... there were plenty of jobs."

"The country's in a recession."

"It's always in a recession for people like me."

"People like you?"

She didn't answer, and he didn't push.

They turned onto a short residential street lined with old, ramshackle houses and vacant lots littered with trash where houses had been torn down. They walked its length, avoiding a small pack of dogs, before they turned onto a main avenue. Half a block down a city tow truck was fastening a chain to the bumper of a rusty old Chevrolet.

Becca gave a small cry.

Immediately Jase knew why. "Your car?"

She managed a nod, but she was coughing again.

"We could try to stop them, but it won't do any good Now that it's hooked up, they'll tow it no matter what. You'll have to go down to the city impound lot and pay the fine to get it back."

She straightened enough to watch, and as she did, the tow truck driver got into his cab and started his engine. In a moment the truck and Becca's car were gone.

There was a church on the corner just behind them, a brick monument to Cleveland's immigrant past. Becca lowered herself to the third step and put her head in her hands. "That was my place to stay."

"There were better choices for a front yard than a no parking zone."

"It stalled there."

"The friends? The apartment? Lies?"

"I had to tell Red something. No one hires a waitress who lives in a car."

"Do you have money to get the car back?"

"I don't have money for a piece of gum." She looked up at him. "But I will. I'll find a way."

"Not tonight you won't."

She rested her head in her hands again. "Maybe not tonight."

Jase was torn about what to do. His plans had not included taking care of someone else. Yet what could he do? She was already sick. A night on the streets could kill her. A glance at the digital thermometer at a bank they'd passed had confirmed his hunch that the night was getting colder. She could not spend it outside without protection. Even her car could have been a death trap.

"There's a mission not too far away," he told her. "I heard about it from another man this evening. They serve soup if you go to their service first."

"I'm not hungry."

"Look, you don't have to feel like you're taking charity. From what I hear, the soup's payment for listening to the preacher's wife sing."

"You go on. Thanks . . . for everything you've done, but I want to be left alone," she managed, before another cough began. He sat quietly until she looked up from her coughing spasm. "You're still here."

"I'm not leaving until you're warm and fed."

"Go on and get out of here."

"If I was sensible, would I be out on the streets in the first place?"

She stared at him. "Why are you doing this?"

"Because apparently you're too tired and too sick to make a good decision by yourself."

"I can do anything by myself! Nobody has to help me!" She began to cough again. When she had stopped, she put her face in her hands.

"Becca, you'll die out here."

She realized that this stranger, who didn't seem to have his own life in order, might be right about hers. Fear curled inside her, more powerful than the pain and the despair. She had reasons, two of them, to keep on living. "Okay. I'll go. But it's my decision."

"Sure." He stood. "We'll walk slow."

She followed the pace he set. The route was an unfamiliar tangle of rights and lefts, but she stopped caring immediately. She no longer had a car she had to get back to. Anywhere was as good as anywhere else. There was no feeling in her feet or her fingers by the time she saw a blinking neon cross at the end of a block of dingy storefronts.

Jase stopped and pointed. He wasn't sure if she'd seen the mission or not. He wasn't even sure she would make it that far. "That's it. Think you can sit through the service? It should be starting pretty soon."

She tried to rally. "I can do anything I have to."

"Good girl."

There were two lines spreading down the mission steps and onto the sidewalk. They were divided by gender. Becca joined one, Jase the other. The lines were moving slowly, and when Jase was halfway to the steps, he saw why. Each person underwent a brief search before he was allowed inside.

"What are you looking for?" he asked when it was his turn.

"Drugs, knives." The old man doing the honors gave him a quick smile. "You're clean. Welcome, Brother."

Jason nodded. Becca was waiting for him inside, and they found a seat in the chapel. Throughout the drawn-out service he kept an eye on her. Her eyes stayed closed after prayers. When she stood for hymns, she swayed on her feet. Even the relative warmth of the barny old chapel seemed to have little effect on her coughing. More times than not, Jase

couldn't even hear the preacher—which was its own kind
of blessing.

When the service had finally ended, the hundred or so
who had gathered filed into a large dining hall. They stood
in line for a bowl of soup and a plate of bread. Jase gave
Becca his bread and carried the soup. He knew there
wouldn't have been a drop left if she had been forced to
carry it herself.

The soup looked watery and the bread dry. After they
were seated at a long table, he crumbled his bread in his
soup, solving both problems. He had rarely tasted anything better. He watched Becca choke down half a dozen
bites. "How long since you've eaten?" he asked.

"I don't know."

He believed her. He already knew she wasn't the kind of
woman who dwelled on her misery. "Keep eating slow.
You'll fill up too fast if you haven't eaten in a while."

"I'm already full." She lifted her spoon to her mouth,
anyway, and he guessed she wasn't going to waste a drop,
full or not.

"They have beds here," Jase told her.

"Fifty beds," the man next to him said. He was clean
and shaven. The only thing to identify him as poor was the
disrepair of his clothing. "The first fifty in the door,
twenty-five men, twenty-five women, get 'em. They stamp
your hand?"

Jase looked at Becca. She shook her head.

"You won't sleep here, then," the man said philosophi-
cally. "Have to find another place."

"You're sick. Maybe they'll make an exception," Jase
told her.

"I couldn't ask for someone else's spot."

He wanted to shake her. What did she have to prove,
anyway? And to whom? She was nothing more than a
homeless waif, and nobody, nobody, cared if she had pride
or not. "Suit yourself," he said. "But before you die from

exposure, be sure you leave a note telling the city you plan to pay for your own funeral...just as soon as St. Peter hands over your paycheck.''

"What I do's none of your business," Becca told Jase. "If I didn't do what I thought was right, I wouldn't be any better than a critter."

"You'd be alive." Jase put down his spoon. Without her coat, he could see that Becca was as thin as he had guessed. Her cheeks were rosy again, but not from the wind. This time he was sure the cause was fever. She was in her early twenties, give or take a year or two, but she looked like she'd seen a hundred years of bad luck. "Proud and dead is nothing to brag about. You've got to sleep somewhere warm tonight."

"I'll find a place."

He had learned long ago not to waste his time. He finished his soup and waited for the plastic cup of pudding that volunteers were passing out. Then, when he and Becca were finished, he followed her to the door.

The preacher and his wife were waiting there to speak to each person as he or she passed through. The preacher frowned when Becca began to cough. "You're sick," he said. He touched her forehead with the palm of his hand. "You've got a fever, Sister."

"Couldn't she stay the night?" Jase asked.

"I'm not taking anybody else's bed," Becca said between coughs.

"Her best bet is an emergency room, anyway." The preacher named two hospitals in the vicinity. "One of them may admit her. And even if they don't, the emergency room will be warm and safe. As sick as she is, no one will make her leave before morning."

"Thanks," she said.

Outside Jase took one look at her and knew that, grateful or not, Becca was going to ignore the preacher's advice. He attempted some himself. "I meant what I said about the women's shelter. I know someone on staff. I'm sure they'll find a place for you. They can help you get back on your feet.''

"I don't want charity! I'll take care of myself."

Jase realized he was stuck with Becca for the night. Every attempt he had made to foist her off on someone else had been in vain. She was too full of spirit. She would harm herself rather than let anyone help. Reluctantly, he admired her as he considered what to do.

"Are you looking for a job?"

The question surprised him. He wasn't, and he couldn't think fast enough to concoct a good lie. "No."

"Well, I'm not going to stop until I find something!"

"More power to you, but right now, let's just find you a place to sleep tonight."

"I'm fine."

"There's a construction site not far from here, and the basement level is completed. It won't be as warm as a shelter, but it's out of the wind. We'll go there."

"I'm not going anywhere with you. You've done enough."

He clamped fingers that were already growing numb again over her shoulder. "You're coming with me. I'll hound you all night until you do."

For a moment she wondered if he intended her harm. So far he had been nothing but kind. She met his gaze and tried to read his motives.

"I'm not going to let anything happen to you," he promised. "Let me do this much. Okay? I just want to get you out of the cold and the wind. And I want some sleep."

What choice did she have? She knew she was sinking fast. She couldn't make herself say the words, but she nodded.

He smiled a little. "Good."

By the time they reached the site of what was obviously going to be a new landmark for Cleveland's skyline, she knew she had no strength left. Jase seemed no worse for the eight block hike, but Becca's knees were shaking. She followed him along the side of the building, shivering as wind blasted around the corner. He seemed to know exactly where to go, and she guessed he had slept here before.

"There's a security force," he said. "Don't worry about them. They usually let people sleep inside on cold nights."

She thought that very odd, but she was too exhausted to comment. She followed slowly, her lips in a grim, determined line. They wound their way through construction debris and makeshift plywood tunnels. Finally he led her to some steps. "Can you make it?"

She nodded. He held out his hand, and she took it, afraid that if she fell, she would be a real burden. The stairwell was dark, and she was momentarily frightened, but he squeezed her hand as if he knew. "We're almost there."

At the bottom of the stairwell they stepped through a doorway. There was some light from the street lamps filtering through the unfinished panels of the floor above, but the basement resembled a huge, dank cave. She couldn't go on.

"There's a room at the back with some light from above. The last time I was here there was a kerosene heater for warmth."

"I don't like this."

"I don't blame you."

She began to cough. Jase put his arm around her to help keep her on her feet. She was shivering.

"You'll be safe. I promise. Would a maniac try so hard to get you to go to a women's shelter?"

"Let's go."

He guided her carefully. He knew the whole floor like the back of his hand, but the eerie mottled light distorted everything. Halfway across he looked up and saw a man with a flashlight in his hand. Jase blocked Becca's view. The beam traced the contours of his face. He waved it away. The man melted into the shadows.

"Jase?" she asked.

"It's all right. I told you, they don't mind us sleeping here. They've seen me before."

"They really don't." She was amazed.

"Let's go."

The room in the back was just as he had described it. And the heater took only a moment to light. She stood next to it to warm her hands. Jase watched her for a moment. When he was sure she wouldn't bolt, he went to the door. "I know where there are tarps and pads we can sleep on. I'll be back in a minute."

He was back before she had time to be frightened. "This isn't going to be terribly comfortable, but it will be better than sleeping in an alley somewhere." He spread a tarp on the floor and covered it with two pads that until a moment ago had protected some of the thousands of dollars worth of equipment stored in the next room. He rolled one into a pillow and saved two for cover. "There." He stood. "See what you think."

"You've done so much."

"Do me a favor in return. Get some sleep. I'll stand guard."

"But you have to sleep, too."

"I sleep in the daytime," he lied.

"What do you do at night?"

"Look for ways to stay out of trouble."

"You seem so..."

He watched her search for a word. "Normal?" he supplied.

"No. Efficient. I bet there are a lot of things you could do."

"Go to sleep, Becca. We can talk in the morning."

She went to the makeshift pallet and lowered herself to the floor. He watched her curl up on one side, her hands under her cheek. Her handbag was nestled against her chest, less from fear of theft, he supposed, than for the comfort of having something she owned close by. She didn't move for a moment; then she sat up and fished around inside it.

He wondered what she was looking for.

She pulled out a scrap of paper. From his limited perspective, it looked like a photograph.

She stared at it, as if it could give her solace. His curiosity was already racing full speed. She was young and probably attractive when she was well and well-fed. What had brought her here, and what had put her on the streets?

"Can I show you something?" she asked.

He was surprised. "Sure." He joined her on the pad, kneeling beside her. "What is it?"

She held out the photograph. He squinted in the darkness, just able to make out two shapes. Two small, pig-tailed shapes in pink overalls. "Who are they?"

"They're mine."

"Where are they?"

Becca shook her head. The photograph disappeared back into her handbag. She lay down again and clasped it to her chest.

She wasn't sure why she had shown the photograph to Jase. It was her most precious belonging. If it had been in the car when they'd towed it away...

She shuddered. Then she shuddered again. The heater might warm the air eventually, but she was afraid the cold seeping through the tarp and pads was never going to go away.

She felt a hand on her shoulder. "You're freezing," Jase said.

She was as close to tears as she had come in a year. She was as close to giving up as she had ever been in her life. "I'm all right."

She wasn't all right, and he could only think of one more thing she might accept from him. "I'm getting under the covers. I have no intention of forcing myself on you. Shivering, coughing women have never been an interest of mine." He lay down under the cover. Then he inched toward her until her back curved against him. Surprisingly, she didn't move away. "You'll warm up faster this way," he said against her hair.

She lay in the circle of a ragged stranger's arms and thought of all the things that had brought her to this place and moment. The last man to sleep beside her had been her husband. Tears tickled her eyelids, but she was too exhausted and the pain was too old to make her cry.

The man beside her was not her husband, but he was kindness and strength. She had almost forgotten that either of those things existed. "Why are you being so nice?" she asked.

He had been called many things in his life, but nice had rarely been one of them. His arms tightened a little. "Because you deserve to have someone be nice to you."

"I . . . we shouldn't be here."

"It's okay. Tomorrow we'll go somewhere else."

She thought about tomorrow. For once there was no small surge of hope that tomorrow would be better. She couldn't expect anything from the future. The best she could do was think about the present moment and a stranger's kindness.

She placed her hands on his arm. All thoughts faded, and in a moment she was asleep.

Jase stroked her hair. It smelled like soap, not shampoo, but soap, inexpensive and unadorned. He wondered if she had washed her hair in a public restroom somewhere. She would have, rather than be dirty. He knew that much about her already. Tomorrow morning he planned to discover more, right before he told her who he was and what had brought him to the streets.

She coughed, but she didn't wake up.

Tomorrow he would get her to a hospital. Tomorrow he would be sure her pride took a backseat to her health.

Tomorrow. He finally fell asleep thinking of tomorrow.

Chapter Two

"I don't care if it's bad business. Yes, you heard me right, I don't care if I take a loss." Jason Millington switched the telephone receiver to his left ear to give his right one a break. This was his fourth call in fifteen minutes. "I can afford to take a loss. Get me the coffee shop like a good boy, and be sure my old buddy Red doesn't come out of it with anything. Yes, I know he's a bastard. But I'm a bigger one."

Jase hung up with a flourish. At the same moment the door to his office, a door that was as solid and stately as his mahogany desk, banged into the wall. The three Winslow Homers artfully grouped a distance away from it danced uncertainly.

He didn't even look up. "Pamela, I presume."

"Your new secretary was going to announce me. I told her we don't announce family. Now she's cowering at her desk."

He gave her a look that would have made the bravest man uneasy. "I don't raise my voice to her. She has no reason to cower."

"Everybody's afraid of you."

"Except you, apparently."

Pamela crossed the room, bent low and kissed him. "I'm terrified."

"Don't be. You beat me up when we were ten."

"We were eleven. I was taller than you." Pamela found a seat and kicked off her shoes. She was not taller than her twin brother now. He was six foot, and she was six inches shorter, but there was still a strong resemblance between them. Her short hair was as dark as his, her eyes just as green. They both had the stubborn Millington jaw, although Pamela's was a more delicate version.

Jase knew what men thought of his sister. Twenty minutes after she had entered a room filled with more beautiful women, the men gravitated to Pamela. Her eyes sparkled with vitality; her features were mobile and expressive. But best of all, she was never afraid to say exactly what she thought. And Pamela never stopped thinking.

Now she gestured toward the stellar view of a Cleveland April outside Jase's twelfth-story window. "Someday you'll own it all, won't you, Jase? Own it all and change every bit of it to suit yourself."

Since that, or something similar, was her usual opening gambit, Jase ignored it. "Why are you here?"

"Not for your money."

He picked up a pen and tapped Morse code on his desktop. Pamela had said the same thing to him one day in March, and now the words brought back that day as clearly as if he were living it again.

The afternoon had been much like this one. He had been in the middle of a telephone business deal when Pamela walked in, and things had not been going his way. More irritable than usual, he had pulled out a checkbook, but she had waved it away.

"You know, Jase," she'd said, "all the world's problems can't be solved with money. It's so easy for you to write a check. Your funds are virtually limitless. Heck, your pen is worth more than three rooms of furniture at The Greenhouse. When I walk out that door, you won't miss the money. You probably won't even remember you gave it."

"So what *do* you want?" He had shoved his hands into his pockets and gone to the window. The Cleveland he saw was a growing city, rich with potential and energy. Pamela was right; he rarely thought about the other Cleveland, the one where children went hungry, and men and women roamed the streets looking for shelter. That was Pamela's Cleveland. As a social worker at The Greenhouse, a refuge for homeless and battered women, it was the Cleveland she came up against every day.

"I think I want you to escape your narrow little world." She joined him at the window. "I want you to understand, just once, what it's like to be poor. What it's like to be hungry, to have no home to go to. Your money helps now, but maybe if you understood what it's like to have no hope, you could give the kind of help we really need."

"I'm sick of this conversation. I'm sick of you harping at me. I'm not the problem. You grew up with money, and the guilt's eating you up. Millingtons have always given generously to good causes. We have nothing to be ashamed of."

"You don't understand a word I'm saying."

He stared at the street below. Directly under his window there was a man shoving a shopping cart in front of him, one shuffling step at a time. "I don't understand," he conceded. "I don't understand why more people don't help themselves. There are jobs everywhere. Maybe some of those jobs aren't great, but they're jobs. I know some people can't work. They're too sick, or addicted or crazy. But what about others?''

"What about them? Maybe you should find out first-hand.''

"How? Work in a soup kitchen for a night or two?''

"No. *Go* to a soup kitchen for a night or two. Yeah. That's what it would take, Jase. You'll never really understand what it's like to be without hope, but you could try it for a while. You might understand a little better.''

He had learned to understand a little better, all right. After their conversation, he had taken her suggestion—or, more accurately, her dare—and lived on the streets for two nights and a day in between. Now, of course, he realized that he had pretended to be homeless as much for the novelty as to get Pamela off his back. Maybe there had been a little guilt mixed in, too. Everything had always been easy for him. He had been born into a family with assets ranging from steel mills to corporate farms and cattle ranches. He had been a superior, popular student and later, a superior, if not popular businessman. Millington Development was his own creation, and last year the company's financial statement had been solid gold.

But nothing of what he was, of what he had been born to, had mattered for two nights in March. He had learned quickly that one homeless man was the same as another. He had skulked around corners, avoiding places where he might be recognized and picking through trash that others had missed. And on the second and final night, he had met a woman named Becca Hanks.

The Morse code ceased abruptly. It was April again, and Pamela was waiting for his question. "I guess you'd tell me if you'd heard anything about Becca?''

She looked at him with sympathy. "No one named Becca Hanks has turned up anywhere. For a month now I've checked and rechecked every agency she might have gone to, every clinic, every mission or shelter. She just doesn't seem to exist.''

"She exists. Or she did." He leaned back in his chair. "She slept with me in the basement of my new building down on 4th Street. She was sick and proud, and when I woke up the next morning, she was gone."

"I know. I'm sorry." Pamela reached over and put her hand on his. "But so many people pass through the city. They struggle to stay alive while they're here. If this Becca made it through the winter, she'll be safer now that the weather is warming up. Maybe she found a job and a place to stay, or she's just gone back where she came from."

"She never claimed her car. I've made arrangements to be called if she tries to."

"You've changed."

"Not at all."

"You've changed. You're softer around the edges these days. I like you better."

"You liked me all right before."

"I adore you. I survived childhood because of you."

He met her eyes. "We had a good childhood, Pamela."

"We had a rotten childhood, but we had each other."

He ignored that. "Why are you here if you don't have any news and you don't want money?"

"To take you to dinner. At The Greenhouse." She held up her hands. "Don't say no."

"You want me to take food from the mouths of people who need every calorie?"

"Somebody gave us a huge sucker of a ham, and the kids are practicing a play to entertain everyone afterward. It's a festive occasion, and you know you're always welcome there. You practically own the place."

"You'd be surprised if I said yes, wouldn't you?"

She grinned. "Truthfully?"

"I'll be happy to come. I've got something to talk to you and Shareen about, anyway."

Her grin widened. "Much softer around the edges."

"Tell Red that."

"Red?"

"Just a man I know who's going to wish like hell that he never met me."

The Greenhouse was not green. It was a rambling white Victorian with pink and yellow trim and a picket fence that was missing one of every six pickets. The house itself was in a constant state of disrepair. Shutters flapped in the breeze, and pieces of rotting gingerbread fell to the wide front porch every time the breeze turned into a strong wind.

One of the other residents had told Becca that Pamela Millington's brother sent a work crew for repairs every time there was a lull in one of his other projects. Little by little his crew had painted and nailed and shingled until the house was basically sound. Apparently the fence was next on the list, and new gingerbread was on order from a company that specialized in reproductions. Already the house outshone its neighbors, but the renovation had encouraged some other residents of the block to show more pride. Two houses down, new paint sparkled. Four houses down, someone was planting pansies.

Pansies were great, but Becca was in the backyard of The Greenhouse planting peas. The first crop had been planted two weeks before, along with the lettuce. That was a little late, but in March, when she should have been making a garden, lettuce and peas hadn't been on her mind.

"Ma-ar-ry!"

April had been a surprisingly dry month. The black soil crumbled in Becca's hands, rich in humus and earthworms. The soil in Blackwater had not been nearly so rich. To have a garden there, she had hauled rocks and hoed until her back ached. But she'd made a garden, a big flourishing garden. Now, choked by weeds, the asparagus would just be nudging its way through the warming soil. Asparagus never quit.

The Greenhouse needed an asparagus patch.

"Mary!"

She turned, startled. "Shareen. You scared me to death!"

"I've been calling and calling you! Where's your ears at?"

"Glued on the side of my head, same as yours."

"You didn't answer."

"When I'm digging, I'm digging. Nothing gets through to me."

Shareen plopped cross-legged on the grass beside Becca. "What's that?"

"Lettuce. I planted two kinds. That's Black-seeded Simpson, and that's Oak Leaf."

"What's growing next to the fence?"

"Peas."

Shareen made a face, and Becca laughed. "I put in spinach, too."

"Girl, you trying to poison us?"

"I'm trying to save you money. If The Greenhouse grows some of its own food, that's less we have to buy."

"I know what you're trying to do. It's your choices!" Shareen stood and brushed grass off her jeans. The lawn had been mowed for the first time that morning. "Did you know we're having a party tonight?"

"A party?" Becca smiled. Just weeks ago she had wondered if life would ever hold anything for her again. "What kind of party?"

"Doesn't have to be any kind. Just a party. Ham, sweet potatoes, my mama's vinegar pies."

"Is your mama coming?"

"She's bringing the pies. I'm going to talk her into staying. Pamela's trying to get her brother to come, too."

Becca loved Shareen's mother. Dorey Moore was a tiny woman with snapping black eyes and a mouth that could cut the most arrogant down to size. Shareen had more polish, but no less guts. Pamela and Shareen had nurtured Becca during her first week at The Greenhouse as gently and tenderly as she was nurturing her garden. Rarely in the last years had anyone been as kind to her.

Except one homeless man named Jase, who had probably kept her from dying.

"So you got to put on your dancing shoes," Shareen said.

"Are we getting dressed up?" Becca asked.

"Might be nice."

"I found the prettiest dress in one of the boxes of clothes we washed today. I can't imagine why anyone ever gave it away."

"Probably didn't fit them. Did it fit you?"

"It's a little big."

"Everything's a little big for you, except doll clothes. You eat double portions of that ham tonight. And Mama says one of the pies has your name on it."

Becca coughed, but the cough was no more than a tickle now. Weeks of intravenous antibiotics had seen to that. "I bet your mama eats peas."

"You're working too hard."

"This isn't work. It's pleasure."

"Will you go in now? Take a shower and lie down for a while before it's time to change into that dress?"

"I was going to help with dinner."

"No way."

Becca understood strong wills. She stood. "Then I'll help serve."

"Maybe." Shareen slung her arm over Becca's shoulder and gave her a squeeze. "Now, you go take care of yourself. That's the only job you gotta do here."

Becca owed Shareen too much to argue. But Shareen was wrong. Becca had to take care of herself, it was true. But she also had to find a way to pay back the people who had reached out to her and led her, one step at a time, back to some kind of a life. The garden was one way to contribute. In the weeks that were left to her at The Greenhouse, she would find others.

She wished there was some way to find Jase and do something for him, too. She wondered where he was now. Was his life going to be one of these dead-ends that made the papers from time to time? Homeless man found dead in cardboard box? He had told her he wasn't looking for work. What *was* he looking for? Whatever it was, she hoped that he found it.

Jase made a mental note that The Greenhouse fence still hadn't been fixed. The house was looking better, though. He stood in front of it and tried to figure out exactly why.

"No, you may not build a skyscraper here," Pamela said.

"I'm trying to figure out what's different."

"It does look better, doesn't it?"

"Lots better." He realized what had changed. "Who's been doing the landscaping?"

"Nothing gets by you, does it? It's our new resident. Mary Smith."

"Mary Smith?" He glanced at Pamela. "For real?"

"We don't ask too many questions."

"She's quite a gardener. What are the beds along the fence for?"

"Flowers. She's started seeds in the basement under an old fluorescent light."

"I wouldn't have guessed the shrubs could be saved. But she's tamed them."

"Come see what she's done in back." Pamela led Jase through the gate to a flat area behind the garage. "Vegetables."

"She's a paragon."

"She works too hard."

"Is that possible?"

She laughed. "You wouldn't understand."

"Well, if she works this hard, you shouldn't have too much trouble finding a job for her before she has to leave."

"I hope not. But she's like a lot of the others. She doesn't have much education, though she's smart as a whip. Unfortunately, IQ isn't as important as B.A."

Three little girls launched themselves out the back door and headed straight for Pamela. She laughed, delighted, and held out her arms.

"A fan club?" Jase asked.

"One of my compensations." Pamela dragged her clinging friends toward the back door. "Do you want me to find Shareen now for that talk you mentioned?"

"If we've got time before we eat."

"Why don't you wait in the parlor?" She left, walking as normally as anyone could with a child attached to each leg.

The parlor was a hodgepodge of old furniture and unusual, graceful touches. The Greenhouse received donations almost every day from church and civic groups. Some of the residents arrived with no more than the clothes on their backs, but they always left with a complete wardrobe. What furniture wasn't needed in the house went to individual residents setting up their own apartments.

Whimsy and fantasy were in short supply for the women in the house, but the parlor fulfilled some of those needs. There were overstuffed chairs covered in English floral prints, hand-crocheted doilies on polished wood surfaces, silk flower arrangements in vases. No matter that the prints didn't coordinate, the woods ranged from pine to mahogany, and the vases would never hold water again. There was an old Victrola and a supply of 78s for entertainment, and two bookshelves filled with hardcover novels. The children were only allowed here if accompanied by adults, and even then they were required to be on their best behavior.

Jase felt uncomfortable in the parlor. If he had to play along with the Victorian theme, he would much have preferred a room paneled in mahogany and furnished with leather. He paced the small space until Shareen and Pamela arrived.

"The lion in his cage." Shareen went to him and gave him a kiss on the cheek. Like Pamela, she found nothing about Jase frightening.

He admired her, as he always did. She was tiny, with curves in all the right places and a smile that welcomed the world. The smile could change in a moment, though, if she thought anyone or anything about The Greenhouse was threatened. As a black woman growing up in inner city Cleveland, she had bounded over her own share of hurdles. The facts of life she had been forced to learn made her the ideal director for The Greenhouse.

"We're glad you came," Shareen told him. "We like having you here. But I know there's got to be a better reason than ham and sweet potatoes."

One of the things Jase liked best about Shareen was that she never beat around the bush. One of the reasons The Greenhouse continued to survive was Shareen's unswerving, unflinching devotion. "I've bought an old factory not too far from the Flats. The section's not fashionable, and the building's a mess."

"You want condolences?" Pamela asked.

"I want to convert it into apartments. The potential's there. The building will stand forever if someone doesn't take a wrecking ball to it. There's nothing wrong with it that can't be fixed. Right now it's heaped with debris. The windows are all broken, and it's a barn inside. But the floors are solid maple, and the space can be divided any way we want."

Shareen perked up. "We?"

"I could hang on to the property for a few years. I'm betting that there'll be renovation in that area by then, and more buildings will be turned into apartments. It's a gamble, but I win more of those than I lose."

"Modesty becomes you, Jase." Pamela dusted a cabinet top with the hem of her blazer. "What does this have to do with us?"

"I could wait, or I could turn the property into apartments now. Not the same kind, obviously. I wouldn't be aiming for affluent professionals. If I do it now, I do it for people like the women coming out of The Greenhouse, people who are just getting back on their feet and need a place to start. There's money available to provide shelter for the homeless, not a lot of it, God knows, but a little. I'll donate the building and whatever supplies and workmen I can afford. The government will pick up some more of the tab. The rest will have to come from the community."

"You're pushing all the right buttons. You know that," Shareen said. "The hardest thing we have to do is find decent housing for our ladies after they leave here."

"I know."

"What do you mean, the community has to come up with the rest?" Pamela moved on to the Victrola. "How much, and how do we get them to do it?"

"A lot. And getting them to do it is your baby."

"Committees? Fund-raisers?"

"Mother." Jase saw Pamela grimace. "It's right up her alley," he reminded her.

"I suppose."

"Mrs. Millington would be willing to raise the money?" Shareen asked.

"Mother thrives on committees. Jase is right. We'd need someone like her to head this up. She knows all the right people, and they all owe her favors. She sees to it."

"You're just going to give us this building, free and clear?" Shareen asked Jase. "How come?"

Jase smiled. "Ask Pamela."

"A blinding light on the road to Damascus," Pamela said. "He's been converted to good works." She reached out and touched his arm.

He felt her pride, and it embarrassed him. "I'm doing it because it needs to be done. The building's just sitting there. I hate waste."

"Well, whatever the reason, I'm sure glad you thought of us," Shareen said. "We'll do whatever we have to. I know our board will help, and there are some influential folks on it. They'll work with your mama. Maybe we can call some attention to problems while we're at it. The publicity can't hurt."

There was a knock on the parlor door, and a little girl in a green jumper opened it a crack. "Dinner's ready," she lisped.

"We're done?" Shareen asked. "For now?"

"Done."

Shareen scooped the child up and settled her on one hip. Then she led the way into the dining room.

Jase felt the party atmosphere immediately. Shareen and Pamela believed that joy was one of the things the women and children in the house had to be reintroduced to, along with good food and a safe place to stay. There was no occasion too small for a celebration, and crepe paper streamers and balloons were usually part of The Greenhouse decor.

Today the streamers were yellow and the balloons red. There was an arrangement of funereal white lilies on the pine sideboard, but the room was perfumed by the reason for the celebration.

"This ham," Pamela said, "must be fifteen pounds, and Gina studded it with cloves and pineapple. Doesn't it smell fantastic?"

Jase noted the sign on the wall, scrawled and decorated by a child. "I yam happy about ham?" he asked.

"We're happy about the sweet potatoes, too."

The china was mismatched garage sale variety, but it sparkled like the mismatched glassware. There were cloth napkins, and the same child who had made the sign had also turned her talents to name cards at each place.

He really didn't want to be touched. He was not a sentimental man, but he felt something catch in his throat when he realized his place was at the head of the long table. Shareen's mother arrived, pies in hand, and bussed his cheek on the way to the kitchen to deliver them.

He stood politely until she came back and almost everyone was seated. There were still two places vacant when Pamela, who was at his right, ordered him to sit.

"Those belong to Gina and Mary," she said. "They'll be serving."

He winked at a little boy who was missing his two front teeth and sat. They were the only males in the room. "You've got a full house these days."

"We turned away a woman with two children this morning. The city would close us down if we took in even one more person."

"Where did she go?"

Pamela didn't answer.

"Pamela?"

"I'd rather not say."

He put his hand on her arm. "Did you take her in?"

"Well, she's just staying at my place for a few days." She spoke so softly he could hardly hear her. "She has a sister from California who's driving out to get her and take her home."

"And what does Shareen say about that?"

"She didn't ask, and I didn't volunteer the information." She met his eyes. "And you're not going to volunteer, either. Got it?"

"You can't take in the whole world."

"And you can't buy it, but you'll keep on trying, won't you? Even if it's just so you can give it away again."

"Don't get any ideas. The factory is just one building, and I took a liking to it, so I had to think of some way to use it."

She leaned forward. "This Becca person changed you, Jase. You'll never admit it, but she did."

He leaned forward, too, and missed the entrance of the ham until he heard the round of spontaneous applause.

The applause covered the gasp of the woman holding the platter. When Jase finally did look up, he saw her, lips gently parted, eyes greatly wounded. His hand clenched Pamela's arm. Becca stared at him.

Then, as he watched speechlessly, she set the ham on the sideboard and disappeared back into the kitchen.

Chapter Three

The row that would hold carrots had to be double spaded. First the topsoil had to be carefully removed; then the subsoil had to be broken up and mixed with humus before the topsoil was restored. Becca had found an old leaf pile at a nearby vacant lot and hauled wagon after wagon of composted leaves back to the garden. This morning she intended to work them into the carrot row.

Everybody loved carrots, didn't they? Even the pickiest child could be tempted to eat a raw carrot, particularly if she had helped pull it from the garden. When Becca was no longer at The Greenhouse, her carrots would still be growing, nourishing the latest crop of Greenhouse children. For a moment she pictured herself as a New Age Johnny Appleseed, traversing the country, leaving asparagus and carrots in her wake. Johnny had been a homeless wanderer, too, but that hadn't stopped him from making his mark.

She dug the first spadeful of topsoil, but her heart wasn't in it. She felt well enough. If she took frequent rest breaks she would be able to plant carrots today and still have the energy to finish trimming the hedge along the back fence. She had the energy, but not the enthusiasm. Jason Millington, millionaire developer and brother of Pamela Millington, had stripped her of enthusiasm just as surely as Jase, compassionate, homeless man, had saved her life.

She dug the second spadeful of topsoil. What kind of game had Jase been playing that night? Did slumming give him some sort of thrill? Maybe he had been investigating some kind of financial deal, sleuthing for millions at Red's Place. Maybe Red's Place was going to be the site of a new downtown luxury hotel, and he'd been scouting out potential clientele.

She wanted to laugh, but it was tears that clutched at her throat. Tears, and she hadn't cried in years, not since everything that mattered had been taken away from her. Tears watered down her determination to make a new life for herself and her babies. There was no point in crying when there was so much work to be done. And there was no point in crying about a man who had pretended to be something he was not. She should be happy that he wasn't dining out of garbage cans and sleeping in doorways.

The third spadeful joined the others, but she couldn't stop herself from remembering last night's dinner. She had worn the new dress, a lilac floral print with a lace collar that had only needed a little mending. One of the children had tied a purple ribbon in her hair, and she had shined a pair of black pumps that almost fit. The kitchen had smelled heavenly, like Gramma's kitchen had always smelled at Easter, and she had known she was really on the road to recovery when her stomach had rumbled with hunger. It was funny how quickly she had learned to convince herself she didn't need food, how quickly she had learned to ignore her body's signals until one day they hadn't been there anymore. But all her signals had worked again last night.

The party had made her happy; the ham had made her hungry.

And seeing Jason Millington in a suit that cost as much as six months' rent had made her feel like a fool.

She was sure he had recognized her. She hadn't changed as much as he had, after all. Her hair was different, and she had gained a little weight, but she was essentially the same.

He was nothing like the man who had gotten her through a frigid March night. He was a sleek, elegant panther, while that man had been an embattled alley cat. Jason Millington the developer had all that alley cat's power and presence, and he had the clout to use it. She found it no wonder that he had made millions rearranging Cleveland to suit his fancy.

She had nothing but a high school diploma, and hardly that, but it hadn't taken her more than seconds to see the truth and seconds more to act. She had retreated into the kitchen and out the back door. Then she had gone for a long, long walk. She had returned to questions, but not to Jason Millington. He had been gone by then, worried, she supposed, that she might reveal his silly little secret.

There was a small pile of topsoil beside the row, but she was already exhausted. She hadn't slept well. Every time she had shut her eyes, she had seen Jason Millington's face. Every darned time.

"I could do that for you."

She knew who had spoken before she looked up. That voice had stayed with her during her weeks in the hospital. Sometimes she had heard that voice coaxing her to get better, insisting that she fight to stay alive. Twice she had even dreamed that Jase had come to see her and promised he would take her somewhere so they could both make a new start. Crazy, humiliating dreams.

"I'll do it myself, thanks," she said. She raised her head—and her chin. "I don't need your help. I never did."

"Well, the hair's different, and the clothes fit snugger. But the woman's the same."

"Funny thing. The man's not, is he?"

Jase didn't smile. He felt like a fraud, like a voyeur caught in the act. "Same man. Different clothes."

"They say clothes make the man. Even ignorant country folk have heard that one."

"I don't blame you for being angry."

"Angry? Why should I be angry, Mr. Millington? Just because you made me feel like a fool? You sure weren't the first, and you probably won't be the last."

She was angry, and despite his discomfort Jase couldn't help but admire the effect. Her cheeks bloomed with it; her brown eyes sparkled. He hadn't remembered the color of her eyes, but now he saw they were a rich coffee-brown, an interesting contrast to hair that was blond in the sunlight. Someone had cut her hair to her shoulders, and there were bangs caressing her forehead. The simplicity of the style suited her, emphasizing strong bones and a full bottom lip that was not about to curve into a smile.

"Will you give me a chance to explain?"

"I'd love to hear an explanation. My imagination's taken flight."

"I pretended to be homeless because someone close to me—"

"Pamela?"

He refused to implicate his sister. "Because someone close to me suggested that I needed to do more about the world's problems than write checks. So I decided I wasn't going to understand what it was like to be homeless unless I was homeless myself for a few nights."

"How lucky we are! Just think, you could have taken the environment or world peace as your pet charity. Instead you chose to slink around alleys with a bunch of bums."

"I don't deserve that."

"I worried about you! Didn't you even guess when you were playing bum that somebody might just think of you as real? That somebody might care a little or worry a little? You don't know how many times I've wondered what happened to you! I even said a few prayers, and I haven't prayed in a long time!"

Her impassioned speech had taken more out of her than she realized. She began to cough, but when he stepped toward her, she waved him away. "Leave me alone!"

"You're still sick."

"No, I'm not. I'm just not well yet."

While he waited for her to catch her breath, he thought about everything she had said. Life was a chess game to him, a game he always won. Becca had started her chess game with nothing but a pawn or two, but she was still playing hard. For the first time he felt something very close to shame.

"Look," he said when she seemed to be breathing normally again. "I'm sorry. I really am. I was going to tell you who I was the morning after we met, but you left before I could. I would have told you that night, but I knew if I did, you wouldn't have let me help you. And you desperately needed help. I was afraid you were going to go off into the night and die in some miserable corner of the city."

"I trusted you, and you were playing with me."

"I never meant to play with anybody. For my whole life I've had everything my way. I just wanted to see what it would be like if I didn't have anything."

"So what did you learn?"

"I learned what it means to be lucky."

"People make their own luck."

"Not always. Look at you. What did you ever do to deserve what you've been handed?"

"You'd be surprised." She lifted her shovel again and started to dig.

He wanted to jerk the shovel out of her hands and force her to rest, but he held himself back. "If you trusted me, Becca, why did you leave without saying goodbye?"

She wasn't going to tell him it had been pride mixed with a large dose of femininity. She had awakened snuggled tightly against his chest, and she had known that in the light of day neither she nor Jase were going to stand up under scrutiny. She had been dirty, ill, as close to defeated as she had ever come—even though she and defeat were old buddies—and she had not had the courage to face him and let him see the woman he had held in his arms all night.

"I was afraid somebody might find us."

"Where did you go?"

She turned over two more shovelfuls of soil. With the third she decided not to spare him. "It was still dark outside. I was going to sit on a bench somewhere until it was light; then I was going to start making the rounds of coffee shops, looking for work. I picked the wrong bench." She tried to lift the shovel and realized Jase was gripping it so that she couldn't. She stared into compassionate green eyes. "Two fellows jumped me and grabbed my purse. When I tried to follow, one of them knocked me to the ground. I woke up in the hospital."

"Becca."

Her expression didn't change, even though she couldn't remember anyone saying her name quite that way before. "I was there for weeks. For a while a machine did my breathing. When I could do my own again, they told me they wouldn't let me out unless I promised to come here while I mended. I didn't have a choice."

He touched her shoulder. Gently. So gently. "You are one pigheaded woman."

"I guess if I weren't, I'd be dead."

"And Mary Smith? How did she come into the picture?"

"I didn't have any identification. Becca Hanks had three strikes against her. When I woke up I thought maybe somebody might throw a woman named Mary Smith a ball or two."

"I'm so sorry."

"For what? For lying to me? For knowing somebody whose life is as messed up as mine? Don't be."

"I wasn't lying when I tried to help you. I wanted to do it. It didn't matter who I was. I wanted to help."

"You and your sister are two of a kind. And don't think I don't appreciate it." She pulled the shovel from his grasp. "You were kind to me. Maybe you even saved my life. I owe you thanks for that. But I don't want anything except a chance to make my own way. The people here are great, but I've got to leave. And I'm going to, just as soon as I pay them back for everything they've done."

Jase couldn't find the words to tell her that The Greenhouse didn't operate that way. And where were the words to tell her to slow down, to let someone else share her burden? She had gained a little weight and a little healthy color in her cheeks, but she was still a long way from well.

"It's all right to take care of yourself. Stay here until you're ready to face the world again. Let The Greenhouse help you. Let me help."

"You?" She frowned. "Do you own another floor I can sleep on? I'm guessing you owned that one."

"Becca."

"Why would you want to help me?"

"Because I can. Easily. Let me help you make a new start."

She wondered how many people said no to Jase Millington. He was dressed casually today, dark slacks, a green shirt that made his eyes glow like emeralds. But casual or not, he stood like a man who was used to people throwing themselves at his feet. He held himself with supreme confidence, his broad shoulders thrown back, his head cocked. He was a man any woman would feel drawn to.

She had liked him better, so much better, on a dark March night when he had been in trouble, too. "No." She tried the word out slowly, watching for its effect. "No, Jason Millington, the Whatever-You-Are, Third, Fifth, Tenth? I don't care. I've said thank-you for your help, and I'll say thanks for the offer of more. But I don't want anything given to me. Nothing. Not from anybody."

"Why in hell are you so stubborn?"

She thrust the shovel into the ground and whacked the top of it with her foot. Pain shot through her leg, but she didn't care. "Because stubborn is who I am! It's the one thing I've got that nobody can take away from me! The only thing!"

She was almost to the end of the row before he left. She didn't hear him go; she didn't watch him. But she knew when he was gone. Funniest thing, but she knew when he was gone.

Jase and Pamela's parents, Jason Millington the Third and his wife Dorothea, lived in a rambling eighteen-room house looking over five acres of manicured grass and evergreens in Hunting Valley, east of Cleveland. Dorothea suffered from allergies and disliked bees, so every flowering shrub and tree that had once bloomed on the property had been removed the week the Millingtons moved in. Pamela called her parents' estate Sing-Sing. They called it their little country cottage.

Jase seldom visited his parents at home. His work schedule left little free time, and the drive to Hunting Valley annoyed him. He usually met them for drinks or dinner in Cleveland. He liked the city, the smells, the bustle, the energy, the rumble of traffic. He was never certain what his parents had needed to escape from by their move. Their home in Cleveland Heights had been spacious and perfect for the extensive entertaining that they still did. He could only guess that Cleveland Heights, with its mixture of rich and not-so, had become too much like the real world for them to feel comfortable.

On the Saturday evening after his talk with Becca, Jase found himself driving out of the city for his mother's birthday dinner. Pamela had insisted on meeting him there. Even though she had pleaded that a hair appointment was going to make her late, he knew the real reason why she hadn't driven with him. Pamela would not visit their parents unless she had her own car to make an escape in.

By the time he wound his way up the tree-shaded driveway, Pamela was already there. She was minutely examining newly planted juniper when he joined her.

"Have you been inside?"

"Not yet. I was just fascinated to see what new things Mother had allowed in her yard."

"How long have you been out here?"

"A little while."

"In other words, they don't know you've arrived?"

"Probably not."

"You couldn't face them alone?"

"Did I say that? Juniper fascinates me. The variety of plants Mother can find that don't flower or bear fruit fascinates me." She put one arm around Jase's waist. She was clutching a gift in her other. "Let's go."

"It's a party, Pamela. A celebration."

"Yeah. Someone might crack a smile."

"They're not that bad."

"They're worse." She put her finger on her lips to forestall any more discussion. "I'll be good."

"You'd better be."

He rang the bell. He had never lived in this house, so he didn't have a key or want one. Surprisingly, it was his father who opened the door.

"We were beginning to wonder if you were coming." Mr. Millington moved back to let them pass.

"Would we miss one of your wonderful parties?" Pamela asked.

Jase shot her a warning glance, but there was nothing except goodwill visible on Pamela's face. They exchanged minimal small talk before following their father into the garden room.

Dorothea Millington was watering a towering palm when they entered. She was a tall, thin woman with dark hair that she had not allowed to go gray, and hands whose hardest work was holding still for a manicure twice weekly. Her husband was even taller, broad-shouldered like his son and lean from regular workouts at a private gym. They would always be a striking couple.

"I was just about to tell Gladys to hold dinner," she said. She finished watering before she turned. "I do wish you'd let your hair grow out a little, Pamela. It's so wash and wear."

"Practical hair for a working woman. Happy Birthday, Mother." Pamela walked just close enough to hand her mother the gift. "No one will believe you're fifty-eight."

Jase got closer, but his mother was surrounded by a no-man's land into which one didn't intrude. He knew the boundaries. "Happy Birthday." He presented her with his gift. She leaned forward, and he kissed her cheek.

"I'll open these later. Gladys has already set out hors d'oeuvres, and your father made Manhattans."

Neither Jase nor Pamela drank Manhattans, but there was nothing to be gained from pointing that out again. Once Jase had wondered if his parents made Manhattans and graceless comments out of hostility. Now he realized their lack of tact was nothing more than self-absorption. Their world was narrow and comfortable. They had been born into affluence, and they had never balked at it the way he and Pamela had. They did not understand, could not understand, that there were others, most particularly their own children, who viewed the world differently.

He and Pamela accepted the Manhattans and exchanged more small talk. By the time they went into dinner, Pamela had been chided for not attending a benefit dinner for the Opera Society and he for allowing himself to be written up in the city magazine as one of Cleveland's most eligible bachelors.

Dinner was more pleasant, although Jase could not help comparing it to the party the night before at The Greenhouse. Here there were no streamers or balloons, and the dining room wasn't perfumed by the evening's menu. There was beef Wellington and steamed broccoli, and for dessert a chocolate almond torte purchased from an east side bakery. His mother ate only a few bites and looked askance at Pamela's seconds, although she refrained from comment.

They opened presents in the garden room over coffee. Jase's was an onyx brooch with a tiny spray of pearls, expensive, but not expensive enough to be considered in bad taste—the Millingtons didn't flaunt their wealth. Pamela's was an elegant black and white scarf from a Beachwood boutique. As usual, he and Pamela had not coordinated their gifts, but their gifts complemented each other perfectly. One year he had bought perfume and Pamela a crystal bottle to put it in. Another he had bought a blue cashmere cardigan, and Pamela had shown up with a silk shell of the same color to wear beneath it. They did not examine the phenomenon too closely.

"My children buy wonderful gifts," Dorothea said.

"Your children wish you the happiest birthday," Jase answered. He got to his feet, and Pamela joined him. "But I'm afraid I have to go now."

"Don't tell me you're working tomorrow."

"I am."

"It's Sunday, Jase. Neither you nor Pamela should be working on Sunday."

Jase knew his mother's comment stemmed less from religious fervor than from her dislike of her childrens' chosen professions. "Sometimes business can't wait."

"And people are still homeless on Sundays," Pamela said.

"It would be different if you needed these jobs."

"I need to do what I do, Mother," Pamela said. "And that reminds me, I need you to do something, too." Briefly, she outlined Jase's plan for turning the downtown factory into apartments. "Jase and I both think you would be the perfect person to head up our fund-raising committee. You know everybody in the city, and half of them owe you favors. You could make the difference between success and failure."

Dorothea's face was creased by unfamiliar wrinkles. "You want me?"

"Who better?"

"But I'm not even sure I approve of this project."

For one moment Pamela's face showed all her frustration, her hurt; then it smoothed into the expression that Jase had begun to think of as her family mask. Her voice was cold. "I suppose it's asking a lot to accept the fact that Jase is so flamboyantly successful that he can donate entire buildings on a whim, or that I'm mired up to my ears in trying to help people you'd rather I didn't even know, but that's what we are, Mother. And we'd like you to be with us on this. I hope you'll give it some thought."

Their father looked as if he thought he ought to object to Pamela's speech but wasn't quite sure why.

"What Pamela means," Jase said, smoothing the waters, "is that this is important to us, and we'd like to share it with you. But if you're not interested, maybe you can think of someone who might help."

"I don't know."

He nodded and took Pamela's arm. Firmly. "Don't worry. Just think about it." He said enough goodbyes to cover for Pamela's silence, then steered her through the house. At the door he kissed his mother's cheek and clapped his father on the shoulder.

He took Pamela to her car after the door had closed behind them. "Well, you almost got through the whole evening without a scene."

"You think that was a scene?"

"I know it wasn't the one you wanted to make. You're improving."

"I really don't hate them, you know. I just can't understand them! There's as much warmth in that house as in a North Pole igloo."

He watched her struggle for control. He had come to terms with his parents long ago, but he had been luckier than Pamela. As a boy, he had been granted more freedom. He had thrown himself into activities that took him away from home. Pamela had been kept on a tighter rein, and she had been exposed to her parents' rules and expectations until she had been forced to rebel or shrivel and die.

On the surface, their lives had been perfect, but the surface had been all there was.

He put his arms around her now. "It doesn't matter, does it?"

"No. Not unless I'm exposed to them for too long. Then the old longings start. Crazy, huh? I do therapy. I'm not supposed to need it."

"You just need a hug."

"And here you are giving it to me because they can't, and because there's no man in my life to do it. Both you and I are so afraid that if we meet someone and fall in love, we'll end up with a marriage like theirs."

He rejected the on-the-spot analysis, but in the same instant he thought of Becca. Why, he didn't know. "I'm not married because I don't have time."

"You're not married because you're afraid you'll go home to something like that. Both of us compensate all the time. I give other people the warmth and love I didn't get, and you reshape the world to your liking." She shook her head. "Don't listen to me. It's been a long, rotten day, and I'm wiped."

"Anything happen at The Greenhouse?"

"One of the residents' husbands drove back and forth for an hour and shouted obscenities until the police chased him away."

"Not . . . Mary's?"

"As far as I know, Mary doesn't have a husband." She paused. "Are you going to tell me your connection to Mary?"

He leaned against her car. "Mary Smith is Becca."

She sighed. "I figured that out last night when she took off after she saw you."

"I came to the house this morning to see her. She said she changed her name because Becca Hanks had three strikes against her."

"Do you know what that means?"

"I'd guess she has something to hide." He thought of the photograph of two little girls in pink overalls and wondered if they were part of what she was keeping secret. He had never mentioned the photograph to Pamela, and he didn't now. Becca had shared it in an unguarded moment, and she, like everyone in the world, was entitled to her privacy.

"Did she tell you she almost died in the hospital?" Pamela asked.

Something clenched inside him. "No. But she told me enough that I guessed."

"It was touch and go for a week. She had pneumonia, a particularly nasty variety. She was anemic, malnourished, dehydrated. You name it. She's a lovely person, Jase. I can see why you couldn't forget her. And so proud."

"That she is."

"We're having trouble getting her to rest and take care of herself."

"What can I do?"

Pamela joined him against the car. She folded her arms just as he had folded his. "She won't take anything from anybody."

"She's made that abundantly clear."

"What about a job?"

"What about one?"

"Do you have a job in Millington Development that she could do?"

He considered. Many of the jobs were highly technical, and many more required strength and stamina Becca just didn't possess. He could create a position in his office, but somehow he knew she would realize she wasn't really needed and decline. "I can't think of anything," he said. "And I think it has to be something she knows she's qualified to do, or she won't take it."

"You're probably right."

"Even if I found a way to hire her in a low level position, I don't know how she could afford housing." He wished the factory were already renovated. An apartment there would be the perfect start.

"She needs a live-in position. A job that comes with a place to stay."

"I don't need a housekeeper. I'm never home."

"Jase, what about Kathryn's house?"

Their grandmother's house was a subject Jase and Pamela usually didn't discuss. Kathryn Millington had been an eccentric, opinionated old woman, the heaviest cross their parents had been forced to bear. She had castigated her son for his stuffiness and choice of spouse until he had stopped allowing her in his home. Then, from a distance, she had taken her twin grandchildren under her wing and given them everything their parents had forbidden. She had greatly enlivened their childhood.

On her death, Kathryn had left Jase her home in Shaker Heights, a century-old Tudor with walls as thick as a fortress and two acres of elaborate gardens. Pamela had inherited Kathryn's summer home on Lake Erie in nearby Vermillion. Pamela lived there year round, one of the few privileges of wealth that she allowed herself to enjoy.

"What about the house?" Jase asked.

"Don't you think it's time to fix it up and move in? You've been promising you would for three years now."

Jase understood Pamela's attachment to the house. It had been a place of refuge. He was less attached, but still unwilling to sell it. He wasn't sure what the house represented to him, but it was more than an investment. "I'm happy where I am, and I haven't had time to do anything about renovations. What does this have to do with Becca?"

"Becca could supervise the renovations. She could live in the caretaker's cottage. And she could do the landscaping! The place is a jungle, but you've seen what she's done at The Greenhouse. What better recommendation do you need?"

Jase was only surprised that the idea hadn't occurred to him first. The cottage was four rooms, Tudor-style like the house, and quaint, to say the least. Through the years it had been used for guests or household staff, but it had always been called the caretaker's cottage. While the house would not be livable while it was undergoing restoration, the cottage would be more than comfortable.

He realized that if he said yes, he was making more than a commitment to help Becca. Once the house was fixed up, he would have to move in or sell. "Do you think she'd agree to do it?"

"I think she might. It would be something she can really do, and she knows we know it. It's nothing like charity. That's what she's afraid of."

He thought about having Becca so close by, so within reach. He could supervise her recovery, assure himself that she was really going to be all right. He didn't know why that was so important to him. Usually he left those sorts of commitments to Pamela. But this was one commitment he wanted to watch over himself.

"It would only be temporary," he warned. "There's a lot to be done, but it won't take longer than the summer."

"She'll be well by then, more able to cope."

"Can she handle it? Is she well enough?"

"She can handle it better than what the world has in store for her." Pamela faced him. "What do you think?"

"I think we've got a plan."

"You know this isn't like you, don't you? It's very personal, Jase. You'll be seeing her frequently. She'll be hard to ignore."

"Impossible," he amended.

"She's not like the women you know. You can't lose interest and write her off."

"This is hardly the same thing."

She looked at him as if she wondered. "Just tell me why you're doing it."

"Because I hate to see potential going to waste."

"She's not a city block you can level and replace with something new and flashy."

"Go home, Pamela."

She did, and he did, too. But on the way to his penthouse looking over the lake, he wondered what changes both he and Becca had in store for them.

Chapter Four

Among Kathryn Millington's eccentricities had been a reluctance to throw anything away. The house in Shaker Heights was still piled high with books and magazines. Every piece of first-class mail she had received was packed neatly in boxes. Every dress she had worn, every umbrella that had sheltered her gray head, every slipper that her five dogs had chewed, was still somewhere in the house. Each of the fourteen rooms held four times the amount of furniture it should, and when the house started bursting at the seams, she had begun to store things in the cottage.

When Jase unlocked the cottage door for the first time in the three years since his grandmother's death, he thought he was ready for what he would find. He had hired a cleaning service to dust and vacuum regularly, but there was only so much even the most conscientious could do when faced with total disarray. His work crew took one look at what awaited them and went for another pickup to supplement the one they'd driven there.

A day passed before the cottage floor and walls were visible, and two more before the most basic repairs had been made. It was a week before new paint graced the walls and cabinets, and another three days before new floors had been installed in the kitchen and bathroom. Not until that point did Jase feel that he could even bring Becca to see the house.

This time when he got to The Greenhouse, he didn't find her in the garden. She was in the kitchen by herself, working on a stew that looked to be nine-tenths potatoes, carrots and onions. It still smelled heavenly.

From the doorway he watched her work. She was humming as she stirred. Her hair was pulled into a tidy French braid, and she was wearing jeans and a man's flannel shirt. There was nothing boyish about the figure the jeans were molded to. The weight she had gained filled out all the right seams.

"I can see it's going to be hard to get you to leave that stew and go out to dinner with me."

She turned. The hand holding the spoon made slow, steady circles as she examined him. Finally she smiled. The smile disappeared quicker than it had come, but not quick enough to shortcut the leap in his heart rate. "I wondered if you'd come back."

"You didn't scare me away."

"I'll bet nothing scares you."

"I get scared when I think a woman is going to turn down a date."

"I'll bet you've never been turned down."

"There could be a first time."

"Sure could." She turned back to her stew. "This is my gramma's recipe. Only they're fresh out of rabbit and squirrel in these parts, so I had to make do with chicken."

"A pity." He moved closer, encouraged by that fleeting smile. "It smells good."

"You've never eaten stew in your life."

"Sure I have. Stew's not a have or have not issue. I've eaten everything. Name something I haven't eaten."

"Grass."

"Have you?"

"Close. Dandelion greens, poke salad, lamb's-quarter."

"My grandmother cooked dandelion greens with bacon."

"Expect me to believe that?"

"You'll believe it by the end of the night if you let me take you out for dinner and a short drive." He leaned against the counter beside the stove so he could see her face.

The rhythm of her stirring didn't change, but she was completely aware of him. Tonight he was the successful businessman who had come to dinner, the man who had almost made her drop a fifteen pound ham on the dining room floor. He was dressed in a dark suit, but he had removed his tie, perhaps to pretend he was "just folks."

He wasn't just folks. Since their last meeting she had learned everything she needed to know about him. Jase Millington was old money and brand new ambition. He was a ruthless businessman with one chink in his armor. He loved his sister unconditionally, and if Pamela told him to give money to The Greenhouse, he gave. If she told him to send a work crew, he sent. And if she told him to dress up like a homeless man to see how a growing minority of the population was forced to live, he dressed up.

Not without a fuss, she guessed. And not without some feeling that Pamela might be on to something. No one ordered this man to do anything he didn't believe in, not even his beloved sister.

She took her time answering him, because his invitation had caught her off guard. She had also learned he was good at that.

"Now, I'm from the country. You can tell that, I know. I didn't get a lot of education, and some that I got wasn't too good. But my daddy didn't raise any stupid young'uns.

And he taught me real early to ask myself why a man was being nice to me."

"What answer do you get this time?"

"Not the usual. Usually a man wants something I'm not inclined to give out. I'm sure you, in particular, have no trouble getting that in other places."

"Are we discussing my sex life?"

"No. We're discussing what you want from me. You want me to make you feel good. You want to do something for me so you can feel better about yourself. You feel sorry for me, and you don't want to."

"All those deep, dark motives behind a simple invitation to dinner and a drive?"

"Well?"

He took the spoon out of her hand and set it on the stove. Then he took her hand in his. "I do feel sorry for you. What kind of bastard would I be if I didn't?" He squeezed her hand when she started to interrupt. "No, let me finish. I feel sorry for the things you've had to go through, but I don't pity you. You'll find a way to make your life better with or without me. I don't know much about you, but I know that. The thing is, I could make that process a lot easier."

She pulled her hand away. "Thank you kindly. But I don't want your help."

He went on as if he hadn't been interrupted. "I could make your struggle easier, and at the same time you could make *my* life easier, too."

"How?"

"I think you'll have to see for yourself, so you'll know I'm not making any of this up. But I do need your help, Becca."

She couldn't imagine what Jase Millington needed from her. But he had found the one sure ticket into her life. He and his sister had already helped her immeasurably. If he even remotely needed something she could give him, she had to agree.

She picked up the spoon. "What kind of dinner are we talking about?"

He shrugged. "Whatever you'd like."

"I won't go anywhere fancy. I don't want you spending money on me."

"I'm not eating fast-food hamburgers just because you're too stubborn for anything else."

She held out the spoon. "Then think of a compromise while I change my clothes."

She was gone before he realized that he had been left with a kettle of stew to nurture.

Upstairs Becca found Shareen and told her where she would be going. Then she considered what to wear. Her new wardrobe was small, but attractive. As a child she had learned to quilt, as a teenager to sew her own clothes. She could take anything apart, cut it down to size and reassemble it so that it looked like a new outfit. The Greenhouse had a sewing machine, and she had altered donated clothes for herself and some of the other women. In exchange one of them had cut her hair and another, who had worked for years in a department store, had given her advice on the colors she should wear and the kinds of clothes that looked best on her.

Now she chose a plain peach sweater and a patterned turquoise skirt. The outfit was simple and attractive, but not nice enough for the kind of restaurant Jase Millington would normally frequent. She chose her low-heeled shoes to make certain she wouldn't look dressed up.

He was still stirring when she came back downstairs. For a moment she let herself admire him. He looked at home at the stove as only a perfectly confident man could. She couldn't imagine what would ever diminish Jase's masculinity. Even when she had believed him to be a drifter, even when she had been too ill to make sense of a senseless night, she had recognized his strength and allowed him to take control of her life.

She couldn't allow that again. She wasn't ill now, and he wasn't a drifter. He was a man with much of the world at his fingertips. If she let him, he would choose a corner of the world for her, and there would be nothing wrong with his choice. She already knew he would be more than fair. But she had to find her own corner, and she had to get there under her own steam.

"Did you think of a place?" she asked.

He turned. She watched his gaze drift from her newly brushed hair to her shoes. She felt a tingle at the wholly masculine assessment. Once men had thought her pretty. Dewey Hanks had chosen her to be his wife because she was the prettiest girl in Blackwater. Of course, there hadn't been a whole heck of a lot of competition.

By the time Jase's eyes were level with hers again, she knew he approved of her choice of clothing and possibly of more.

"Becca, you look very nice."

"Thank you. But what you see is what you're taking with you, so I hope you've come up with someplace where I'll feel at home."

"I thought we could give old Red another try." He smiled as her eyes narrowed. "A joke. Besides, I've heard Red sold his place. And not for much."

"I might work up some sympathy. In the next century."

"I'm never sympathetic on an empty stomach. Let's go."

She crossed the room and turned off the burner. Then she followed him outside to his car.

She wasn't sure what she had expected Jase to drive, but it wasn't the dark blue sedan he led her to. His car was Japanese, not European, and although it was top of the line, she guessed it was half the price of a more prestigious model. He opened her door, and she relaxed against the leather seats. They were as soft as butter, contoured for every curve of her body. She shut her eyes and cuddled in as Jase backed out of the driveway.

Jase didn't speak until he had wound his way through the maze of residential side streets and onto a main road. Then he glanced at Becca. "Do you like Greek food?"

Her eyes were shut, as if she were enjoying the quiet purr of the engine. When she didn't answer, he realized she was enjoying something else. Sleep.

She didn't rest enough. Pamela had warned him. Here she was, sound asleep the moment she sat down. He gripped the wheel and turned his eyes back to the road. Since Pamela had suggested putting Becca in charge of the renovations and landscaping at the Shaker Heights house, he had given little thought to his decision to do so. Now he wondered. Certainly the job was a better possibility than many. If she was waiting on tables or helping in a child care center, she would be on her feet most of the day. At his house she could rest whenever she felt tired. But would she? Or would she work so hard at any job that she would work herself right back into the hospital? Or worse?

He glanced at her again and shook his head. When she was sleeping she looked young, impossibly so. She looked defenseless and sweet and malleable—which proved the adage that looks could be deceiving.

She slept for the entire twenty minutes it took to get to Constantine's. He had parked and turned off the engine before she stirred. When she opened her eyes she didn't apologize or make excuses. "Where I come from, getting a girl this relaxed is the beginning of a locker-room fairy story."

"What if the girl's been sick and still isn't well?"

"Easier prey."

"When are you going to start taking better care of yourself?"

"Do you make a habit out of worrying about everybody you come across? How on earth do you stay rich? How do you sock it to people like Red?"

"How do you know I socked it to Red?"

"I didn't. Not until just now. You've got a great poker face. It's hard to tell what you're thinking. But there's this little hint of a smile sometimes when you're pleased with yourself." She searched his features. "And there it is. What did you do to the poor man?"

"Poor man?"

"I bet he's a poor man now."

"Not poor. Just not as rich as he might have been if he'd used his head. Red thought he was getting a great deal, but Red didn't do his research."

"And you did?"

"I made it my business to research his block."

"And?"

"When the office building next door decides to build a new parking garage, Red's Place will be sitting smack in the middle of it, unless I get the price I want."

"How do you know they're planning one?"

"I don't. They don't, in fact. But a little research proves they need one badly, and the only likely location is Red's. And since the same corporation also owns a nice little piece of property over on Euclid that I've been itching to own for two years now, I believe a trade will be in order."

"And you knew this when you went after Red?"

He opened his door. "No."

"You went after him just because of the way he treated you?"

He got out, but not before she heard his answer. "No, because of the way he treated you."

She was still mulling that over as he held the restaurant door open for her. Constantine's was red-checked tablecloths and starched white café curtains in the windows. There was a blackboard with the night's specials, and Chianti bottles at each table with well-dripped candlewax decorating the sides. The atmosphere was someone's version of Italian bistro, the piped-in music was appropriate for dancing the Russian bear, and a brief glance at the blackboard testified that Greek or plain old Midwestern American was the cuisine of choice. A glance at the right-hand column on the blackboard reassured Becca that Jase had taken her caution seriously.

"Come on and meet Constantine and Mama."

"Mama?"

"She has a name that no one can pronounce, and she likes Mama better, anyway."

Together Constantine and Mama weighed as much as a Thanksgiving turkey without the stuffing. They fussed over Jase as if he were their first-born son and seated him at the best table in the house, one looking directly over the parking lot.

"Mama likes you. Good," Jase said when Mama had left them to choose from the hand-scrawled menu.

"How can you tell?"

"She'd call you 'Miss' if she didn't. I've seen her do it before. Freezes a woman dead in her tracks."

"I risked that?"

"Mama has good taste."

She favored him with her second smile of the night. She was charmed by Mama and his choice of restaurant. She had already gathered that he ate lunch here often, and that much of the nitty-gritty business of Millington Development was conducted at this very table.

Without waiting for an order, Mama brought them each a Greek salad large enough to qualify as an entrée. "I'm not even growing enough lettuce to fill this salad bowl," Becca said when Mama was gone.

"Save some room for Mama's moussaka."

"You said there was something I could do for you."

Jase was only surprised that she had waited this long to remind him. "I'll show you after dinner. I promise." He watched her toy with a Greek olive. "Should I order you something else?"

"I just hate to eat it. It's so pretty."

He realized she was serious. He wondered when he had stopped paying attention to simple pleasures. "Mama's an artiste with feta cheese and tomatoes."

"You probably think I'm silly."

"No."

"It's just that . . ." She couldn't think of the right words to explain her feelings. Not in a way that wouldn't remind him of what she had endured. "Well, I guess I just appreciate food," she said, because she had to say something.

He was immediately aware of how little he appreciated it. "It tastes as good as it looks."

She sighed and dug in.

She was halfway through before Jase spoke again. "Becca, I had Pamela looking for you after you disappeared that morning. When you recognized me at The Greenhouse, she figured out who you were. She knows your real name."

"I know. We talked. Shareen knows it now, too."

"There's nothing that would shock them. Nothing they wouldn't try to help you with."

"Is this why you brought me here?"

"No. I'm just concerned."

"Don't be."

"You showed me a photograph. Remember?"

She remembered too well. The photograph was gone now, taken from her along with her purse. She had almost lost her life, as well, and for a few days it had hardly mattered to her. "I don't want to talk about that."

"I wish you'd let me help."

"I know you do. What I don't know is why. Why does this matter to you? I'm nothing. Nobody. Just somebody who drifted through your life once."

"You're Becca Hanks. Not Mary Smith, classic nobody."

"I'm Becca. And Becca has to figure out who she is and where she's going. And she has to do it on her own."

"On her own and alone are two different things."

"Maybe."

He realized she had left the door to her life cracked, but just barely. If he tried to storm his way through, the door would slam and never open again.

They talked about The Greenhouse until the moussaka came. Becca promptly asked for half of hers to be packed to take home. Mama refused, promising it was so good, Becca would find room for it somehow. She did, but there was absolutely no way she could manage the devil's food cake that was meant to finish the meal. That, Mama packed up. By that time, she and Becca were firm friends.

"She made me promise to bring you back again," Jase told Becca on their way to the car.

"Speaking of promises, is this where I find out what you want me to do for you?"

"I've never met anyone with less patience."

"Jase . . ."

He opened her door. "This is where you find out. Just give me a few minutes to get you there."

She was silent as they drove toward Shaker Heights. She didn't know much about Cleveland. When she'd still had her car, gas had been too expensive for sight-seeing tours. She had stayed away from the city's better residential sections because there had been no jobs there for someone like her. She knew they were headed for one of those sections now. The streets were wide and tree-shaded, the lawns as green as Jase's eyes, and the houses were stately.

"Do you live here?" she asked at last.

"Not yet."

"You're planning to?"

"I'm planning to live right here." He pulled into a driveway that ended well away from the street.

"This is a mansion."

"Not at all. It's a big old house that needs more work than it's worth."

"That's not possible." She got out of the car without waiting for Jase to come around to her door. "It's a castle."

"Well, it's Tudor design, but that's as close as it gets to being royal."

Becca wasn't sure where to look first. Even though the sun had set, she could see how wonderfully substantial the house was and how individual. This was not one house of many in an upscale development, constructed of particle board and decorative two-by-fours. It was built of stone and brick, with recessed windows of tiny diamond-shaped panes. There were four chimneys pointed toward heaven, and the heavy timbers gracing the upper story obviously had a purpose.

The house was surrounded by trees she wouldn't be able to stretch her arms around. Branches badly in need of pruning scraped the slate roof. The lawn had been mowed, but no one had adequately tamed the shrubbery—and there seemed to be acres of it—for a very long time. The house did not look abandoned; it looked as if no one loved it.

"You want to buy it to save it." She faced Jase, and she was smiling. "You saw it and realized how badly neglected it had been. So you want to buy it to save it. Who'd let a house like this one go? There should be people living here, kids laughing, dogs running through the yard, yappy little lap dogs with squashed-in faces." She gestured to one side. "There ought to be a garden over there. Probably is already, only somebody has to find it again. Can't you see it?

Roses and lilacs and iron tables with pitchers of lemonade? And croquet? This is a yard for croquet.''

He realized that this was the longest speech she had ever made. ''Croquet?''

''Don't sound so disgusted. It's a perfectly good game. We used to play it at church picnics and pie suppers when I was a little girl.''

He grimaced. He ran three miles a day and played tennis or racquet ball whenever he had time. But croquet was a game from another solar system. ''Would you like to see the inside?''

''Do you have the key?''

''I own the key.''

''Then you've already bought the house?''

Jase rarely felt guilty. He was too busy for guilt, and he had a core of beliefs he rarely strayed from, making guilt unnecessary. Why, then, had he begun examining his life so minutely since Becca had appeared in it? Why was he uncomfortable telling her the truth, that he had owned this house for years now and hadn't done a thing to it? That he hadn't bought the house to save it, but had been given the house on a silver platter and paid very little attention to the gift?

''I didn't buy it, Becca. It's my grandmother's house, or was. She left it to me some time ago, and I couldn't decide what to do about it. But I've decided to fix it up and move in.''

He hadn't been sure about the last part until he said the words. The house had to be fixed up even if he sold it. Now he'd made a commitment to keep the house, and he wasn't quite sure why.

''You mean it's been standing empty?''

''Yes.''

''How many rooms does it have?''

''Fourteen or so.''

"Fourteen rooms. Standing empty." She turned away from him and stared up at the house.

He owned an empty fourteen-room house while people slept in alleys and bus stations. He could see her thoughts just as clearly as if she were scrawling them on Constantine's blackboard. "Come on, I'll show you the inside."

She followed him, but he stopped at the brick walkway and held out his arm. "The path has to be leveled and redone. Hold on to me so you don't stumble."

She contemplated the arm, as sturdy and strong an arm as anyone had ever offered her. The man it was attached to was as strong a man as she had ever known. And his strength could be her undoing.

She took his arm and looked up at him, trying to read his expression. "Why are you showing me the house?"

"Give me a chance to explain. First, take a good look." Her fingers were so light against his arm that he could hardly feel them, but Jase knew they were there. He hadn't been this close to her since he had held her in his arms and felt her body convulse with coughing. He had slept an endless night with this woman, but they were still strangers.

"What am I supposed to be looking for?"

"Possibilities."

"I'm not sure I'm the best person for that. I've always believed everything was possible, and look where it's gotten me."

"It's gotten you here. Let's see where else it can take you." He started up the path. At the door she moved away from him, and he felt something very much like disappointment.

Inside he turned on the lights downstairs as Becca followed him. He said nothing, letting her form her own opinions. There were very few places to walk. Paths were cleared through each room, but furniture draped in plastic lined every wall and jutted out into the rooms. Boxes were piled in corners, some towering almost as high as the twelve-foot ceilings.

"Kathryn believed firmly in the waste not, want not, philosophy of life," he said when they reached the kitchen.

"Kathryn?"

"My grandmother. She detested titles. She was always Kathryn to us."

"There's enough furniture here to furnish three more houses like The Greenhouse."

"Some of it's priceless. Some of it I'll have to pay somebody to haul away."

"Can you tell the difference?"

"I'll have to hire somebody."

"Why haven't you done that before now?"

"I really don't know." And he didn't. Even now, talking about getting rid of Kathryn's things made him uneasy. "Do you want to see the upstairs? It's more of the same. Six bedrooms—seven, if you count the nursery—and plumbing so old I could sell it to the Smithsonian."

"Is the upstairs piled high, too?"

"Higher."

She leaned against a linoleum counter that had skipped kitchen redecoration fads as it gracefully flaked and peeled. "So why are we here?"

"If I'm going to renovate—and I am—I have to hire somebody to oversee the job. I'm not talking about the actual work. I'll use people I trust, and I'll check up on them from time to time. But somebody has to be here to be sure things get done, to answer phone calls, unlock doors, run errands if need be. Somebody's got to consult with the decorator, take messages, be sure I'm getting what I pay for. Up to that point, I just need a warm body with a brain and a finger to punch buttons on the phone. Beyond that point, I need someone who can help oversee the outdoor work, supervise landscaping crews—"

"Landscaping crews? Are you kidding, Jase? You're talking about those companies with the trucks filled with chemicals to kill everything in sight? I know what they'll do. They'll take one look at that jungle out there and pull out their chainsaws. You'll be left with some new seedlings they cart in from who knows where, and the yard will look like somebody scalped it!"

"Well, what do you suggest?"

"You don't need new landscaping. I didn't get to see everything—"

"You're right. You didn't. There are over two acres exactly as overgrown as what you've seen."

"That's even better. Somebody had a plan for this house. I could see that, even though it's dark outside. Somebody loved that yard. Under all those shrubs and vines and ground cover are gardens. They don't need a chainsaw. They just need a loving hand."

"Will you be my loving hand?"

She didn't speak for a moment. She'd had an inkling he was going to propose that she be the warm body with the button-punching finger and the brain, but she had gotten too worked up to realize he was leading up to asking her to do the landscaping, too.

The soil here would be rich and black. There would be lily of the valley. She just knew there would. And lilacs and mock orange, hydrangeas and rhododendrons. There would be perennial beds with day lilies and bleeding hearts and daisies. There would be places for annuals, and maybe even a vegetable garden with decade-old plantings of rhubarb and raspberries. Somewhere there would be a sturdy clematis vine twining its star-shaped purple flowers round a trellis. All hers to guide and design.

"Why?"

Jase knew the most decisive moment had come. Becca could not be fooled. If he was not perfectly honest with her, she would know, and she would refuse. If he *was* perfectly honest with her, she might still refuse.

"I'm trying to think of something to convince you," he said.

"How about the truth?"

"You need a job, preferably one that includes room and board. I need someone like you to live here and help get this property in shape. I could find someone else, but I don't see why I should bother. You're perfect for the job, and I trust you. If you let pride stand in your way, you'll be doing us both a disservice. But if you have another reason for not wanting it, just say no and I won't bother you again."

"Did you make up this job for me?"

He hesitated for a moment. "I don't know how to answer that. I was wishing I had a job for you, and Pamela suggested this. She's wanted me to fix up the house and move in since Kathryn died. I've put it off. I'm comfortable where I am."

"Where are you?"

"I have a condo on the lake. It's very different. Modern, efficient. Chrome and leather." She made a face, but he was encouraged. "Will you do it?"

"Where would I stay? In one of the bedrooms upstairs?"

"Nobody can live here while the renovations are going on. The house hasn't been painted in years, and I know the paint's lead-based. There'll be lead contamination when they scrape to repaint. And that's just for openers. It'll be dusty and dirty and inconvenient. Luckily there's an alternative. Would you like to see it?"

A few minutes later she stood in the newly painted living room of the cottage. She turned around slowly, taking in the stone fireplace and cherry mantel, the diamond-paned windows with the wide sills, perfect for African violets.

She thought of all the nights she had lived in her car and the endless nights she had lived in a worse place. With its antique furniture and floral print curtains, the little cottage was a slice of heaven. The room smelled of fresh paint and fresher air, and for a moment she was aware of a lump in her throat.

"You would more than earn what I pay you," Jase said. "And if I have to look for somebody else, it will take me longer to move in. The house shouldn't stand empty any longer."

The man knew how to push all the right buttons. "I can see why you're such a walloping success," she said.

"Will you do it?"

"You forgot to mention the chainsaws again."

"You're right. I'm manipulative, and I suffer from tunnel vision. When I want something, I go for it until it's mine." His gaze didn't leave her face.

For just a moment she wondered what Jase was like if it was a woman he wanted. The thought rippled down her spine.

"I'll do it," she said at last. "Soon as I'm done at The Greenhouse, and soon as I've trained someone there to watch over the garden. But only because I know there's no one who can do this better. I'm going to earn every penny you pay me." She paused. "What are you paying me, by the way?"

He named a sum that was more than fair, but she knew she was going to be worth it. "Okay. But when the job is finished, I leave. You can only invent so many things for me to do."

Since he knew that even the best work crews could find reasons to delay, he wasn't worried. The renovation was going to take just as long as it needed to. The house would be ready when Becca was well, and not a minute before.

He drove her back to The Greenhouse, but only after she'd had a moonlight tour of the grounds. He left her on the front steps talking to Shareen, but it was a moon-speckled wraith kneeling on the ground at the house in

Shaker Heights that he thought of as he drove home. As he'd watched her, Becca had pushed aside a thick mat of vegetation and peered into the darkness with a practiced eye. "Peonies," she'd said. "Peonies, Jase. And they'll bloom again once I've trimmed everything back so they get some sun. Imagine these peonies here all this time, just waiting to be reborn."

Chapter Five

Cara Preston had legs no company had enough assets to insure and breasts as perfect as a plastic surgeon's dream. She also had a breathy, quicksilver laugh she timed with the precision of a stand-up comic's punch line. Tonight the laugh was getting on Jase's nerves.

Cara's apartment looked over the lake with a view much like the one from his own. He had spent many pleasurable hours here. He had known Cara for two years, and he admired more than her impeccably constructed body parts. She was intelligent and ambitious, the vice-president and marketing manager of a Cleveland-based catalog company. Cara's plan for her life did not include a husband, at least not right away and not one rooted in the Midwest. She planned to serve out her time in Ohio, then move east to New York or Boston, where she would settle down to real success. In the meantime, she was content to enjoy a more-than-casual-but-not-truly-intimate relationship with him.

That arrangement had been more than satisfactory for Jase, too. They both saw other people. Sometimes they didn't see each other for a month or more, and he was hardly aware so much time had passed. When they were together they shared mutual interests and friends, but rarely their feelings.

Tonight Jase stood on Cara's balcony, a drink in one hand and Cara's hip in the other. They had gone out to dinner and shared a perfectly grilled rack of lamb and a lemon soufflé. Then they had gone to Severance Hall to hear the symphony. If the night followed classic lines, he would finish his drink, then Cara would lead him to her bedroom. He would leave her apartment in the early hours of the morning and finish the night's sleep in his own bed.

"You seem far away," she said.

"Do I?"

"You have all night."

"I guess it's been a busy week."

She moved away to freshen her drink. "You haven't said anything about your house. How is it coming?"

"Fine, I'm told. I haven't found the time to get by there often. I spent one afternoon going over the furniture with the appraisers."

"Didn't you say you're selling most of it?"

"That's what I'd planned, but now it looks like I'm keeping a houseful."

"Why? Was it worth more than you'd thought?"

"In a way." He thought of the afternoon he had spent with Becca and the appraisers. It had been one of those surprisingly warm spring days that sometimes occurred right on the tail of a frost. Becca had worn shorts, revealing legs that rivaled Cara's. He couldn't remember what she'd worn with them, but the shorts had definitely made an impression.

Ten minutes into the furniture tour, the appraisers were ignoring him and consulting Becca. He had hired a simple country girl to oversee his renovations—or so he'd thought—but the woman he had gotten knew volumes about antiques. More important, Becca had a feel for each piece, as if she had personally collected it. He'd had the strangest sense that Kathryn was in the room, nodding in satisfaction as Becca pointed out how perfectly a table fit into a nook or cranny, how wonderfully well a shelf fit in front of a window.

Of course, Becca had a ruthless streak that Kathryn had never had. By the time the appraisers arrived she had already cleared the house of much of its rubbish. Clothes, slippers and umbrellas had been given to The Greenhouse or thrown away, depending on condition. Phone books and magazines dating from the forties had also been culled. Kathryn's personal memorabilia had been sorted and boxed. Becca had saved all his grandmother's letters and thrown away all bills and junk mail. Now there was a manageable amount for him to go through with Pamela.

He still wasn't sure why he had given in to sentiment and refused to sell so much of the furniture. Without junk filling every corner, he had seen the majestic lines of the antiques, the patina from age and years of loving care, the tasteful beauty of the dark and light woods. Some he had sent to be refinished. Some he had just shifted into areas of the house that would be the last to be renovated. Perhaps the decision was only good sense. His collection of chrome and leather would be as out of place in the old Tudor home as a woman like Cara.

He glanced up at her and realized where his thoughts had led him. "Do you like antiques, Cara?"

She wrinkled her delicate nose. "I'm a tomorrow person. Not a yesterday."

"What would you do if someone left you an old house that needed thousands of dollars' worth of work?"

"Sell it to the highest bidder, contents included. Invest the profit in high-yield bonds."

"What if you were sentimentally attached to it?"

She laughed, and he felt another twinge of annoyance. "Not possible, dear. Don't you know me better than that?"

He did know Cara. He didn't know Becca. There was still much about her that had never been revealed. But he did know how Becca valued the past. He had watched her touch his grandmother's furniture, watched her discuss the merits of each piece with the appraisers. Briefly he wondered what Cara would do if she suddenly found herself penniless, with no place to live and no job to go to. Would she show Becca's courage and determination to succeed on her own?

He didn't know Becca, but she occupied his thoughts more and more. And Cara and the other women he knew occupied them less.

Cara put down her drink and slipped her arms around his waist. "I always thought we were two of a kind, Jason. But maybe I don't know you as well as I thought. Sentimentally attached? The man I thought I knew didn't have an ounce of sentiment anywhere in his body."

He set his drink down, too, and put his arms around her. "Not an ounce? You don't think I'm sentimentally attached to you?"

"Truth?"

"Truth."

"I think when I move to New York, you'll forget you ever knew me."

He pulled her closer and laid his cheek against her dark hair. But when Cara suggested they go inside, he remembered that he had an early appointment in Toledo the next day. The evening ended sooner than either of them had planned, and Jase, at least, didn't regret it.

Among other things, Becca's car needed a new transmission, brake pads, four new tires and a body job. Jase's me-

chanic went over the car thoroughly and grumbled when
Jase didn't take his advice to sell it for scrap.

Becca didn't know that Jase had paid her fines, and he
didn't plan to tell her until the work on the car was completed. So far she had shopped for necessities by bus and on
foot, but he knew that not having a car was a major incon-
venience. If she had waited until she could afford the fines
and the work herself, it would have been months before she
had transportation.

The afternoon the car was ready, he drove it to Shaker
Heights himself. It sputtered a little, almost as if it was
surprised to be moving again, but halfway there it settled
down to burning oil and guzzling gas. He parked on the
street in front of the house. He planned to gently ease Becca
into the subject of her car, then inch her toward the street.
He doubted she would make a scene in public.

Two weeks of concentrated man—and woman—hours
hadn't made too many changes in the exterior of the house,
but the yard was already showing signs of Becca's efforts.
She had deigned to allow an arborist and crew to prune
trees and large shrubs, but she had directed every swipe of
the saw and clippers. There were signs that beds were being cleared and edged, also under her direction. The result
was a pleasing trim and not the military crew cut that had
so worried her.

Inside the changes were more evident. In the front of the
house, floors had been sanded and sealed, new wiring installed and walls scraped and replastered. There were still
sections where woodwork had been removed for refinishing, but the rooms were taking shape. He talked to a man
who was repairing the fireplace and another who was re-
moving a chandelier. The mystery of where the rest of the
crew had gone was solved by a third man who was heading
out the kitchen door toward the cottage. Jase followed him.

He heard laughter when he was still twenty yards away.
The cottage door was open, but he heard men's voices. He

stopped in the kitchen doorway and watched four men get the scolding of their lives as Becca poured them coffee.

"Now I'm telling you good gentlemen, I might not know much about wiring walls or putting in a floor, but I do know that buying lottery tickets with your hard-earned money is no way to get rich quick!"

"Come on, Becca," a man Jase knew as Roy said as he held out his cup for more. "We're each putting in ten dollars. That's not our life savings. Besides, with six of us doing it, that gives us sixty chances at the pot each week. This week the pot's twelve mill. Split twelve million six ways, and that's still a whole lot of cash."

"More likely a whole lot of nothing. You're throwing your money away. If you put ten dollars into the bank every week, you'd have over five hundred dollars in a year's time. That's a couple of weekends away from the young'uns with your wife."

"You haven't seen my wife." Roy held up his hands. "Okay, okay. But I'm a gambling man. If it's not the lottery, it's the races or betting on the ball game. I'm going to hit it big someday. I know I am."

"Don't be handing in your resignation too quickly," Jase said. "Jobs where you can sit and gab all day don't come along too often, even when you've won the lottery."

The men grumbled, but they stood, snatching pieces of coffee cake from a plate in the middle of the table before they filed past Jase on the way back to the house. They were all gone by the time Becca spoke.

"They weren't goofing off. They work hard. I'm a terrible hard taskmaster. This was the first break they've had all day."

"I've heard what a taskmaster you are. Word filters up to the top."

"They grumble a lot, and sometimes they get fresh. But they keep on coming back every day."

Jase reached for a piece of cake and took Roy's seat. Becca had coffee in front of him before he could ask for it. "I hear you won't let them cuss."

"I sure won't."

"I hear you climb ladders when they're done to inspect every little detail."

"I pretend. Half the time I couldn't tell bad work from good."

He sipped his coffee. It was the best he'd had all day, including a cup in one of the city's finest restaurants. "I hear they're telling you the stories of their lives."

"They've had interesting lives."

"They've gotten a lot done. You've gotten a lot done." He studied her. She was dressed in pale green, just a T-shirt and skirt, but she looked as fresh as spring. As the sun tanned her face and arms, it bleached her hair to the color of wheat. She no longer looked tired or drawn. He realized that he hadn't heard her cough since the day he'd confronted her at The Greenhouse.

"I haven't gotten nearly enough done, Jase. I work and work, but this is a major project."

"I don't want you to work and work. I'm not paying you to slave. Take your time. I haven't even put my condo on the market yet. I'm not in any hurry to move."

"I don't want to take advantage of you."

"I'm taking advantage of you. Can't you tell the difference?"

She poured herself a cup of coffee and sat down across from him. "I've been thinking about what you said last time you were here."

He admired the curve of her wrist as she lifted the cup to her lips. There was nothing studied about Becca's movements. There was none of Cara's languid grace, nothing to indicate she had ever thought about what a man might find attractive. She moved with purpose, each gesture the shortest distance between two points, yet watching her gave him a deep satisfaction.

"Jase?"

"What did I say?"

"About the yard. What you wanted me to do."

He tried to remember that conversation. "I wanted it to be practical, easy to keep up."

"That's right."

"And?"

"Well, if I give you what you asked for, I'll have to dig out everything your gramma spent her life planting and start all over again."

"As a master at using guilt, I recognize it when I hear it."

"Lord, I'm not trying to make you feel guilty. It's your house, even if it did used to be your gramma's heart and soul. And so what if a whole lot of thought and work went into it? If all you're interested in is a yard that a lawn service can mow and edge and maybe trim twice a year, you can sure have it. Only I can't give it to you."

"You can't?"

"No. I've tried. The first day I had a chance to work in the yard I walked over to that bed of peonies we found, and I told them they had to go because they were going to bloom, and Jase Millington the Whatever doesn't want flowers."

"I don't?"

"Don't you?"

He had a fleeting vision of his parents' house. "I never said that."

"Well, you said easy upkeep, didn't you? Flowers take work, Jase. No lawn service is going to do flowers. You'd have to have a gardener come in, or you'd have to get your own hands dirty."

He backtracked. "Just what did the peonies say when you told them?"

"They said thank you, but they'd been there a lot longer than you have, and they weren't going to move out. I reasoned, but by the time I'd weeded a little, they'd convinced me."

"They sound persuasive."

"Little red shoots coming up all over and not a thing I could do about it." She got up to refill his cup.

Becca always seemed to be in motion. He liked the way her skirt skimmed her hips and backside. All that purpose gave her the nicest little wiggle. "I guess the peonies will have to stay," he said.

"See, the problem is they started a rebellion. They've got all the perennials on their side."

He liked the way she said "p'rennyawls." He was beginning to wish he had spent more time in Kentucky. "A rebellion?"

"I tried to dig up one of your gramma's perennial beds. Same thing happened."

"One of the beds?"

"There are a mountain of them, Jase. Your gramma was fond of perennials. See, I think she liked things that lasted, things that she could pass on to the people she loved."

"When you're done with this job, I'm going to give you a new one collecting all the money I'm owed."

"I'm not trying to change your mind. I'm just reporting."

"Let's hear it all."

"Do you like the cake?"

He hadn't had a chance for a bite. Now he ate a piece while she watched him intently. It was wonderful, sweet and sour with a flavor that was vaguely familiar. "What is it?"

"Rhubarb cake. And guess where I got the rhubarb?"

He supposed it hadn't been at the store. "Kathryn did grow rhubarb. I remember it now. And she made pies, or rather, someone made them for her. Whenever we could sneak over here in the spring, she'd feed us rhubarb pies."

"Sneak?"

"My parents thought Kathryn wasn't good for us. Rhubarb, either. It needed too much sugar to make it edible."

"Why, that's terrible! Family not good for you?"

"What about your family, Becca?"

"All dead." She toyed with a fork, the first time she had purposely looked away from him since he'd sat down at the table.

His stomach clenched. "The little girls in the picture, too?"

"I meant the family I came from. Parents, grandparents. I had an older brother killed in a fire on a navy ship and another in Beirut. The service was their ticket out of... the town where we grew up."

The knot in his stomach eased, but he knew better than to ask about the children again. "What did you find besides rhubarb?"

"Raspberries."

"Kathryn made jelly. We were only allowed to eat it here."

"And asparagus."

"I refused to eat it. She rolled it in sugar once to make me taste it."

"Do you like it now?"

"If I say yes, am I going to inherit an asparagus patch?"

"You did inherit one. You just have to decide if you're going to sow it over with worthless old grass seed."

"What else?"

"Well, just the most important thing of all." She stood again and took his cup, although it was half full.

He leaned back in his chair and watched her clean up the other cups and take them to the sink. She ran water in a dishpan and added detergent and dishes instead of stacking the dishwasher. He had never found dishwashing intriguing before. She was much more fun to watch than a machine.

"You use guilt like a pro, and now you've added suspense to your repertoire," he said when she was almost finished.

"And you're a waiting champion."

"I can wait forever if I have to, but I never have to."

"Have you always gotten everything you wanted?"

"No. I can't get you to take it easy and stop buzzing around here like a workaholic bee."

"Then maybe we've both met our match." She was silent for a moment, as if she were listening to her own words. "I mean, in terms of stubborn."

He couldn't see her face, but he could almost swear she was blushing. She *sounded* like she was blushing. "I have no match. You're a beginner compared to me."

She dried her hands on a dishtowel and faced him. If she had been blushing there were no traces. "Let me show you what stubborn is, Jase."

"You can try."

She favored him with one of her rare smiles and nearly bowled him over. She smiled so seldom that each time he noticed just what a cataclysmic experience it was. She was a pretty woman, but when she smiled, damn it, when she smiled she was absolutely radiant. He had the strangest feeling he didn't know her at all.

"You might get your feet wet and your hands dirty," she taunted, still smiling.

"My butler and valet will clean me off when I get home."

"You don't have a butler. Nobody in the whole U. S. of A. has a valet. Except when they park."

"How do you know?"

"My vast acquaintance with rich folks." She threw the towel on the counter. "Ready?"

"For anything."

Anything was the side of the house that had inspired visions of yappy little dogs and endless croquet games. Becca and Jase passed under a weeping willow tree that Jase had fallen out of once at age eight and through a slim gap in a newly clipped boxwood hedge. "What do you see?" Becca asked before Jase had even made it to the other side.

"More yard. A buildable lot or two. If I had a mind to do it and it was zoned accordingly, I could probably put two houses here."

"Don't even think about it!"

He didn't point out the irony of her response. If anyone understood how desperately housing was needed, Becca should. On the other hand, anything he would build in this neighborhood was not going to help the homeless. "What was I supposed to see?"

"Look around."

There were very few people he would waste so much time for. But this was Becca asking. He shook his head as he skirted the area. At the border of his property he found a deep, wide bed, newly weeded and layered with cypress chips. Thorny shrubs clipped a foot or two above ground level were beginning to sprout branches and leaves. "This?"

She slapped her hands on her hips. "Don't you know what they are?"

He tried to remember what Kathryn had grown here. There had been a swing in the corner by the boxwood, an old-fashioned porch swing hanging from a wooden frame. And there had been a table to hold lemonade and picture books. Once a bee had stung him. There had always been swarms of bees because of the roses.

"Roses."

"Good for you." She came to his side. "Jase, I can't dig these up. I really can't. Regular roses take a lot of work. I know they do. They have to be babied to grow, fertilized and sprayed for bugs and leaf spot and mold. But these aren't regular roses. They're the old-fashioned kind, the kind that grew in gardens all over the world for centuries before somebody started dickering around to make them bigger or prettier.''

"How do you know? They're sticks in the ground right now. Sticks with thorns, the worst kind.''

"Because they're still here. Nothing's still here that wasn't hardy. Your gramma's been dead for three years now. And all anyone's done to this yard is cut the grass and cut off a branch or two that hung too low. That's it. Anything that needed care is gone now. But the roses are still here. Nobody fertilized or sprayed. They made it through the winters without being mulched or protected. I pruned them back a lot, because they were going wild, but look how they're taking off again. They'll be beautiful when they bloom, Jase, the centerpiece of the yard if you don't dig them up.''

He sensed more than just a passion for gardening in her plea. "Where did you learn so much, Becca?''

She turned back to the roses, squatting to smooth the mulch. "My gramma had old roses, too. Some of them came over to this country with her grandmother, from England. She tended them like they were her babies, only they don't need much tending, so mostly she just talked to them because she loved them so much. She told me stories about them.''

"What kind of stories?''

"There was one I remember, a poem, about a man, Sweet William, and the woman, Fair Margaret, who loved him. William married another woman, and it broke Margaret's heart. On his wedding night she appeared to him in a terrible dream, and he, being sure it was a bad omen, went to her house and found her dead.''

"I hope this ends happily.''

"Mercy no. He was so sorry for what he'd done that he lay down and died from it. He was buried beside Margaret.''

"I thought this was about roses?''

"It is. The story says that out of Margaret's breast sprang a rose, and out of William's, a briar. I still remember the next part exactly. 'They grew till they grew unto the church top, And then they could grow no higher; And there they tied in a true lovers' knot, Which made all the people admire.'"

"There have to be happier stories."

"There are. But even better I remember a little game we played. Every summer I'd go to Gramma's house in the morning and help her with the chores she couldn't do alone. Then, when we were done, we'd take iced tea out to the rose garden and look for one perfect rose. We never found one. There'd always be a petal that was bruised, or maybe a bee had spread pollen over a petal and turned it yellow. Some were too big, some were too small. Some weren't white enough or red enough. Never a perfect one. But it didn't matter. They were all wonderful, every single rose. Gramma used to say the roses tried harder for us because they knew we were going to look at them every day."

"My grandmother loved these roses, too."

"I know she did. I can feel it." She stood and wiped her hands on her skirt. "The roses just want a chance to grow, Jase. That's all. They don't want to be fussed with or interfered with. They just want a chance."

Just like Becca. He was not oblivious to the parallel. Becca wanted a chance. That was all. No fuss, no interference. A chance to grow and flower, and maybe someday to produce one perfect rose.

"How could I dig them out?" he asked. She was standing within touching range, and it seemed the most natural thing in the world to touch her. He picked a boxwood sprig from her hair, and his hand lingered there when the sprig was gone. Finally it dropped to his side. Her gaze had never left his face. She seemed to be holding her breath, waiting for something to happen. He knew the feeling.

"Then they can stay?" she asked.

"I wouldn't want it any other way. Will you teach me what I have to know to take care of them?"

"Just visit them every day. That's all. They'll do the rest if you let them."

"I don't think . . . that will be hard."

"Thank you." She reached for his hand and squeezed it, then dropped it immediately. "I'd hoped you'd understand."

"I think I understand too well."

She didn't ask him what he meant. She just smiled again. He felt the impact for the rest of the day, even when he was miles away.

Chapter Six

Jase visited the roses as frequently as he could. They grew inches every day, sturdy and thriving. Becca didn't grow inches, but she thrived, too. Sometimes he and Becca were so surrounded by workmen that they hardly had a chance to speak; sometimes he caught her alone and got a private tour of the work on the house or grounds. Inside, the work was progressing faster than he had planned, but outside it was moving slower. Reclaiming the gardens and the lawn was a lengthier process than digging up and replanting would have been, but since his intention was to keep Becca on the payroll as long as possible, both her stubbornness and perfectionism suited him.

On the Saturday of Memorial Day weekend, Jase spent the morning having brunch at Pamela's house in Vermillion, along with his parents. His mother had agreed to organize the party to raise funds for converting the abandoned factory into apartments, and talk of the gala evening dominated the conversation. For once she and Pamela were not at odds, and the morning passed pleasantly enough.

Jase drove almost all the way home before he realized he had no other plans for the day. Cara had invited him to take the ferry to Put-in-Bay on Sunday to visit friends who were opening their island home for the summer, but the rest of this day was his. No one was working, and although there was always paper to push, a holiday weekend seemed no time to push it.

Briefly he considered going home to begin the process of deciding what he would take when he moved and what he would sell or give away. He had a collection of contemporary art chosen almost entirely by a former woman friend who had owned a small gallery, and he couldn't imagine it hanging on the walls of the house in Shaker Heights. He had never loved any of it—although for a while he had thought he loved the woman—and he imagined that Marnie would be glad to sell it again and make them both a profit.

The late spring sunshine heated his car, and with his windows down to catch a breeze, he could hear the shouts of children and the screeching of crows. He couldn't imagine cooping himself up inside his penthouse. The sun was too bright and the air too magnificent. He wondered what Becca was doing on this nearly perfect spring day. He could almost imagine her in the side garden near the roses, drinking lemonade and watching the world go by.

The picture appealed to him. After changing lanes, he chose the exit that would take him to his grandmother's house. He supposed that soon he was going to have to start calling the house and the exit his.

When he reached the house he parked in the driveway. There was a truck at the far end, but Becca's car was nowhere in sight. She had fussed about the car repairs, just as he'd known she would, and demanded that he take fifteen dollars a week out of her salary to cover the cost. But she had opened the trunk immediately to be sure her few possessions were still there. Nothing had been removed, and the look of pleasure on her face had been all the gratitude he'd needed.

He went to the cottage first to find that the door was locked. Inside the house he encountered the owner of the truck, a plumber who was obviously using the quiet Saturday to finish some work. Jack Ferris looked as out of sorts as a man could look.

"Even I don't expect people to work on a holiday weekend," Jase said.

"Every time I turned off the water to fix this, somebody complained. I got sick and tired of hearing them—" He looked around, as if he expected to see his mother standing in the doorway, hands on her hips.

"Complain?" Jase suggested.

"Yeah. So I came in today. Nobody around here to...complain today."

"Becca's not here?"

"Nah. She left yesterday, after everybody but me was gone for the day."

"Did she say when she was coming back?"

"Nah. Just that she wouldn't be here today, so she gave me a key."

Jase went back to his condominium to begin sorting his possessions and settled for a lonely whiskey and water instead of lemonade with Becca.

For the next twenty-four hours he wondered where she might have gone. He sat with Cara on the deck of their friends' island home and considered that Becca might have run away. If so, from what? He knew little about her, not nearly enough to put clues together, but obviously something had driven her to Cleveland. Could the same force, benign or malignant, have driven her away?

He smiled and chatted with his friends. He strolled around downtown Put-in-Bay, a tiny town preparing itself for an onslaught of summer visitors, and helped Cara choose a birthday gift for the mother she rarely saw. But Becca was in the back of his mind the entire day. By the time he dropped Cara off at her apartment and pleaded another early morning appointment as an excuse not to linger, the sun had gone down.

He wasn't far from the house in Shaker Heights. Ten minutes and he could be there. He weighed the peace of knowing Becca was all right against the guilt of knowing he was checking up on her. She owed him no explanations. She was doing a wonderful job of watching over the renovations and landscaping the yard. No one could, or should, work constantly without a break. If she had gone somewhere, she had the perfect right. There was no reason why she should have consulted him.

Ten minutes later he was at the cottage.

Becca wasn't there; the absence of her car in the driveway was the only proof he needed. Still, he parked and unlocked the cottage door. Inside, the three rooms were as neat as a museum. Not a piece of furniture was out of place. The first roses of the season in a vase on the table were still fresh; the faint scent of fresh-baked bread lingered in the air.

He went from room to room looking for proof that she would be returning. Some of her clothes were in the closet, but not the peach sweater and turquoise skirt, and not the spring green outfit she had worn the day she had told him about the roses. She hadn't taken the book beside her bed, a four-inch-thick encyclopedia of gardening, or the notebook with diagrams of the house and yard.

But why would she have taken them if she never intended to come back?

He wondered why he hadn't pushed harder to learn more about her past. As it was, he knew nothing about her except her name and the state where she had been raised. Was Hanks a married name or the name she had been born with? He might be able to trace her if Hanks was her maiden name, but even then he didn't know if Becca was short for Rebecca or if it was a name indigenous to the area of Kentucky that she came from.

A more important question was why he cared so much.

He settled himself in a comfortable armchair and put his feet up on a matching hassock. Becca wasn't there, but the same imagination that conjured visions of skyscrapers where vacant lots stood brought her to life for him. He remembered the first time he had seen her. She was hardly the same woman now. Along with gradually blooming health and beauty, her spirit had bloomed, as well. The same qualities that had ensured her survival made her a woman worth knowing. She had maintained her independence in the face of all odds. She was intelligent, lively, not afraid to speak out for what was important to her. She was not afraid of him.

And why should she be? Who had he become? He wasn't sure, but he knew who he wasn't. He wasn't Jason Millington, hard-nosed developer with a bad case of tunnel vision and a worse case of self-righteousness. Somehow, somewhere, his view of the world had changed. It no longer consisted entirely of skyscrapers and million dollar deals. Now it included people and causes and a house he had never expected to live in. It included Becca.

From the table his grandmother's roses were sweetly fragrant. The scent brought back memories of the lazy summer afternoons of his childhood, and he shut his eyes to enjoy it.

Becca pulled her car into the driveway beside a dark sedan. Late at night, distinguishing features were at a premium. The car looked like Jase's, but she couldn't be sure. What reason would Jase or anyone have to be here at this time of night? Jase certainly had a right to be at the house anytime, but she doubted he had used the weekend to move in. The repairs weren't completed, and he wasn't given to impulsive actions. When he moved, it would be according to a well thought out timetable.

She got out of the car reluctantly. She doubted anyone who meant her harm would park in the driveway, but the night was dark, and she was too exhausted to think sensibly. At best she suspected a confrontation ahead, and all she really wanted was sleep.

She checked the house first, although she refused to climb the stairs and check the bedrooms. She called Jase's name, but when there was no answer, she locked the doors behind her and went to the cottage.

In the living room she empathized with the shock of the three bears who had found Goldilocks asleep in Baby Bear's bed. No porridge had been touched here, but there was obviously a stranger asleep in her house. Except, of course, that this particular cottage belonged to the stranger, who wasn't really a stranger at all.

Jase didn't wake when she approached him. He was dressed casually, as if he had spent the day somewhere other than his office. From the knees down, his legs were bare, and she admired the tanned, muscled length of them before she turned her eyes to his face.

His hair fell over his forehead boyishly, but there was nothing else boyish about Jase Millington the Whatever. Even asleep he looked exactly like what he was, a one-step-from-ruthless businessman, the modern version of a riverboat gambler whose luck with the cards was legendary.

She moved closer. "Jase?"

He stirred, but he still didn't wake up. She touched his shoulder. "Jase?"

His hand covered hers, and his eyes opened. He smiled, and the slow, sleepy grin was like a caress. "Becca?"

"Well, who else did you expect to find here?" She knew she should remove her hand, but it didn't seem to want to drop back to her side. Before she could give it an order,

Jase stretched his other hand toward her. She felt it slide along her waist and press against the small of her back.

"You're here."

"That seems obvious."

He pulled her closer. "Not obvious enough."

She resisted, but only long enough to make a decision. Then she was in his lap and in his arms. She had never dared imagine what it might feel like to have Jase hold her again. Even before he had come back into her life, she had buried her memories of the man who had protected her from the cold, memories of his arms around her, the warmth of his body against hers.

Jase's hand slid up her back, and she knew that the memories had never been buried at all. He felt familiar, but familiar was oh-so-different from ordinary. He felt like a thousand promises and a million dreams. Her body resonated in ways she had forgotten it could. Every place he touched absorbed his heat, until it felt as if he were touching her all over.

He lowered his mouth to hers, and she lifted hers to meet him. His lips were as warm as his hands, and as tempting. Her lips parted. His parted, too, and the kiss became a slow dance, a prelude to something yet to come.

Only when his hand spread welcome heat to her breast did she pull away. In the dim lamplight his eyes were the green of a tumultuous sea. She gazed at the man who had given her so much and knew she could not take another thing from him.

She slid off his lap, and he didn't try to stop her. But when she tried to walk away, he stood and took her arm. "It's time, don't you think?"

"Time?" She played for more of it.

"You don't owe me any explanations about where you went. I'm not buying explanations when I pay your salary. But I was worried about you."

"You shouldn't have been."

"But I was." He touched her chin, hoping to make her look at him. "I care about you. I guess I just made that known."

"You were half asleep. Maybe you thought I was somebody else."

"Maybe I didn't."

"I think you'd better go home."

"Why did you pull away?"

She still hadn't looked at him. "Things were getting out of control."

He touched her chin again. This time she complied. "No, they weren't. I could show you what out of control means, Becca."

Her eyes widened, and he knew she was seeing the same visions that he was. "Things can't get out of control," she said at last. "You don't know me, Jase. You only think you do."

"I can only know you if you let me."

She stared up at him and realized she had no choice. Jase had cared for and about her in a way that no man ever had. She owed him the truth about herself, even if it meant that he would see her differently afterward.

She turned away. "I'll make coffee."

"It's the middle of the night."

"I'll make tea." She started toward the kitchen. He followed close behind.

"I'm going to tell you a story," she said, refusing to look at him again. "It's not very pretty, and it's not easy to tell. But you should hear it."

"It never occurred to me that your story might be pretty. Pretty stories don't have chapters like yours did."

"No. I guess not." She heard the slide of a chair and knew he was sitting at the table. She ran water into the tea kettle and set it on the burner. She prepared the teapot before she spoke.

"I come from a place called Blackwater. Ever heard of it?"

"No."

"'Course not. Nobody's heard of Blackwater. I don't know why I asked."

"Maybe to make the story easier."

"Maybe. Anyway, I was born and raised there. My mother died early on, and my father raised me and my brothers. He worked in a coal mine, and he died from it, choking and coughing until there wasn't any room for air in his lungs. I was seventeen. My brothers were gone by then, and one of them was already dead. So I went to live with a cousin of my mother's who lived on the other side of town. I'd always wanted to go to college. Our school wasn't good, but I was a good student, made straight A's except in gym. I never could serve a volleyball."

He heard pride when she reported her grades, and he was touched by it. "I'm sure you were the kind of student any teacher wishes she had."

"Matty, my cousin, was good to me. Don't think she wasn't. She had three kids of her own that needed watching, but she never once took advantage of my being there. She and her husband didn't have much, and I strained what little they did have. Matty wouldn't touch the money I got from the mining company after Daddy died. She wanted me to save it all for college and be somebody. I'd wanted that, too, only after Daddy was gone, I didn't seem to want it as much. I was sad, and I stopped working so hard in school."

"But it was natural to be sad, Becca. Your whole life had changed."

"Well, I went and changed it again. I stopped wanting to leave Blackwater. It seemed like the only place for me. After Daddy died, everything was different, but Blackwater was still the same. There was a man, Dewey Hanks, who wanted me to stay, too. Dewey was the son of Bill Hanks, the man who owned the Hanks Hardware Store, and he was about five years older than me. The Hanks were good people, church-going and upstanding, but Dewey was wild. When you're seventeen you want somebody wild, because you think you can tame him.''

"And did you?"

She busied herself with the tea. The kettle had boiled, and she took her time pouring water over the tea bags. She only spoke when the lid was back on the pot.

"Nobody could have tamed Dewey, only I was too sure I was 'somebody' to realize that. I thought I had something special, some kind of magic that would make him quit drinking and running around with his buddies. Dewey told me I did. We ran off and got married, and I quit school at the beginning of my senior year. Matty cried for two days, and Bill and Alice, Dewey's parents, like to have had a fit. But they got used to the idea after a couple of weeks and let us move in with them. Dewey said it was only going to be temporary. He was going to find us a place of our own just as soon as he got a better job than the one he had at his father's store.''

Jase watched her fill a plate with gingersnaps. He had no intention of eating even one, but he knew she needed something to do with her hands. "So far nothing you've said is much of a shock, Becca. Girls . . . women make mistakes like you did all the time. That's what divorce is about.''

"I didn't divorce Dewey." She set the gingersnaps in front of him. "He tried to be a good husband at first. We worked together in his father's store. Bill had had a heart attack a year before Dewey and me got married, and he never recovered the way he was supposed to. He let Dewey take over the store a little at a time, until finally there was hardly a day in the week when Bill was there for more than an hour or two. But as soon as Dewey realized everyone was counting on him, he just kind of went crazy. It was like the pressure was too much. He started staying out nights. Sometimes I didn't see him for days at a time. I worked at the store, trying to hold things together and making excuses for Dewey, but his parents knew something was wrong."

"You were still living with them?"

"We had a little apartment on the side, in the old carport. They'd come visiting, and they'd ask where Dewey was. I'd tell them he was out running errands or fixing something at the store. They got so they didn't believe me, of course, but at first they did. They wanted to so bad, that at first they believed anything I said. By the time they stopped believing, things were really awful. When Dewey was at the store, he made mistakes. He could never figure how to use a cash register, and when he'd come in after a drunk, he'd push more wrong buttons than right. It got so coming to Hanks Hardware was better than going to the bank.

"And that was just one thing. He'd forget to order things. Then, if I wanted to keep customers satisfied, I'd have to drive over to the next town and buy whatever they wanted retail, come back and sell it for the same price. Sometimes he'd just take whatever was in the register and leave. We weren't making money, and Dewey was as good as giving away or stealing what we had. Some days he'd be so charming customers would stay and gab with him for hours. Some days he'd be so rude, they'd swear they were never coming back."

Jase was getting a clear picture of the man Becca had married, but one thing was still unclear. "You said you didn't divorce him. Are you still married?"

She shook her head. "After we'd been married almost a year, two of the mines in the area shut down. People started moving away to find new jobs. By that time Bill knew what had been going on. He figured if he didn't go back to work, between Dewey and the mines closing, his store was going to close, too. He was shocked when he saw what a state things were in, and he blamed it on me. He and Alice always blamed Dewey's problems on me.''

He was surprised there was no self-pity in her voice. ''Why?''

''I guess they couldn't face what Dewey was. They'd done the best they knew how when he was growing up, but Dewey wasn't the son he should have been. They couldn't accept any of the responsibility, and they couldn't give any of it to Dewey. So they blamed me. Bill was blaming me at the top of his lungs one day when he had another heart attack.''

She poured tea that he wanted as little as he wanted the gingersnaps. He touched her hand. ''It wasn't your fault.''

''I know. Dewey knew, too. When he found out about his daddy, he cried. He said everything was going to change. While Bill was in the hospital, Dewey came back to work, but I think he saw it was too late. There wasn't anything anybody could do by then to save the store. But Dewey never took no for an answer, so he came up with a plan.''

She sat down across the table from him. For the first time she looked at him. ''A couple of nights later Dewey asked me to take a ride. It was the first time in a long time that he'd asked me to do anything with him. It was like we hadn't really been married for a long time. When Dewey was drinking, he would get mean. Sometimes he'd hit me or call me names. After his daddy's heart attack he seemed to sober up. I was happy, real happy, he wanted me with him that night. I had something to tell him, and the time just hadn't been right.''

''What happened?'' He reached for her hand. She let him take it.

''Dewey asked me to drive. I should have figured that was strange, but I was just so happy he was being nice to me. When we were out on the highway he told me to drive over to Baldwin, the next town. He wanted to get a six-pack of beer to take down to the river. I didn't want to do it, but Dewey said it would be like old times. It was a chilly night, so when we got to the convenience store, Dewey told me to keep the engine running so the heat would stay on. Then he got out and went inside. I wasn't paying much attention. I was thinking about what I had to tell Dewey. But when I looked inside, I saw a man with a ski mask and a gun robbing the store. That man was Dewey."

"Becca." He turned her hand palm up, lifted it to his mouth and kissed it.

"Before I really understood what was happening, Dewey came running out and pushed me into the other seat. I was so scared that all I could think about was getting out of there. I let him take off for Blackwater, but I screamed and screamed at Dewey that I was leaving him that night. I screamed so loud that I didn't hear the siren until the highway patrol was almost on top of us. There were two cars, coming at us from both directions. Dewey pulled over and jumped out before the car had even stopped completely. He fired his gun at one of the police cars, then he took off running. One of the police fired back. I don't think he meant to hit Dewey, but he did. He died right away."

Jase couldn't imagine what purpose would have been served if Dewey Hanks had lived, but his thoughts were colored by the agony in Becca's eyes. "He made a choice and he paid the price," he said.

"No. I paid the price." She pulled her hand from Jase's. "They charged me as an accomplice to the robbery, and to the attempt on the policeman's life. By the time I came up for trial, I was six months pregnant. That was the secret I hadn't had time to tell Dewey. He died not knowing. I didn't have money for a lawyer. I'd put all the money I'd got when Daddy died into Hanks Hardware, paying back money Dewey took or gave other people by mistake. Matty didn't have any money to help me, either, so the court appointed a public defender. He had a lot of people to take care of, and he wasn't very interested or very good.

"There'd been a lot of robberies—always are when times get tough and folks get desperate. They decided to make an example out of me. I was sentenced to three years, and the defender thought that was pretty light, considering. After all, I sure had the motive to help Dewey rob the store. I was pregnant, married to a good-for-nothing, and scared to death I wouldn't be able to take care of my baby.

"They let me stay in Blackwater to have the baby. It turned out to be more than one. I had twin girls, Amanda and Faith, and I got to spend four weeks with them. Then they gave custody to Bill and Alice and put me in jail. I served a year before they let me off on parole."

"You were railroaded!"

Becca was gratified at the fury in Jase's eyes. She had been so frightened she would see pity or distaste. She had even slipped her hand away so he wouldn't have to hold it. Now she covered his. "No. I wasn't."

"You had nothing to do with it, and if you'd had a decent lawyer, you would have gotten off scot-free!"

"I didn't know anything about Dewey's plans beforehand. I really didn't. But when Dewey came out of that store, I knew what he'd done. I should have gotten out of the car then, but I panicked. I let Dewey take the wheel. I was terrified, and I wasn't thinking straight. But those seconds cost me my babies, a year of my life and what little self-respect Dewey left me."

"The way you acted was understandable. You didn't have time to make a decision!"

She stood to fuss with the teapot again, although neither of them had taken a sip. She just couldn't sit still. "I made a decision. Just not the right one. And until I make something of my life and get my girls back, I won't be able to forgive myself."

"Were you in Blackwater this weekend?"

"I went to see my babies."

"How old are they now, Becca?"

"Three. They're beautiful." She swallowed. Hard. "Sometimes I miss them so much I could die."

He was up, and his arms were around her in seconds. "Becca."

She wanted to resist. But she found herself slipping her arms around his waist. "The Hanks love them, but the girls are a strain. Bill's totally disabled now, and Alice has to take care of him, too. They don't have much money, just what they get from social security. Alice feeds the girls too many sweets, and Bill gets mad when they do something wrong. I have to get my babies out of there."

He held her tighter. "Will they give you custody?"

"I think so, even though they hate me. They know I didn't have anything to do with the robbery, but they still think Dewey went wrong because of me. If I hadn't married him and forced him to take on a role he wasn't ready for, then Dewey would never have robbed the store. If I'd been a better wife, I would have known what he was planning and talked him out of it." She gave a bitter laugh. "As if I could have. But they think I should have settled him down and made a good husband out of him. They think if I'd told him he was going to be a father, that would have made a difference."

"What do you think?"

"I think it would have made him more desperate."

"I think so, too."

She pushed him away because he felt too good and it was too tempting to lean on him. He resisted for a moment, then let her go. She turned away from him, because it was easier. "By the time I got out of prison, Blackwater was almost a ghost town, and there weren't any jobs. I knew better than to look for anything in the next town, where the robbery took place. My parole officer got me a job in a laundry a hundred miles from Blackwater. But the laundry closed down after a few months. I started traveling, look-ing for work. I could have gotten in trouble for going out of state, but my parole officer looked the other way. He knew how badly I needed money. I took anything I could find and sent as much as I could of what I earned back to the Hanks for the girls. I lived wherever I could. I never had the money to rent a real place of my own because I had to send money back. I knew if I didn't, the girls would suffer, and nobody would believe I really wanted them. Things just got worse and worse."

He could imagine the rest. Unskilled and undereducated, only rarely did someone like Becca make more than minimum wage. Even with overtime, there wouldn't have been enough money to support herself and the girls. So she had stopped supporting herself. Eventually she had succumbed to illness and exhaustion. And she had almost died.

"I have pictures." She faced him and smiled tentatively. "The Hanks have an instant camera, and they let me use it this morning. I took two. Would you like to see them?"

"Of course."

Her smile broadened a little, but he saw it tremble. "Prepare yourself for the prettiest babies in the world."

He expected her to find her purse, but she lifted the photographs out of the pocket of her blouse. He realized she had kept them next to her heart. She held them out to him. "You have to hold these by the edges."

"I promise." He took the first photograph. A blond-haired urchin with jelly on one cheek grinned at him. The resemblance to Becca was there. Something grabbed at him. The girls were real. Becca's story was real. She had lived through hell, and these children were on this earth to show for it. "Which one is this?"

"That's Amanda." She traded photographs.

An identical urchin with jelly on her chin was sticking her tongue out at him. "Faith?"

"I should have come up with something a little livelier. Like Scarlett."

"They are beautiful." He watched her put the pictures back in the same pocket. He realized it must have broken her heart to leave her children this morning. His own heart felt suspiciously weakened after the horror story she had just told him.

He had imagined a better history, and he had imagined worse. But at no time had he imagined anything with the pathos of this tale. Becca had been abandoned after her father's death, abused and neglected by her husband, vilified by his parents and dragged into a robbery resulting in the death of her husband and her own prison sentence. Then, when life could hardly have looked blacker, her new twin daughters had been taken from her and given to the very people who had refused to acknowledge the kind of son they had raised.

And through it all, somehow, she had remained determined to make the best of what she had been handed. She had struggled through her marriage, lived through her prison sentence, and worked her hardest to support the children she was not allowed to keep. Worked so hard, in fact, that she had almost worked herself into the grave.

"How long did you live in your car?" he asked. "You said you could never afford to rent a place. How long were you living in that car?"

"On and off."

He gripped her arms and made her look at him. "How long?"

"A lifetime."

He dropped his hands. "You could have died."

"Sometimes I wanted to. I would have gladly, if I hadn't had my babies to think about."

He wanted to grab her again, to hold her against him, but he knew she would reject him now. He didn't know what he was feeling other than anger at a justice system that could imprison this woman and anger at all the people who had watched Dewey Hanks ruin her life. Unless he sorted out all his feelings, Becca would believe that whatever he offered her sprang from pity.

He ran his hand through his hair. "Why didn't you tell me this earlier?"

"I'm sorry. I should have."

"You're damned right you should have."

"I'll pack my things and be gone by morning."

He stared at her. "What?"

"I'm a convicted felon. I had no right to drag you into my life. I should have told you the truth right away." She tried to smile, but she couldn't. "It's just that..."

"What?"

She flinched a little at his tone. "I wanted to start over. I wanted a chance. And I took one. At your expense."

"Are you done yet?"

She nodded.

"No, you're not. Before you pack and leave, why don't you tell me what I've done to make you think I'd turn you away! What was it I said, Becca, that convinced you I wouldn't want you to stay? Aren't I paying you enough? Haven't I shown you enough concern? Was it the scene in the living room a little while ago?"

"No, I—"

"My turn! You've said enough. You're not leaving. Is that clear? You're staying. I'm going to raise your salary, and we're going to buy children's furniture for the other bedroom so your daughters can come here to live. I'll hire a lawyer for you to get custody. You can finish high school and get some job training. I'll pay whatever tuition costs there are."

His words fell into empty space. She stared at him, absorbing what he'd said. "You would do that for me?"

"I'm going to do it for you. You can stay here forever, as far as I'm concerned. I don't need this space."

"No."

"No what?"

"Thank you, but no." She waved her hand to stop him when he started to argue. "I finished high school in prison. I even got a college credit. I'm going to straighten out my life the same way, with my own hard work, not with anyone else's. Do you think I lived all those months with Dewey and didn't learn anything? Every day was a lesson, Jase! I tried to change Dewey. His parents tried to change him. We bribed him. We threatened. We cried. Dewey didn't change because Dewey didn't want to. And even if he had, he didn't know how to work for anything. If change had come easily, maybe he would have tried it. But change comes one tiny little step at a time. I know. God, how I know."

"I'm not trying to change you, Becca, I'm trying to help you!"

"You're trying to do the work I have to do. If I'm ever going to have any self-respect, I have to change myself and my life. Can't you understand that?"

"You almost died trying to change your life. When are you going to realize that you're not the problem? Life's handed you nothing but bad breaks. Now I'm trying to hand you a good one!"

"I made choices. I quit school and married Dewey. I stayed with him. I sank my money into Hanks Hardware to save Dewey and his parents. I didn't get out of the car when I should have! I made those choices. And I'm making another one. I can't take what you're offering. I thank you for it, from the bottom of my heart. But I can't take any more help from you."

He was speechless. He could think of nothing to say to refute her. He didn't agree, but there was no point in telling her that. She believed every word she'd uttered, and her decision was carved in stone.

"Then you're leaving?" he asked at last, when the silence had stretched forever.

"Not if you don't want me to. I'll stay and finish the landscaping. I'm earning my way here."

Relief filled him. "More than earning it."

"But I won't let you send me to school. And I won't let you pay me a higher salary. And I won't let you help me get custody of my girls. I'll find a way to get them back, and soon, but it will have to be by my own hard work."

He had never been faced with a situation he couldn't change. He had never been faced with a person he couldn't sway. The world had always been putty in his hands. Becca was granite.

"How could you ever have believed I would want you to leave?" he asked.

"I don't think much of myself, I guess. Prison does that to you."

Once again he was filled with the urge to pull her against him and keep her there. She needed protection and hope, and he needed ...

He didn't know what he needed, except that he needed Becca. He didn't know how, and he didn't know why. But he had learned tonight that she was much more than a cause, much more than someone who was just wandering across the edges of his life.

"You can think what you want, but I hope you'll hear this." He put his hands on her shoulders, but gently, carefully. He didn't push or pull, and he didn't grasp. "I think enough of you for both of us."

"I can't think about anyone but myself and the girls, Jase."

"Is that a warning?"

"I'm pleading," she said softly. "I don't need any more hurting. I'm still trying to get over the first time."

"Not all relationships bring hurt."

"Maybe I'll have to learn that, too. But not now. I'm not ready."

He wanted to kiss her again. She badly needed kissing and holding and reassurance. But he knew better than to try. She would be stubborn about that, too.

Jason Millington the Fourth had learned to bide his time when ambushes or stampedes didn't work. He could bide his time now. His hands fell to his sides, but his fingers were clenched. "Will you tell me before you go trotting off to Blackwater next time? I was worried about you."

"It's nice to have someone worried."

"Will you tell me? Just so I'll know?"

"I will."

He bent forward and touched her cheek with his lips. Gently, carefully. Then he straightened. "I'll be moving in soon."

"Already?"

He thought of all that still needed to be done in the house. "It's the right time of year to sell my condo. I'm putting it on the market tomorrow. I'll probably move out in the next few weeks."

"You don't have to be here to check on me."

"That never entered my mind." He turned away, but not before she had seen his smile.

"It *is* because of me."

"I heard every word you said, Becca. And I'm willing to comply."

She heard the "for now," even though it was unspoken. She watched him leave. She was still in the same spot, staring at the doorway, when she heard him start his engine and back out of the drive.

Chapter Seven

"Relax. There's not a thing in the penthouse that wouldn't benefit from the mover dropping it to give it some character."

Jase shot Pamela one of the looks he was renowned for, but she only smiled and continued. "I can take care of everything here, Jase. I really can. I'll be sure everything's safely loaded on the truck before I go home. You go on over to the house and make sure everything's ready for the arrival."

He watched the movers exit his building with a couch that he planned to put in the study of the house. They were using extreme care. Someone—himself, he supposed—had scared them to death. "All right. I'll see you over there later. Thanks for helping."

"I'm so glad to see you moving into Kathryn's house, I'd carry your furniture by myself if I had to."

On the drive to Shaker Heights he considered his decision to move. The house wasn't finished, but enough living space had been cleared to make him comfortable. The decorator had clucked and chortled, but he had managed to finish Jase's bedroom so that at least at night he could pretend there wasn't going to be a troop of workmen going through the house for the next three months.

He liked the bedroom. In fact, he more than liked it. He had grown used to wide open spaces and sleek, contemporary lines, but now he found the smaller, cozier spaces in the Tudor house appealing. He had made some structural changes. His bedroom had once been two smaller rooms. Downstairs, a tiny breakfast room and pantry had become extensions of the kitchen. He had degrees in both engineering and architecture, and by nature he was unsuited to leave anything exactly the way he found it. But much of the house was still as it had been when Kathryn had lived in it. The wallpaper and paint, the drapes and some of the furniture, were different, but Kathryn would recognize and be comfortable in the house if she came back from the grave to visit. And knowing Kathryn, she might just try.

Becca had wielded a surprising amount of influence on the decorator. The first decorator, highly recommended by Jase's mother, had wanted to paint the walnut and mahogany paneling in the den and dining room blue and white, like Wedgwood. Becca had told her that she didn't know what kind of trees Wedgwood came from, but it sure wasn't walnut and mahogany trees, so kindly keep her paintbrushes to herself. The next decorator and Becca had been able to compromise. Jase had been consulted frequently at first, but less frequently as it became clear he was perfectly happy to let the two of them make decisions.

What Becca didn't know about Tudor homes and architecture she had learned from reading every book available. When she wasn't working, she read constantly. He had discovered that her knowledge of antiques had been gleaned from books she'd read in prison and a class she had taken there on furniture refinishing. She was like an empty sponge, soaking up every bit of knowledge that came her way. She asked his work crew questions, then got them to demonstrate. She was picking up knowledge about electricity and plumbing, and she could already rewire a socket and unclog a drainpipe like a pro.

He had never met anyone so eager to learn, so determined to make something of herself. He couldn't tell her that she was already something. She wouldn't believe it. Since the night nearly two weeks ago when she had told him the circumstances that had brought her to Cleveland, he had understood her better. But he still couldn't comprehend why she wouldn't let him help her. She was so bright, so filled with potential, but she had tied his hands. She could be in college, studying physics or Greek, yet she dug weeds and learned to nail shingles on roofs instead, because that was available to her and she could do it on her own.

Her refusal to accept his help both infuriated and intrigued him. She was the only woman he had ever met who not only had no interest in his money but would probably appreciate him more if he didn't have it.

At the house, he went inside to inspect the areas where his furniture was to be stored until all the rooms were ready. He ended up on the sunporch. Everything was prepared, but he had known it would be, because Becca had been in charge.

"What do you think?"

He turned and found her in the doorway. "I think I'm moving."

"Looks that way."

He admired her. Her legs were long and tanned, and her shorts fit almost as well as his hands would in the same place. Her bright gold T-shirt proclaimed Fun and Sun in Miami, straight across her breasts. He wished he could take her there.

"I guess you'll be unpacking most of the night and won't have time to make yourself dinner."

He wasn't going to admit that he never made himself dinner, unless warmed-over coffee with bologna sandwiches qualified. "Probably not. But there are plenty of good restaurants nearby." And he was on first-name basis with the hosts and hostesses at every one, he frequented them so often.

"I'd like to make you dinner, if you'll let me."

He heard her struggle to sound casual. He would almost bet that she wanted very much to cook for him but was trying not to sound too eager, in case he refused. She still couldn't, didn't, believe that he wanted her company. Visions of Becca in his lap, being soundly kissed, filled his mind. He wondered what other proof she needed.

"I'd love that," he said, "if it's not too much trouble."

"Are you picky?"

"Not a bit."

"I'll make something that can sit on the stove until you're ready to eat it." She left, and he admired the back of her shorts until she was out of sight.

Becca was sure she could make a mean spaghetti sauce. There had been cooking classes in prison, and she had taken every one of them. In fact, she had taken every class she had been allowed to. She wanted to know things, everything, but that had only been half the reason. The other half had been to keep herself from going crazy.

She tried not to think about prison, about what it had been like to wake up every morning knowing that someone else was holding her babies, someone else was feeding them, watching them sit up for the first time. But sometimes the memories invaded anyway. Barren, sterile rooms lined with beds and windows so high that what light they let in faded before it reached the floor.

She supposed she had been lucky. She had been assigned to a minimum security prison. No one had seriously believed she was a threat to society. She had been sentenced by a hanging judge, to show the world he meant business. And she couldn't blame him, not really. There were a lot of people out there like Dewey, people who thought they were owed something for nothing. Of course, not everybody in prison was like that. Some of them, a surprising amount, really, had been more like her. Dragged into committing crimes because they didn't think hard enough. People who had made mistakes, then let the mistakes build on each other, over and over, until society shoved them out of sight for a while to think.

She'd had plenty of time to think, more time than she could handle. So she had taken classes, gone to rehab groups, started with A in the prison library and read clear through to H. Somewhere in the midst of all that she had seen what she had to do to change her life. She had to take responsibility for herself in a way she never had before. She had given responsibility to Dewey when he was alive, and she had allowed him to manipulate and abuse her. She would never give responsibility to anyone else again.

She added canned tomatoes and fresh herbs to the ground meat and chunks of hot sausage that she had browned with onions and bits of green pepper. The man who would eat the spaghetti sauce tonight wanted to take responsibility for her life. He was nothing like Dewey. Jase would hold her life carefully in his hands, mold it with skill, and probably leave her a better person for the experience. But any success she achieved would belong to him. She couldn't, wouldn't, let that happen.

The sun was going down by the time she brushed fresh Italian bread with melted butter, garlic and cheese. The movers had arrived an hour ago, and through the cottage kitchen window she had watched them carry Jase's possessions into the house. Now, as she looked on, they slammed the back doors of the truck and drove away. She turned up the heat under the water simmering in wait for the spaghetti.

Jase arrived ten minutes later looking disgruntled. She plopped the spaghetti in before she greeted him. "All done?"

"Whose idea was this?"

"What, the move or dinner?"

"The move." He collapsed into a chair to watch her bustle around the room. "I can face citizens' committees and city government hearings and angry contractors without blinking an eye. But I'm never going to move again."

"You'd better not. I'm not doing all this work in the yard so some bull goose loony can move in and chop it all down."

"Your work is safe." He propped his feet up on another chair.

"Is everything in?"

"Everything I'm moving. The rest goes other places."

She stole a glance at him as she went to the refrigerator to get the salad. He looked tired, disgusted and thoroughly masculine. He was wearing jeans, well-faded jeans that would have suited the Jase she'd met on a cold March night. His polo shirt was an eye-catching jade that stretched across a chest and shoulders that would have suited the men who had done his moving. All of it suited Jase Millington the Whatever.

"Would you like a drink? I have club soda, and I bought some beer in case you wanted it."

He was pleased she had thought so far ahead. He took a beer and let her bring him a glass. "Dinner smells wonderful."

"I hope you like it." She stirred the sauce, keeping a close eye on the spaghetti.

"Your grandmother's recipe?"

"No. Yours. I found it when I was cleaning out the house. I copied it and saved the original for you."

"I can't believe it was Kathryn's. She never cooked. She'd eat everything raw rather than bother with a stove. She had a woman who cooked for her sometimes. I don't know her first name, but we always called her McDaniels. McDaniels probably forced the recipe on Kathryn."

"You called your grandmother by her first name and the hired help by her last?"

"McDaniels was never thought of as hired help. She was more of a companion to Kathryn, a friend. She spoiled Pamela and me rotten. And now that you mention it, I remember her spaghetti, and it smelled just like yours."

"What was growing up like for you?"

He was so used to denying that his childhood had lacked anything that for a moment he almost did it again. But Becca's story had made him confront some of his own past. Maybe honesty about who you were and where you had come from was part of what Becca called taking control of your life.

He tried to be honest, now. "Good in some ways, not so good in others. My parents don't show their feelings. Pamela and I were close to compensate. We escaped to Kathryn's every chance we got."

"That's what it's supposed to be like to grow up rich. That's one of those stories the rich spread around so that poor folks will feel happy they're poor."

He laughed, and she granted him one of her extraordinary smiles. "I had mountains of friends, as rich as I was," he said, "and about half of them came from intact, loving families, and the other half didn't. Was everybody you knew happy and loved?"

"Not hardly. Most of them were so busy trying to make it from day to day, they didn't know how to be happy. A lot of them were sick and dying from working in the mines."

"But the government has programs to help black lung victims."

"Sorry, rich man, but the government gives money to less than ten percent of the people who need it. You've got to be half dead to get it, and then it doesn't mean much."

"I didn't know."

"Most people don't. Who's going to speak for a bunch of Appalachian nobodies?"

"You're not an Appalachian nobody."

"I told myself that every day when I was living in my car. It helped, but not a whole lot." She turned and leaned against the stove, crossing her arms. "You know what I want to do?"

"What?"

"I want to be somebody important enough to speak out. I want to be somebody who people listen to. I want to tell people what it's like to be poor and hopeless, not so everybody can throw money, then forget the people they throwed—threw—it at, but just so people will know, and knowing will change them."

He couldn't think of a word to say. She had exposed her heart.

"I guess that's silly."

"No."

"Well, that's what I want to do." She turned back to the stove. "And I will, but whether it will change anybody or not depends on them, doesn't it?"

"Do you believe people are good?"

"I think we all have a chance to be, but some have a better shot at it than others."

He watched her drain the spaghetti and put the finishing touches on the rest of the meal. He tried to imagine anyone he knew—with the exception of Pamela or Shareen—making such an impassioned statement. Passion, at least this particular kind, was out of favor these days. The people he knew gave money to causes—or threw money at them—but rarely gave more than a passing thought to the people the money would help. Becca gave more than a thought. She had been one of those people, and could be again if no plan was made for her life after the summer.

Becca set the meal on the table and took a seat across from Jase. As he took his first bites, she tried not to watch his reaction, but finally she had to admit his opinion mattered to her. Jase mattered to her. She didn't want him to. Her life was far too complicated, and Jase's ideas for simplifying it didn't agree with her own. But no matter how many times she told herself not to think of him, she still did.

"This is terrific. McDaniels would be proud."

She nodded, trying not to let him see how pleased she was. "Good."

"Is there anything you don't do well?"

"Dewey would have named a few things."

"From what you've told me, Dewey wasn't much of a judge."

"He thought he was. I thought so, too."

The statement was provocative. Jase imagined that since she didn't elaborate, she was talking about something highly personal. He guessed she meant her performance in bed.

He tried to imagine a man not being satisfied with Becca. From everything she had said, he knew she had been young and inexperienced when she'd married. But she was warm and passionate and sensual. No woman who cupped the earth in her hands and kneaded it as she did could be cold. No woman who surrounded herself with flowers and herbs and sunlight could be an unresponsive lover.

"Do you still love Dewey?" he asked. "Or can you let go of him and what he thought about you?"

"I don't think I ever loved him. Not the way a woman loves a man she really believes in. And it's what I think of myself that matters, isn't it?"

"If that's what you really believe."

"I've thought myself right into a new job, Jase."

He put his fork down—which wasn't easy, since the spaghetti was every bit as good as he had said. "What?"

"A new job. At Constantine's. Now, don't look at me like that. I'm not leaving here. But my nights are free, and I don't work more than half a day on Sunday in the yard. I realized I could be waitressing then. I won't be taking even a minute away from the time I'd be working here."

"You know that's not what's worrying me."

"Nothing should be worrying you. Now eat your spaghetti before it turns into slimy little worms."

"I don't want you doing this."

"You've said what's in your heart, and I've listened."

"Not well enough."

She set her fork down, too. "Better than well."

"Look, Becca. You're not recovered, not completely. You still need a couple of pounds and a lot of rest. You bustle around here like someone putting out fires, but at least in the evening and weekends you can take it easy. You need to take care of yourself. You need to watch TV, listen to music, read something for fun."

"And you do those things?"

"That's different."

"How? Don't shake your head at me, Jase Millington the Whatever."

"The Fourth, but don't ever, ever, call me that."

"Jase Millington the Whatever, then. I like that better, anyway. You don't know whatever you are. One minute you think you're my father, the next minute my lord and savior, the next minute you're kissing me!"

"You need kissing!" He was on his feet and around the table before she could respond. She jumped to her feet to confront him. "You need kissing and shaking, mountain girl. You can't take the world on your shoulders. It's not a very nice world. You should have learned that by now. One person can't butt it in the head and make it change. Everybody needs help, only you won't let anybody help you. That's as crazy as anything, crazier than not getting out of the car the night Dewey robbed the store, crazier than marrying him in the first place!''

"Who do you think you are, telling me what's crazy. Let me tell you what crazy looks like. It looks like a man pretending he's a bum just to see how the other half of the world lives. It looks like a man who thinks he's so perfect he knows everything about everything and everybody. It looks like Jase Millington the Whatever!''

"You're going to tell me you feel great? That you feel like you can lick the world? That working two jobs isn't going to run you right back into the ground again?''

She opened her mouth to tell him just that, then snapped her lips together.

He was triumphant. "See?''

"I'm going to tell you to go sit back down and eat your spaghetti before I take your plate away!''

He stroked her hair. He hadn't intended to. One minute he was angry enough at her stupidity to shake it out of her, the next he was caressing her hair. He supposed it was his own well-bred version of shaking. God knows it was shaking him up, touching her that way. "I care about you.''

"Don't.''

"It's too late.''

"You feel sorry for me!''

"Ridiculous. Maybe I did once, but who can feel sorry for a feisty Kentucky hellcat who does whatever she wants, whenever she wants to?''

"You shouldn't be touching me that way.''

"Why not?''

"Because it's just another way to get me to do what you want.''

"I'm touching you because I can't seem to help myself.''

"Let's both sit back down and pretend this never happened."

"As long as we're pretending." The hand that had been stroking hauled her toward him. Her eyes were defiant, but she didn't resist. His mouth came down on hers like a hawk swooping for its prey, his lips as heated as his words had been. She knew she should be angry, but all she could feel was desire. It swept through her in a wave, dark and flowing, until she was nothing but desire and need.

If their last kiss had been sweet, this one was anything but. This was what the books claimed a woman *could* feel, if she was really a woman. This was what she hadn't even known how to dream. She fell into the kiss as if she were free-falling into clouds. Her arms circled his waist, and her body ground against his. She could feel his arousal, feel exactly how much he wanted her. That knowledge sent her soaring almost as high as the kiss. Jase wanted her. Badly. And everything he did to prove it made her want him just as much.

Finally he pushed her away. "Now you can start pretending!" He stalked back around the table and took his seat. His fork was clenched in his hand as tightly as a sword, but he began to eat.

"I can save some money this way," she said when both of them had choked down most of the rest of their meal. "I can send money home and put some away for the deposit on an apartment. By the end of the summer I'm going to have a place to live and a permanent job. I want my babies with me!"

He kept eating.

"You don't understand," she said when he didn't answer.

"I understand what you're up against, and I understand how you could make it better. How can you save enough if you don't let anybody help you? The tips at Constantine's aren't going to be much. You'll need a thousand dollars to get into a decent apartment, and after the girls are with you, you'll have to hire child care for two. The court is going to look at that when you go for custody."

"I can do it."

"If anybody can, you can."

"What?"

"You heard me right." He looked up and saw one of the smiles he had learned to hope for. "Do you think I want to help you because I don't trust you to do it on your own? I have more faith in you than in almost anybody I know. I just know how hard it's going to be. And I don't want it to be hard."

She couldn't swallow. She stood and took what was left of her dinner to the sink. She hadn't been there for more than seconds when she felt Jase's arms around her.

"I don't know what to think about you," she said.

"Do you think about me?"

"More than I should."

"Likewise."

"I made raspberry cobbler."

He stood there and held her in his arms. She didn't lean against him, and she didn't turn. Had she done either, he didn't know what would have happened.

"I'm going to Blackwater tomorrow," she said after he finally forced himself to step back. Even to herself, she sounded breathless. "I won't be able to go very often once I start working weekends."

"Do the girls know?"

"I write them every day. I think the Hanks read them my letters. They don't like me, but they love Amanda and Faith. They wouldn't hurt the girls to get even."

"When are you leaving?"

"Late afternoon. After your crew's gone home."

"Go in the morning. I'll be here all day tomorrow getting unpacked. I can give orders for a change. They'll find it refreshing."

"No, I have things to do in the yard before I go."

"Go." He turned her to face him. "Give the yard a rest. Let it grow a few new weeds. Go to Blackwater. You've earned a day of vacation by now, don't you think?"

"You're sure?"

No one would ever have to tell him what hope looked like. "I'm sure."

"Thank you."

"It's a little thing."

"Not to me." She touched his cheek, just a whisper-soft brush of her fingers. "Nothing you've done is a little thing. You've given me a chance. Don't think you have to give me more."

He pulled her to rest against him, but he didn't kiss her again. There was so much more he wanted to give her. He just hoped that someday she would accept it all.

Chapter Eight

Jase awakened to the sounds of hammering. As the sole resident of the house, he wanted to wrench the hammer from the hands of whoever was using it and toss it out a window. As the man paying whoever was using it for putting in a full, productive day, he wanted to applaud. Instead of either, he showered and went down to the kitchen to make coffee.

It was the kind of day that Clevelanders dreamed about through every long, gray winter. Outside the kitchen window he could see artfully trimmed evergreens and borders of annuals, gold and pink and white flowers of various sizes and shapes, none of which he could identify. By summer's end they would be wide drifts of color. The sun was shining brightly, though the air was still cool. The day was perfect for Becca's trip to Blackwater. He wondered if she had already left.

He took his coffee outside to get away from the noise. The woman wielding the hammer was relentless, one of the best carpenters he had come across in his search for top-notch work crews. She was the only person he would have trusted to repair and replace the ornate woodwork in what would be his study, but right now he wished she was a little less conscientious.

At Becca's insistence, a brick patio had been laid across from the rose gardens. It was a herringbone design master-piece, and he had to admit it was going to be a welcome addition. Becca and John, the decorator, had purchased graceful iron furniture—next he expected a perfectly level croquet lawn—and now Jase decided to try it out.

He had settled down with his coffee before he realized he was not alone. He sat forward and peered into the roses. "Becca?"

She stood, dusting grass clippings off the knees of her jeans. "Hi."

"What are you doing here?"

"This and that."

He took his coffee and started toward her. "You're supposed to be on your way by now. It's a long drive to Kentucky."

"I know." She held up a book. "I got this at the library yesterday."

He saw it was a book on old roses, but he couldn't imagine what it had to do with her trip to Blackwater. "Becca—"

"I'm trying to identify these, now that some of them have bloomed. I'm making a list for you."

He wanted to know why she wasn't in her car on the highway, not the names of his rosebushes, but he recognized her reluctance to talk about the trip. He bided his time. "So you've had some luck?"

"More than I thought. I've narrowed down several of them and definitely identified two." She was talking fast, as if she didn't want him to interrupt. "I'll show you."

He followed her into the midst of the rosebushes, trying to figure out how to turn the conversation back to a more relevant subject. "Show away."

"Old-fashioned roses are divided into classes. The first class is—"

"Spare me a horticultural lecture."

"You're not being very nice. I wanted to show off. Anyway, this mess in the corner against the fence is a wild rose."

"That's a class?"

"Technically it's a species rose. Variations grow all over the world. Most people weed them out of gardens. Your grandmother kept this one to fill this corner. Take a deep breath."

The rose was huge and sprawling, despite the pruning Becca had given it early in the season. Covered with hundreds of small white blossoms, it had a light, sweet fragrance.

"A lot of the climbing roses started from this old honey. Over here's a different kind. It's a damask rose. It's called Gloire de Guilan, or I think it is, anyway."

He had never heard French spoken with quite that accent. He stepped closer to hide his smile and buried his nose in a light pink blossom. The flower was intensely fragrant, and the bush was covered with more just like it.

"This one was discovered in Persia in this century, but damask roses have been around since the Roman Empire. Imagine, Jase."

"Have you found one perfect rose this season?"

"I'm still working on it. This one comes close. Isn't it pretty?"

"Beautiful."

"It comes from China, if it's what I think. Old Blush— at least, I hope it is. They were growing in Europe before this country was founded."

He saw a back door into the subject he really wanted to talk about. "What ever happened to your grandmother's roses, Becca?"

"They're still blooming away at the home place. Matty lives there now. Someday when I'm settled, I'll take slips, so I'll have them with me, too. There was one bush, Gramma called it a pillow rose. It's in this book, only it's really called American Pillar. I want to have it growing against a fence of my own someday."

"Why don't you see if you can get a cutting while you're in Blackwater this weekend and start one here? There's room."

She scrubbed her foot against the wood chip mulch covering the rose bed. "I'm not going."

"Why not?"

"I can't."

He debated whether he had the right to push her. He decided he didn't, then pushed anyway. "Why can't you? You have the day off and the desire to go. You have the transportation." She looked up, and he saw that he'd discovered the problem. "Your car?"

She sighed, and it was answer enough.

"Why didn't you say so? Let's take a look at it."

"Mary Lou already did. She says it won't be going anywhere for a long time."

Jase knew enough to trust Mary Lou, the carpenter who had awakened him so early. The day Mary Lou decided to retire her hammer, she could get a job in any auto shop in the city. "I'm sorry. My mechanic did what he could. We'd hoped it would be the end of the year before the engine needed to be rebuilt."

"I guess I was just lucky I wasn't out on the highway."

She didn't look as if she thought she was lucky. She looked ready to burst into tears. He had only seen her this defeated once befo.·e, and he couldn't bear it. He put his arms around her, although she tried to push him away.

"Don't you ever cry?"

"What good does it do?"

"For one thing, it washes away that lump in your throat."

"I wouldn't know what to do...without it." She relaxed and let him hold her. It was a mistake. The moment she gave in that much, the dam shattered, and tears began to course down her cheeks. She had forgotten what it was like to cry, what a devastating assault on her will tears could be. Jase held her tighter as she soaked the front of his shirt.

When the tears were finally cried away, he reached inside his pocket for a handkerchief and came up empty. Becca moved away. He stripped off his T-shirt and gave it to her. "Here."

"I couldn't."

"Why not? You already have."

She glared at him, then she took the shirt and wiped her eyes and cheeks. But not before she'd gotten a good look at his bare chest. She was in no shape to think about bare chests or Jase, but the image of tanned skin stretched across broad, square muscles was imprinted in her mind to think about later. "Thanks."

"You can take my car."

"No."

"My parents have a car I can borrow for the weekend. It won't be any trouble."

She realized she was holding his shirt to her cheek with the affection of a child for his favorite blanket. She thrust it toward him. "I'm not driving your car to Blackwater."

He refused to take the shirt. "Good, because I have a better solution. I'll drive it."

She stared at him. It was exactly like Jase to fix everything for her.

"Before you say no," he continued, "listen. I haven't taken a break in over a year. I didn't even take off Memorial Day weekend. I sorted and packed. Now, I've just made a move, and maybe it's not the best time to leave town, and maybe it is. But I've always wanted to see Kentucky."

"Sure you have."

"Almost more than the Orient or Tahiti."

She sighed, then smiled a little. He smiled back, and her heart sped an extra twelve beats to the minute. "You know I can't let you do this."

"No, I don't. You're not letting me do anything. I want to do it. I want to see Blackwater. I want to see Amanda and Faith. If they're anything like their mommy, they're little girls worth knowing."

"They're wonderful."

"Let me judge for myself. I'm an expert at quality assessment."

"You're just doing this because..."

"Yes?"

She couldn't accuse him of trying to change her life. The trip wouldn't change her life; it would only make the next months bearable. She supposed she would work harder and be more pleasant if she let him do this. In the long run it would benefit him. "Who am I trying to fool?" she asked at last. "I want to go, Jase. I've never wanted anything more. You can't tell me this is something you're dying to do, but I can't tell myself to say no. I'd be proud to have you take me to Blackwater."

"Give me an hour to pack a few things. And I've got phone calls to make before we leave."

"I'll be waiting. Whenever you're ready."

"Bring what you need to make those cuttings, too. The house won't be a showplace until I have a pillow rose in my garden."

She told herself not to get used to being treated this way by a man. Not to get used to one caring enough about her to put his busy life on hold. She told herself not to fall in love with Jase Millington the Whatever. But as he walked away she realized she was fast learning what the Whatever stood for, and the variety of adjectives that came to mind made Jase Millington unforgettable.

Blackwater was a hole. By moonlight it was nothing more than a moonlit hole. Nothing was softened; nothing was improved. The houses had been hastily constructed, and now they were slowly dilapidating. Vines covered one house on the main street, and Jase was sure they held the place together.

Farther away, after the road dipped and shuffled a bit, there were several sturdier homes. Becca pointed to one. "That's the Hanks' house."

Even in the darkness Jase could see that by Blackwater standards, the Hanks were rich. The house was a neat brick ranch, with trimmed evergreens and an enclosed carport. There were two little plastic tricycles parked on the porch under the outside light. He imagined the sight of them broke Becca's heart.

Becca turned her face away, as if she couldn't bear to look. "What you see now is all that's left. Blackwater was never much, but at least it used to be alive. Now half the houses are boarded up. You'll see that tomorrow. The other half have been let go. Nobody's going to paint a house if they have to worry about what they're going to eat tomorrow."

"Two mines closed?"

"Nothing's open around here anymore. Men have to drive so far to work, they just up and move. There's a woodworking plant over in Baldwin. Some people work there, though it doesn't pay too good. But some people have lived here forever. It's home, and they don't want to move on, even if they don't make much money."

Jase found that hard to understand, although he wasn't going to tell her so. "You're sure you want to stay at Matty's tonight? I'm sure there's a room for you in Baldwin, too."

"No, I'd like to stay at the home place. Matty'd make room for you, too. I know she would."

"How many kids does she have now?"

"Six."

"And you think there'd be room?"

"There's always Jimbo's bed. But he's not potty trained exactly."

"A motel sounds good."

"You know, you don't have to go with me to see the girls tomorrow. You could just enjoy Baldwin."

"I'll tour scenic Baldwin another time. What time should I pick you up?"

"Come for breakfast. About seven."

"Seven?"

"Rich tycoons aren't the only folks who work hard. Matty's husband Syl drives fifty miles to his weekend job. That's mountain miles."

He dropped her off out in the country a bit—although distinguishing between town and country was all a matter of judgment—at a sprawling white house with a wide front porch and a junk car in the side yard. The house had its own kind of tin-roofed charm. He refused to go in, since it was so late, but he waited until she was safely inside before he followed the road to Baldwin and the twelve-room motel that was the finest Baldwin had to offer.

He was up earlier than he needed to be the next morning. The motel walls were thin, and the couple in the next room had to be honeymooners. He had listened to their groans of pleasure most of the night, and he had thought of Becca.

He wasn't oblivious to the differences between Becca and himself. There couldn't be more, and driving through Blackwater had rubbed it in. Neither was he oblivious to the troubled roots of their relationship. When they'd met she had been beaten down and desperately ill, and he had been neither. He had wanted to help her. Even Prince Charming had first seen Cinderella as a beautiful princess, not a cinder-covered scullery maid. Love had preceded compassion.

But even if the fairy tale was reversed, hadn't he still seen the princess under the rat-brown coat and dangerous cough? Right away he had felt more for her than pity. He had felt admiration, a large helping of it, and the more he knew her, the more admiration he felt. Slowly, over the months, admiration had magnified to something brighter and surer until he wanted to be with her, groaning and sighing like the honeymooners next door. He wanted to feel the sweetness of her kisses all over his body. He wanted to caress her new lusher curves and rosier skin.

He was a man with a woman on his mind. A very special woman, who made staying in the room another minute unbearable. Silently he bid farewell to his amorous neighbors, showered and took an early morning tour of Baldwin before he started back up the road to Matty's house.

In the sunshine, the home place had even more charm than he'd given it credit for. Morning glories twined around the porch pillars, and roses—*the* roses, he supposed—bloomed profusely in a neat garden far to one side. By the light of morning he saw that the junk car wasn't. It was an old station wagon, but it was parked, not abandoned. Someone kept it free of the dust of narrow mountain roads.

Matty was dark-haired and pale-skinned. Poverty and too many children too close together had heaped eighty pounds on a frame as fine-boned as Becca's. He understood the reasons for the extra pounds as soon as she ushered him to the family table. The meal was heavy on biscuits and white bread ladled with sausage gravy. Some of the children were barely a year apart. They were clean, bright and certainly not hungry, but the oldest boy needed to see a dentist, and all the girls shared their mother's appetite for sugar and fat.

He listened to the banter and heard the love as clearly. Syl said little, but when he did, everybody jumped. Jase sensed not fear but a profound respect in the family's response. And who wouldn't respect a man who worked seven days a week to provide for his brood? He was thin to Matty's thick, gnarled and grizzled and old before his time. But he was a man with a funny little smile and the occasional wry comment, and by the end of the meal, Jase wished Syl lived in Ohio and worked for him.

He and Becca left after each of the children had showed him the gifts Becca had brought them. They were little things, Cleveland Indians keychains for the boys and magic slates for the girls, but the children were thrilled to have them.

In the car driving toward the Hanks' house, Becca watched Jase for a reaction. He had seemed perfectly at ease, but she had been aware of all the things that had probably been new to him. The chipped dime-store crockery, the jelly glasses filled with powdered fruit drink instead of orange juice, the faint odor of wet mattresses and mildew. She was ashamed of none of it. Not of the sofa with springs that protruded, not of Matty's poor grammar—the same grammar Becca still worked so hard to chase from her own speech. Matty and Syl had always stood by her, and the children were almost as dear to her as her own. She wasn't ashamed, but she wondered if Jase now saw more clearly how different they were.

If he saw it, he gave no sign. He caught her watching him, and the intimacy of his smile bounced her heart rate up another notch.

"Bill and Alice know we're coming," she said as she turned away. "Usually they leave after I arrive, and I have the girls all to myself."

"That's nice of them."

"I don't think they do it to be nice."

He waited for her to elaborate. But he didn't have time to question her when she didn't. He rounded a corner, and the Hanks' house was right there. He pulled up in front, and Becca got out of the car before he'd turned off the engine. He followed her up the path.

The door opened before Becca got to the porch. Two pigtailed whirlwinds came barreling toward her. She knelt and scooped them to her, one in each arm. He hovered a good distance behind, reluctant to interrupt the reunion.

Finally one of the little girls noticed him. She stuck two fingers in her mouth and peered over Becca's shoulder. "Who zat?"

Becca swung around and beamed a teary smile in his direction. "Come here, Jase, and meet my babies."

He started forward. Only then did he notice the woman standing in the doorway. She had a permanent frown etched into her forehead under steel gray, tightly permed hair. Her arms were crossed, and she watched every move that Becca made.

He stooped beside Becca. He didn't know much about kids, but he'd visited The Greenhouse often enough to learn that his height scared some of them. He didn't touch, and he didn't talk loudly. He'd learned that, too. "Okay, who's who?"

"This is Faith."

"Good morning, Faith."

She giggled.

He turned his attention to the other. "Good morning, Amanda." He studied her for a moment, then turned back to Faith. "Now I can tell."

"Can he?" Amanda asked her mother.

"Probably not. Shut your eyes, Jase, and I'll mix them up."

He obeyed, to a chorus of twin giggles.

"Okay, open your eyes."

He did. He squinted at the girls. "Amanda here and Faith here." He pointed as he spoke.

"How'd he know?" Faith asked.

"How did you know?" Becca asked. "It takes most people weeks to tell."

"Magic."

Becca stood the girls side by side and looked at them. "Amanda has blue barrettes, and Faith has pink."

"And I thought I could fool you."

Becca stood, balancing Faith on one hip. Amanda held tightly to her other hand. "Jase, come meet Alice Hanks."

He noticed that she didn't add "My mother-in-law." He guessed that Becca had stopped thinking of this stern-faced woman as any kind of mother a long time ago.

Becca introduced them at the doorway. Alice held out her hand with little enthusiasm. "Didn't know you were bringing anyone," she said to Becca.

"Jase offered to drive me. My car didn't want to make the trip."

"Dewey always took good care of that car."

"The car is four years older now," Becca said.

"Well, you both might as well come on in. Bill and me were fixing to go out."

"I won't be staying," Jase assured her. "Becca needs time alone with the girls."

Becca shot him a grateful smile.

"Come on in for a minute anyhow and meet Bill."

Jase followed them into the living room. Inside, the house was much the same as it was out, neat and uninspired. There was a large, paint-by-numbers portrait of a matador over a fireplace that looked as if it had never been used. The furniture was the gold and avocado green of the sixties, and the carpet had seen considerable wear.

When they walked in, Bill Hanks got slowly to his feet. Jase watched him struggle to straighten, and any animosity he had felt for the man lessened. Dewey's father had paid his own price for the life his son had led.

Bill's hand wasn't steady when he held it out. Jase grasped it firmly and murmured the appropriate greetings. "The girls've had their breakfast," Bill told Becca. "Don't let 'em fool you into giving 'em any more of that chocolate cereal."

"I won't," Becca promised.

"And they need a nap at two, or we'll pay for it tonight when you're gone."

"I know, Bill. I always give them a nap when I'm here."

"Well, you're not here much, are you?"

There was a moment of total silence. "I'm not here much because I'm working eight hours away," Becca said evenly. "And that's only because there are no jobs here."

"Cincinnati's a hell of a lot closer."

"We've been over this. I had a job in Cincinnati, and the laundry closed down. They said they could hire me in their branch in Cleveland. So I went there."

She didn't add that the Cleveland branch hadn't been interested in her, or that once she was there she didn't have the money to move back to southern Ohio or Kentucky. Those were stories she kept from the Hanks so that when the time came to ask for custody of her daughters, no one could throw homelessness up at her as a reason to say no.

"Seems to me you'd find your way back more often," Bill said.

Jase watched Becca closely. Her expression didn't change. It hadn't since the conversation began. "I find my way back every chance I get. Maybe soon I won't need to."

"What's that mean?"

"It means that I'm going to court to seek custody of the girls just as soon as I've got all the resources to support them. Then you'll have to find your way north to visit." She paused just long enough to make the next statement significant. "You would always be welcome in my house."

"I wouldn't count on anything, missy."

"I've already learned that, Bill. From Dewey."

Alice made a sound deep in her throat. Jase couldn't fathom what it meant, but he did know he wanted to add something. He struggled to sound calm. "Becca's had more bad breaks than anyone is entitled to, Mr. Hanks. She has friends now who are going to make sure she gets good breaks from now on."

"*I'm* going to make sure I get good breaks," Becca said. "And I'm going to support my daughters and raise them. Don't think I'm not grateful that you and Alice were there for them when I couldn't be. But I need my babies now, and both of you need time alone, and rest."

Bill might appear frail, but Jase could see an iron will, with no touch of goodwill to soften it, in the man's eyes. When the time came for a custody battle, Bill Hanks would pull out all the stops. He wondered if Becca knew.

The Hanks left. Becca didn't seem particularly flustered by the confrontation with them. Jase waited until the girls were settled at coloring books Becca had brought them before he spoke.

"Are the Hanks always like that?"

"No. They're—Bill is usually much worse. Bill was on his best behavior because you're bigger and younger than he is, and because you look like somebody important."

"He's a cheap-trick bully."

"He taught his son well. But most of the time he's good with the girls. He has a soft spot for them that he doesn't have for me. I remind him of all his failures. The girls give him hope."

"You're generous."

"I'm resigned. I change what I can and accept what I can't."

"There's more to the prayer that's from. Do you have the wisdom to tell the difference?"

"I think so. Do you think I do?"

"Not always."

"That's something we'll always disagree about."

He thought about the "always" as he headed toward Blackwater to look around. He liked the sound of that "always" more and more.

Chapter Nine

Blackwater proper was little more than two gas stations, a grocery store with a post office in one corner and a pharmacy in the other, plus a community center with a library, a rec hall and a medical clinic that was open twice a week. If a Blackwater resident was sick on Tuesday or Friday, he was lucky. If he was sick on any other day and couldn't wait, he drove to Baldwin, or beyond, if the illness required a specialist or sophisticated technology.

The community center was a converted church, staffed and run by volunteers. The rec hall was open on Wednesday nights for adults and Saturdays for children and teenagers. There were two Ping-Pong tables and a billiard table that had seen more games than a professional hustler. There was a television set and a video recorder with a small collection of donated tapes. With the dearth of commercial entertainment in Blackwater, Jase imagined every citizen had seen the tapes a dozen times.

He had never felt more like a stranger. He was dressed casually, and there was nothing flashy about his car. But he had not grown up here; he had not been married in one of the two tiny churches bordering the road a quarter of a mile from town or buried his parents in the cemetery behind the community center. He was a stranger. He walked like he owned the world, because in fact he owned a pretty damned big piece of it. He had never known defeat or hunger, or what it was like to be sick on a schedule.

He wasn't sure how the people he passed on the sidewalk knew that about him. No one smiled or nodded. His face might as well have been on wanted posters plastered all over the post office for the suspicious looks that were thrown his way.

He started his tour at the grocery store. Small, with a small selection, the store smelled like ripe bananas and bug spray. There was a line at the post office window and another at the pharmacy. He bought an apple and took it to the cashier, a pretty young woman whose hair was already streaked with gray. She checked him out without a word.

His luck was no better at the community center. Children ran from end to end of the rec hall in sync to a video tape of *The Jungle Book*. The apes in the cartoon had more self-control than the children and were friendlier than the man and woman watching them run. He visited the library and asked if the librarian could recommend any good books on the area, but her response was limited to "nothing we have."

His tour had taken him an hour, largely because he had strolled the equivalent of several city blocks to see if there was anything he had missed and because he had visited the cemetery. The cemetery had been the most enlightening stop. Back in the eastern corner he had located Dewey's grave. According to the headstone, Dewey had been the beloved son of Alice and William Hanks. No stranger reading it would ever know he had also been the husband of a woman named Becca or the father of two beautiful little girls.

With nothing else to see and no one who would talk to him, he got back in his car and decided to take some of the side roads to see where they led. Two hours later he was back on the main road heading toward a ramshackle café between Blackwater and Baldwin.

As he drove, his mind was reeling with possibilities. As he and Becca had driven into town last night, he had been oblivious to the scenery. The mountains had been an obstacle and nothing more. This morning he had been so intent on taking the pulse of Blackwater that he had missed the obvious. The pulse wasn't a few buildings set along the road. The pulse was the mountains, the exquisite scenery that had finally shaken him out of his complacency, the Blackwater River that wound its way through upland and hollow and carved out a path that even ruthless mining companies had never quite managed to destroy. There was potential here. There had to be.

He parked in the dirt lot of Better'n Home, next to six pickups and two cars that reminded him of Becca's. Inside he was met with the same suspicious stares that had greeted him everywhere. Most of the tables were taken by groups of men. There were only three women in the room, and one of them was the waitress. Smoke swirled to the beat of a window fan, the only ventilation in the room.

He sat in a booth, a neatly patched vinyl seat with a sparkling clean table. The menu was simple; the day's special was ham with red-eye gravy. He waited to be served.

The waitress, an aging blonde with too much eye makeup, found every excuse not to visit his table. Finally, when no more excuses seemed to be left, she ambled over, but she didn't seem pleased to see him. He ordered the special and watched her amble away. Like the woman at the grocery store, she had managed it all without a word.

He had heard of the reticence of people living in the Appalachians. Kentucky, after all, was the state where the Hatfields and McCoys had carried out their feud. A man either belonged or he didn't. And quite obviously, since no one had ever seen Jase before, he didn't belong. He was surprised, though, that everyone seemed suspicious of him. He wondered what the whole town was worried about.

The waitress returned with ice water and a salad. He decided to take his chances with her before she left. "Miss?"

She waited.

"I'm visiting for the day, and I'm trying to see as much of the area as I can. Is there anything I should do, anywhere I should go?"

"I don't know."

He was encouraged to find she could speak. "Well, if you'd never been here before, what do you think you'd most want to see?"

"I've always been here." She turned and was gone. He watched her stop by a table at the edge of the room where three burly men smoked and shouted at each other. All three men turned to look at him as the waitress walked away from their table.

He was halfway through his salad before one of the men came to stand beside his table.

"Hear you're looking for places to go."

He eyed the man and saw trouble. "Not hell, if that's what you're about to tell me."

"We don't need no smart-mouthed strangers here."

Jase gestured to the bench across from him. "Look, friend, why don't you have a seat and tell me what's going on? I'm not in town to cause anyone any trouble."

The man didn't move. "S'pose you tell me why you're in town, then?"

Jase weighed that possibility and decided he liked it. What better way could there be to find out how much support Blackwater might offer Becca if a custody battle was to take place? He pushed his salad bowl away. "I'm a friend of Becca Hanks'," he said, watching the man's face. "A very good friend. I came with her to see her daughters for the weekend. I wanted to see the kind of place where they've been raised."

The man's expression didn't change. "Becca Hanks?"

"That's right. Do you know her?"

"Everybody knows Becca. Where is she now?"

"With her girls."

"Cute little rascals."

Jase realized he had been ready to leap to his feet and throw the first punch. He relaxed, gratefully, since he wasn't sure this man wouldn't have flattened him to the ground. "Cutest I've ever seen. Matty and Syl's kids are cute, too. I was there for breakfast."

"You a friend of theirs, too?"

Jase had the feeling he was passing the test, and, more important, so was Becca. "I hope I am now."

"Damn." The man turned and motioned to his friends. In a moment all three were hovering over the table. Jase slid over, and in a moment they were all seated in the booth.

"I want to know what happened to Becca here," Jase said. "And I want to know how it happened."

If he had wondered if anyone in Blackwater knew how to practice the fine art of conversation, he stopped wondering immediately.

Becca had been everybody's friend; Dewey, on the other hand, had been an arrogant, spoiled good-for-nothing who used everybody he came in contact with. Not a soul in Blackwater believed that Becca had had anything to do with the robbery. Her only fault had been blind loyalty to a man who hadn't deserved it.

The parole board had been flooded with letters and calls from Blackwater citizens, so flooded that Becca had made parole on her first try. There wasn't anyone in town who wouldn't have given Becca a job, if there had been a job to give her. And wasn't it a crying shame that the Hanks were raising her kids? There wasn't anyone in town who wouldn't go to court to have their say about her character.

By the time Jase had finished his lunch he knew more than he'd ever expected to learn. He heard about Becca's brothers and the time she had locked them in a basement until they said they were sorry for taking her bicycle apart. He heard how well liked her father had been, and how he had led the local union in a confrontation over better benefits. He heard how many Blackwater boys had been in love with her and how many of them she had kissed.

He also got an earful of what it was like to live in a town where there were no jobs and no hope of jobs, only mountains, a narrow, winding river and roots that went back generations. After lunch one of the men took him on a tour, a wild joyride around mountains and through hollows he hadn't found himself. The man's love for the mountains, for this land claimed by his ancestors, was tangible to Jase. When he finally said goodbye, he had been given a view of Becca's life. Blackwater was a place out of time, and although he would never fully understand its draw for her, he understood a little more of it.

As arranged, he arrived at the Hanks' house about dinnertime. Becca had just finished giving the girls their meal when he walked in. Faith was dancing from foot to foot as Becca washed her face. Amanda had obviously already received the same washcloth treatment.

"Good day?" he asked when Becca looked up.

"Wonderful." She tried to think of a better word. Perfect? Not quite. It would be perfect when she and her babies had their own home, and naps, meals and face-washing were just daily occurrences.

He sat down, and Amanda skirted his chair, as if trying to get up enough nerve to approach him. He was sure there was a way to encourage her without scaring her to death, but he didn't know what it was. When he sat forward, she backed up three paces.

"Bill and Alice should be home any minute." Becca got to her feet. "I called the motel in Baldwin and got myself a room too. Syl's family's coming in tonight, and the house will be bustin' its seams. I don't want to put them out." She smiled. "Besides, I might have to sleep with Jimbo."

He wondered if she was giving the real reason for not going to Matty's house, or if the thought of facing that exuberant family when her own children were just a mile away under someone else's care was too much for her tonight. He had little time to wonder. Bill and Alice arrived, and there was a flurry of goodbyes. Both little girls cried when Becca left, even though she promised she and Jase would be back the next morning to take them out for the day.

"Is it always like that?" he asked when they were halfway to Baldwin.

"Sometimes it's worse."

He didn't know how to console her. He had tallied up what she would have to earn to support them. Even if she saved enough money to get into a shabby apartment and took all the aid a working woman was eligible for, she would still need more money than someone with an equivalency degree could probably earn.

"I saw a restaurant in Baldwin that looks decent," he said.

"I'm not very hungry."

Jase knew Becca well enough to suspect she had barely touched any food at the Hanks'. She would not want to be beholden to them for anything, and Bill Hanks was just the kind of person who would remind her of anything she took, even a sandwich.

He didn't mention the restaurant again. When they arrived in Baldwin he scanned the main street until he found it. Then he pulled into the parking lot. "You might not be hungry," he said, "but I'm starving."

She got out without a word. Inside she picked at broiled fish and cole slaw, shredding more than she ate. She tried to make conversation, but more often than not she stopped in midsentence.

At the motel she was given the room next to Jase's—he hoped the springs on the bed hadn't been damaged by the last occupants. The door closed behind her, and he was left with an evening of television or paperwork he had brought with him. He alternated between the two until ten-thirty, when he finally called it a night.

Without the honeymooners next door, the motel was quiet. He lay awake, hands behind his head, and stared at the ceiling. Everything he had ever touched had turned to gold, yet now, when he wanted to touch Becca's life, she wouldn't allow it.

He pictured the way she had looked with the twins. He saw the graceful swirl of her hair against her cheek, and her huge, earnest brown eyes fixed on Faith and Amanda. Now she was lovely, but never more so than when she had held one of her daughters at the window this afternoon, sunlight streaming around them both like an Appalachian Madonna and child.

As if he had conjured the woman from the vision, he heard her moving around her room. He waited for her to settle down, but there was no reassuring squeak of the bedsprings. He heard footsteps, something that sounded like a shoe hitting the floor, then the rattle of a chain and the scraping of a door. He was out of bed in a second, pulling on shorts.

When he opened his door she was beside the wall between their rooms. "Go back to sleep," she ordered. "I didn't mean to wake you."

"I wasn't asleep." He noted that she was fully, if casually, dressed. She was not going down the covered walkway for ice. "Did you decide you were hungry after all?"

Her gaze swept him. Bare chest, bare feet, denim shorts riding low on his hips and a ten dollar bet there was nothing underneath them. "No."

He lounged in the doorway. "Looking for a nightlife?"

"The nightlife in these parts isn't safe for single women."

He didn't like guessing games. He waited.

"I was going for a walk," she admitted. "I couldn't sleep."

"Are walks safe for single women?"

"Probably. There's a road over that way that leads down to the river. It's not even half a mile. I thought I'd go down there."

"Would you like some company?"

"The first time we met you didn't think I should be out walking by myself, either."

"I was right."

"You usually are, aren't you?"

"May I come?"

"You should be asleep. You don't have to worry about me."

"Okay. I'm not worried. May I come?"

He expected resistance, but the smile she flashed was grateful. "All right."

"I'll be right back."

She was sorry to see him leave. She had liked the view, more than she knew she should. She stood outside his room and thought about the hours she had lain awake considering her life. She had been acutely aware of Jase's presence in the next room. He was a recent addition to her years of memories, yet when she had tried to think of Dewey and what had gone wrong between them, it was Jase she had thought of. Dewey had taken; Jase gave. Dewey had made her feel smaller than a pinprick; Jase made her believe in herself. Dewey had told her repeatedly that she was not much of a woman; Jase told her with every admiring look, every passionate kiss, that he thought she was all woman.

She felt all woman when she was with him. Tonight she had longed for his arms around her. She didn't want comfort. It was never easy to leave her babies with the Hanks, but she could do it because she knew that soon, somehow, she would have them with her permanently. She had been through much worse and survived it without comforting. Tonight what she had yearned for was affirmation. Was she the person, the woman, she wanted to be? Was she a woman Jase Millington could fall in love with? Because somewhere along the way she had begun to fall in love with him.

He came back out, his chest and legs no longer bare. "You'll have to lead the way."

She wondered if he had been reading her thoughts. Then she realized he meant to the river. She held out her hand. "I don't want to lose you in the dark."

He squeezed it in his own. He had been afraid to touch her, not because he was afraid she would crumble, but because he was afraid she was too caught up in her children to think of him. Her hand was a gardener's, not baby soft like Cara's or the other women of his acquaintance. Firm and slightly callused, the hand was as substantial, as capable, as the woman.

She led him to the river. A full yellow moon lit their path, and they were guided by the sound of water rushing over rocks. It was obvious she had visited this spot before. She tugged him into the center of a clump of evergreens, and he realized they were in a cove, protected by tree branches. She pulled him down beside her on a flat grassy area that curved against the water. The dark ribbon of river reflected moonlight in shimmering, mystical patterns. He could understand why she had wanted to come.

"Sometimes when things would get too bad with Dewey, I'd come here," she said. "I'd borrow Alice's car if she was in a good mood, and I'd drive down here, away from Blackwater. It was like leaving all my problems behind. I'd pretend I never got married, that I'd graduated from high school and was on my way to college. I'd picture myself on a boat on the river, drifting off to a new life." For a moment she couldn't continue. "That was silly, I guess."

"It sounds like something any of us might do if we were desperate."

"Did you have a place like this?"

"Kathryn's house. I didn't have to be perfect there. I could get dirty and eat candy and climb trees. Pamela and I used to have a system. Right before we snuck off to Kathryn's, Pamela would inspect me, and I'd inspect her. We'd notice everything. Then, when we were ready to go home, we'd inspect each other again. If something was dirty or wrinkled, we'd fix it the best we could so our parents wouldn't know where we'd been or what we'd been doing."

"When I was little I was always dirty. And I practically lived in trees. I only got candy for special occasions, though. My daddy said he'd save money on candy and dentists at the same time." She leaned back until she was lying flat, looking up at the moon. Jase reclined beside her. "I wouldn't trade with you, Jase. It was good growing up here. I had people who loved me. I had the mountains and the river. I had friends who believed I could be somebody. Where did I go wrong?"

He touched her cheek, trailing his fingers slowly down the side of it. "You didn't."

"Didn't I? Then how come somebody else got my kids and I ended up living in a beat-up Chevrolet? No, don't say it. I'll tell you what happened. I went wrong when I thought I needed a man to run my life. I was little when my mama died, but I still remember how she'd wait for Daddy at the end of the day. Whatever she couldn't take care of while he'd been gone, they'd take care of it together when he got home. I grew up thinking that when I got married, I'd be more than I could ever be by myself."

"I grew up thinking that when I got married I'd become half of something."

"Like you'd shrink?"

"I suppose."

She turned on her side so she could see him better. "Is that why you never got married?"

He had never thought about it, but he supposed that was the reason. His parents had always seemed half of something instead of individuals. He had never wanted that. He liked his power, his control. He had never wanted to share who he was or alter the balance in his life. He had never wanted to become less than he had always been.

Until that moment he had never realized how his view of his parents' marriage had colored his life, just as Becca's had colored hers. "What did you find out from being married?" he asked.

"I had a lot of time to think about it in prison. I figured out that marriage can make you half of what you were or three times as powerful and happy, just depending on who you pick. If you pick somebody like Dewey, it's the same as taking one of those shrinking pills, like in *Alice in Wonderland.* If you marry somebody like my daddy, then you just grow and grow until you're just about too big for the White Rabbit's hole."

Their faces were only inches apart. He saw wariness in her eyes, and right along with it a determination not to let it control her life. "Then you'd risk it again?"

"I didn't say that."

"Would you?"

"How about you? Are you going to be Cleveland's oldest living eligible bachelor?"

He smiled and moved a little closer. "No woman has ever questioned me about marriage and lived to tell the tale."

"Would you swallow a woman up, Jase?"

"I'd probably try."

"And if she wouldn't let you?"

"I'd probably be glad."

"Probably."

"I'm new at this, Becca. I don't know."

"What are you new at?"

"I'm new at you." He leaned forward and kissed her. Her lips were soft and yielding, and the first taste of her made him realize just how much he wanted her. He made a sound low in his throat and kissed her again.

She lay back and slid her arms around his neck. Thoughts of that, of him, had intruded all day. She had thought of Jase as she fed her daughters lunch, thought of him as she read them a fairy tale before their nap. She hadn't wanted to, but she had found that thoughts of Jase were one thing she couldn't control. She worried about it, just as she worried about the way her body was melting into his, but she didn't worry enough to stop him from kissing her.

His lips trailed to her ear. She could feel the warmth of his breath against her earlobe, and something inside her struggled for freedom. She let her hands drift down his back, kneading his taut muscles until they flowed under her fingers. He gave a groan of pleasure as she touched him. Something similar escaped her lips as he kissed the side of her neck, the hollow of her throat. He was in no hurry to give her pleasure or to take his own. He seemed to want to know every inch of skin, to test it for its pleasure potential and gauge how his touch there affected her.

Her eyelids fluttered shut as he kissed her ear. He stroked her hair and whispered encouragement, flattery, words of affection that were as devastating as his touch.

When he lifted her shirt, her heart sped faster. She had never been kissed or touched this way. His lovemaking was a gift, not something he was taking from her. His hands and lips lulled her, like the hypnotic rhythm of the river; they excited, like the cool mountain air against her skin.

She had dreamed on this piece of ground, but nothing she had ever dreamed had been this impossible. It was impossible that Jase wanted her, impossible that she wanted him. After everything that had happened to her, she still wanted him. After everything he'd had, he wanted her. Her. "I'm dreaming again," she whispered.

"It's not a dream. Not a—" He cut short his own reply by kissing her again. Her skin was so warm, so smooth. He found her bra clasp, and his hand closed over her breast, warmer and smoother still. He savored her soft moan and the rush of heat between his legs. Sensation seemed to pool each place she touched and each hidden place she didn't. His body was taut with yearning. He undressed her slowly, not because he wanted this to last forever, but because his hands were suddenly uncoordinated. He was no longer the man who controlled his world. This piece of it was beyond his control. Becca wasn't his for the taking. She was giving herself, and he was the blessed recipient.

He stripped off his own shirt so that he could feel her breasts against his bare chest. She was slender—he doubted that would ever change—but she was all woman, with breasts that swelled against his hand and hips that curved gracefully from a tiny waist. He kissed her eyelids and watched her smile. He cupped her breast and watched her eyelids part.

"Better than a dream." She threaded her fingers through his hair and pulled him back down to her. "Much... much..."

The Kentucky night air rolled over them, and spray from the river dampened the grass. Nothing could cool the warmth surging through Becca. She was coming alive after months, years, of suffocating her feelings, imprisoning her heart. She didn't know if she was ready for this, but Jase had forced her rebirth. In this one thing he had given her no choice. Fear warred with joy, but joy won easily. No promises had been made except that he wanted her. And she wanted him. More than she had known a woman could want a man.

His hands were magic. He touched her breasts as if he knew just how and where he could give her the most pleasure. He stroked and molded her flesh as if it were his to mold. His lips were magic, too. He kissed her breast, just over her thundering heart. She lifted herself to him as he took more of her in his mouth, then more.

She moaned her pleasure as he unlocked all the secret places inside her where yearning and need had been hidden. She moved against him as if unlocking his secret desires, too. Her legs twined with his; her arms held him; her lips explored what they could. His lips left her breast. He kissed her as if he knew exactly what would excite her now. Her lips parted easily beneath the thrust of his tongue; her legs parted and wrapped around him as naturally as if they had always been lovers.

Somewhere beside the river a bobolink called to his mate. She called to hers by pushing away the final scraps of cloth between them. With her naked flesh against his, she felt fully alive. Heat magnified heat. Flesh called to flesh. He was hard against her, hard and probing and much desired. Still, he didn't enter her. His hands slid to her hips, then one hand to the place where all sensation focused. She held her breath and forgot she was anything but a woman being loved, forgot she was anything but a woman falling in love.

His arms circled her at last, and he held her tightly against him, as if savoring this last, precious moment before everything changed. When he finally made them one, she gave herself up to his passion. She knew that he was a man who had forgotten everything except love.

Chapter Ten

Becca woke up the next morning wrapped tightly in Jase's arms. For a moment she thought they were still on the riverbank. Then she remembered that they had gone back to the motel and fallen asleep together in Jase's room. But not before they had made love again.

She wondered how she had dared to allow this to happen. Loving Jase could change the entire focus of her life. But what room was there for a man like Jase in a life such as hers?

"You're awake?"

She couldn't pretend. "Just."

"And you're lying there having regrets?"

"Not exactly."

"Then what, exactly?"

"I'm lying here thinking how hungry I am. And wishing that I'd eaten that fish last night. I guess that counts as regrets."

He knew that wasn't true, but he didn't want to push. He wanted to remember last night and the woman who had twined herself around every part of him, the woman he had fallen in love with. The woman who would put up every roadblock to love that her pigheaded, shortsighted, thank-you-very-much-but-I'll-do-it-myself brain could come up with.

"There's a room service menu. We can eat here."

She wondered about the pure indulgence of eating in bed, of punching out a number or two so someone could come running with hot coffee and omelets. Jase took room service for granted while she thought a fast-food breakfast was an unbelievable extravagance. It was a reflection of the differences between them.

When she didn't respond, he guessed what she was thinking. "Let me explain something about the financial system in this country," he said, pulling her closer. "Those who have money have to spend it, otherwise those who don't will never get any. Now, that may not be fair, and it may not be pretty, but it's realistic. If I don't pick up that phone, some employee, maybe somebody from Blackwater even, maybe somebody with kids—lots of kids—won't have anything to do this morning. And if he doesn't have anything to do, then pretty soon he'll be let go. And if he's let go, he won't have any money to spend, and pretty soon the man at his grocery store and maybe his gas station will be let go, too."

"So if you don't call for room service, pretty soon the whole town, maybe the whole region, has to move away to find a job?"

"And they move to Cleveland, where the whole cycle continues until I'm out of work, and then you're out of work, too."

"And pretty soon everybody's out of work."

"Now you've as good as got a degree in economics."

She wanted to lecture him for joking about something so serious, but she found herself laughing instead. In a way he was right. Jase had money to spend, and when he spent it, someone benefitted. In this case, she benefitted most of all, since she wouldn't have to get out of bed and get dressed quite yet. She pushed all her doubts about their differences aside for the moment. She was in bed with the man who had taught her what pleasure could mean. She was in bed with the man whose green eyes were sparking warmth in places he had already thoroughly explored. She was in bed with a man who was teaching her that she could love again.

"I've never had room service," she admitted.

"Then it'll be a treat."

"Will they wait and bring it when you ask them to?"

"They will."

She ran her fingers down his chest. "That would be a treat, too."

He made the call, then he gave his attention to more important matters.

As if Alice and Bill wanted to avoid having Becca come into the house, the girls were waiting on the porch when Jase and Becca arrived to pick them up. Today Jase couldn't immediately tell them apart, since their barrettes were the same color, but he was beginning to see differences between them. Faith was quicker to smile and quicker to pout. Amanda was more serene. Their personalities were often reflected in their expressions and in the way they moved. He suspected that by the end of the morning they would not be able to fool him.

Becca had suggested a picnic, and before leaving Baldwin he had bought a bucket of the chicken Kentucky was known for. Now Becca guided him up into the same hills that he had toured yesterday at breakneck speed with one of her many admirers.

"Do you like waterfalls?" she asked.

He wasn't going to admit that when he saw waterfalls he thought of raw power just waiting to be developed and channeled. Pamela had been telling him that he was myopic for years. He was only just beginning to see what she meant.

"Doesn't everybody like waterfalls?" he countered.

"I'm taking you to a bitty one. It's nothing fancy, but hardly anybody knows about it, so we'll probably be alone. First you've got to swear you won't tell where it is."

"Who would I tell?"

"I don't know. You might decide to build a hotel there someday. No restaurant. Nothing but room service."

She flashed him one of her uncommon smiles. He reminded himself that he was a well satisfied man with enough self-control to get through the next hours without making love to her again. Then he reminded himself once more.

They parked and walked to the waterfall, with everybody toting something. He brought the chicken and a blanket; Becca brought the bag with soft drinks, salads and napkins, and each of the girls brought a canvas bag brimming with toys. The fall was a sparkling spray of water cascading over a cliff into a shallow pool. The girls could run carefully beneath the fall to cool off and did so half a dozen times while he and Becca set up the picnic.

"Hasn't anybody told them it's still early?" he asked.

"*They* didn't stay up most of the night playing patty cake."

"Is that what we did?"

"Close enough." She smoothed out the blanket. "You don't know much about kids, do you?"

"Not much."

"Don't you want some?"

He had given it little thought. "I don't think I'm father material."

"Maybe not."

He looked up from unpacking the chicken. "Nobody says you have to agree."

"Well, if you don't think you'd be a good father, you probably wouldn't be. Fathers have to have confidence. They have to enjoy taking charge and making things right. We both know how you hate that."

He smiled at her, although she was bending over and couldn't see him. "I get the point."

"You know what I think? I think you've been so busy moving Cleveland around to make it prettier and grander that you just pushed the idea of kids somewhere far away."

"Maybe."

"It's too bad, too, because you could be a happy man if you'd just let yourself."

"How do you know I'm not a happy man?"

"I didn't mean you weren't happy. I just think you could be happier. You could have something more than a view out the window."

He wondered how she had managed to put his life and everything he had ever strived for into five little words. "A view out the window." It fit. He'd spent his life changing that view, but only rarely had he reached for anything he saw.

Dripping wet, the girls came back to flop down on the blanket. Jase had no idea what three-year-olds ate, but after he'd watched these particular three-year-olds make a mid-morning snack of drumstick after drumstick, he guessed anything that had ever been alive was on the list. He watched Becca dole out potato salad and coleslaw as if it were candy, until each girl was begging for more. He watched her make a game of wiping hands and faces and cleaning up.

They were back scampering under the waterfall before he commented, "How often do they eat?"

"About as often as they can."

"You're wonderful with them."

"Do you think so?" She stopped cleaning up and met his eyes. "Do you think when I'm gone they remember the things I've said to them? Do they remember I love them?"

"From the way they greet you, I'd say they do."

"I've got to bring them to live with me soon. Before they start to doubt it."

He wasn't going to repeat his offer. The time wasn't right, and he was a master of timing. He was going to offer again, though, and soon. The more he saw Becca with her daughters, the more convinced he was that she had to let him help her.

She stood and fumbled through one of the canvas bags the girls had brought with them. "Here, look at this." She came to sit beside him. He noticed the way her leg stretched along the length of his, the way her breast brushed up against his side. The intimacy went along with the sound of children's laughter and falling water, with summer sunshine and clear Kentucky mountain air. Something almost like a shudder passed through him. He wanted to stop time and keep that feeling passing through him forever.

He forced himself to stretch out his hand. Unbelievably, the spell wasn't broken. "What's this?"

"It's a kin doll. Don't rack your brain. You've never seen one before."

"Isn't Kin Barbie's boyfriend?"

She poked him. The poke went along with the moment. He grabbed her fingers and brought them to his mouth for a kiss.

"That's Ken. This is a kin doll. Far as I know, they're just made in Blackwater. It's a tradition. Started a long time ago, I guess, because I have a whole set that were mine when I was little. Matty's keeping them for me."

He examined the doll, a fanciful ten-inch rag doll that was beautifully crafted and realistic. "Definitely not Raggedy Anne."

"How old do you think she is? I mean, how old a person is she supposed to be?"

The plump, smiling doll was clad in a plain blue dress with a white apron and sturdy-looking shoes. Her hair was gray, pulled back in a tidy bun.

"She has glasses somewhere, only Amanda always loses them," Becca said.

"I'd say she's supposed to be a woman in her sixties."

"That's right. It took the Ladies Guild a while to get the wrinkles right on this one. Alice and her friends at the Baptist Church make them. Women there have been making them for years for the Christmas bazaar."

"What does 'kin doll' mean?"

"She's kin to a whole family of dolls. She's a grandmother. Alice always lets one of the girls take her when they're going away for the day. That way, if they miss Alice, they can pull out the doll. There's a mama doll, too, only there's no reason to have it here today, since I'm with them."

He imagined the girls with their mama doll when Becca was away. "And they keep it with them when you're gone?"

"There's a whole family. Fathers, grandfathers, aunts and uncles, cousins, babies. Every year the guild makes somebody new. About ten years ago the men got into it and made little books with leather covers that said Family Bible. When you open them, there's room to put the name of every kin in that family and their birthdays. The men make furniture for them, too, rocking chairs and beds and trunks for their clothes. They make more than they can sell."

She busied herself putting the doll back in the bag. "When I leave the girls I tell them that I'm giving their mama doll all my love to keep there with them. Any time they miss me they're supposed to find their doll and give her a hug, and then some of my love will be touching them. I don't know what people do who don't have kin dolls."

He didn't want to think about Becca parting from her children. He felt a rush of anger at her stubbornness, and the magic spell disappeared. "Not everybody has to worry."

"Not everybody has to leave kids behind. I know that. But a lot of people do, Jase. Daddies who are divorced and don't have custody, mamas who have to put their kids in day care for most of the day, grandpas and grammas who live far away and only see their grandbabies on holidays. Seems to me a lot of people could use kin dolls."

He didn't want to talk about dolls. The idea was cute and, to his knowledge, highly original. But it wasn't important. What mattered was Becca bringing her children to live with her so that they no longer needed dolls to remind them of their mother.

He would have told her so, too, timing be damned, except that the twins tired of the waterfall again and came back to see what else there was to do. Becca suggested a walk. They followed a path so old it might once have been used by the Native Americans who had roamed the land. Wildflowers grew deep in woods that loggers had never touched, and Becca taught the girls their names.

They walked farther than they had intended, caught up in the cool beauty of the path. The girls, hungry again, began to whine. Amanda found a rock she liked and refused to walk any farther. Becca picked her up to carry her, and immediately Faith wanted the same.

Jase held out his arms as Becca stooped to put Faith on her other hip. "Let me carry her," he said. "They're too heavy for you to manage."

"No, they're not. I—"

He felt another flash of anger. "Let me do something to help."

This time she heard the anger. Startled, she stared at him, but he was already scooping Faith into his arms. Faith went without protest, as if she thought the idea of having this strong, handsome man carry her was a good one.

"I just didn't want you to feel you had to do it," Becca said.

He bit back his reply because he didn't want to argue in front of the girls. Faith settled against him as if he had been carrying her since birth. She put her chubby arms around his neck and leaned her head against his shoulder. He wondered why he had never thought about having children.

It was midnight by the time they got back to Cleveland. They had stopped for dinner along the way, but neither of them had eaten much. He had listened to music on the drive, and Becca had slept. Jase didn't know which had tired her more, the pleasures of their night together or the trauma of leaving her children again.

In the conversational void he had been given lots of time to think, more than he needed. But even with all that time, he knew he still wasn't thinking clearly. His motto had always been Watch and Wait. He almost always got what he wanted because he knew how to bide his time. Emotion had never come into it. He had never wanted anything so badly that he felt any impact if he didn't get it. That objectivity had always served him well, because it meant he could not be manipulated. He had a reputation as a man of ice in business dealings.

He was not a man of ice where Becca was concerned. Something vital inside him had been shredded to pieces over the weekend. If he didn't know which had tired Becca, their lovemaking or parting from her daughters, he also didn't know which had affected him more. He was a man who'd had his share of women, though he had never been indiscriminate. Singles bars weren't his style, and even as a young man fresh out of college he hadn't kept a black book of his conquests. But he hadn't been celibate, either. At no time, in all the years he was fighting his way up the ladder of success, had anyone like Becca come into his life.

It wasn't her vulnerability. God knows, the word must have been invented with Becca in mind. She was vulnerable to life in a way that no one else of his acquaintance had ever been. The simplest things had been denied her, yet still she fought for those things, things everyone unquestionably deserved. Simple things like a home and the right to care for her own children.

Her vulnerability had touched him, but it was her strength, her determination, that had grabbed him and never let go. And now there was so much more. There was the way her dark eyes sparked with life when he touched her, the way her skin flushed, the way she moved when his body was close to hers. Nothing in his life had been so sweet, so powerful, as making love to her. They had not had sex. He'd had sex before, and now he knew the difference. They had made love.

And even if they had not made children together, he had felt some of Becca's pain when she had been forced to leave her girls crying in the Hanks' doorway. Hell, he had felt his own pain. Children grew fast. He knew that much. What would they look like when he saw them again? What new mischief would they have invented? And wasn't there always the chance that he might never see them again, that Becca might not? Becca had to consider that every time she left Blackwater. She could not be there to protect her daughters, and even though the Hanks obviously cared greatly, wasn't it always in the back of Becca's mind that something might happen while she was gone?

He had turned those thoughts over and over as he'd driven the miles between Blackwater and Shaker Heights. In between cycles he had reached for his famous objectivity, but there had been no trace of it.

Now, parked in the driveway of Kathryn's—no, *his*—house he had told himself to let go of it all, to wake up

Becca and escort her to the cottage—or into his bed—
without telling her about his turmoil. They could talk later,
when the time was right. He knew better than to talk now.
He knew better.

"Becca?"

She stirred but didn't wake up.

He touched her shoulder, and without conscious per-
mission his hand slid to the back of her neck, warm, soft
skin, druggingly sweet. "Becca, wake up. We're home."

Her eyes opened slowly. She turned and smiled. Not fully
awake, she touched his cheek. "Where are we?"

"Back in Shaker. Home."

"That's right. I was dreaming about the girls. But we left
them, didn't we?"

His hand tightened on her neck. Then he pulled it away.
"We did."

"Amanda cried." She rested her head on the back of the
seat and stared straight ahead. "Faith is learning not to."

"Let's go inside." He got out of the car before she could
answer and came around to open her door.

She was out by the time he got there. "You must be exhausted. I didn't help with the driving at all."

"I didn't mind."

"But I should have helped."

"No, you shouldn't have." His tone was sharper than he
had meant it to be.

"What's wrong?"

"Don't you think you're carrying independence to extremes?"

"Sounds to me like we're not talking about who drove
and who didn't."

He jammed his hands into his pockets in frustration.
"We can get our suitcases tomorrow. It's late now. Let's
just go to bed."

"Whose bed? Is that what's bothering you?" Becca realized she was wide awake now. "Are you afraid I'll ex-

pect more from you than you want to give me? You didn't make any promises, Jase. I'm not expecting—"

"You don't expect a damn thing, do you?"

She leaned against the car and stared at him.

"Do you?" he repeated. "You don't expect anything. Not room service, not a ride to Blackwater, not help with your kids, not even an explanation of what I'm thinking. What is it, Becca? You talk about my view out the window, but I'm not the only person around here who settles for a view when they could have so much more."

"A view is more than I've had at times."

"So?"

"You wouldn't understand. You haven't understood before when I've tried to tell you how I feel about being helped."

"You want to know what I understand? I understand that I could make a difference in your life, only you're not going to let me! And you know why? Because you're afraid you're going to be let down again. It's not pride, it's fear that keeps you from taking my help."

"I don't need anybody's help. I'm going to make it on my own. And if you can't understand that, then you can't understand me."

"Maybe I don't. But I understand your little girls. They need their mother. I can give them their mother. Do you know what a drop in the bucket it is for me to help you? Do you have any idea what I'm worth? I can't find enough ways to spend my money, Becca. And here's something good, something that can really make a difference, and I'm not allowed to help. Do you know how that makes me feel?"

She stared at him for a moment before she spoke. "I can't imagine."

"It makes me feel more frustration than I knew I had in me."

"It's good for you."

"What?"

"I said it's good for you. Most of the world feels frustration every day. So maybe, just maybe, Jason Millington the Whatever ought to feel a little now and then, too. Maybe there ought to be some little corner of the world, some little speck in Jase's view out the window, that he can't change! Maybe it'll build his character!"

This time he stared. "So it's my character under discussion? Not the fact that your children are eight hours away in another state when they could be here with you?"

"They will be! The minute I can make it happen. Are you questioning how much I love them? I love them enough to give them a mother who can take care of them! Not the two-bit mistress of a rich man!"

His hands shot out of his pockets, and he took a step toward her. "What's that supposed to mean?"

"It means that last night has nothing, *nothing,* to do with what I'll take from you and what I won't. I won't let you keep me, Jase, no matter how good you think your reasons are. I slept with you last night, but it was a one-night stand. One night. That's it. I won't do it again, not if you think it gives you rights to my life! I don't need any man poking around in my heart trying to figure out what I need and for what reasons! And I won't have any man telling me I'm not a good mother because I don't want his charity!"

"Charity? You call it charity?"

"Char-i-ty. When one person rescues another. Only I don't need rescuing. I might have once, and thank you very much for everything. But I don't need it again!"

He leaned closer to her, propping one hand beside her head. "Let's try another word. How about love? Maybe I want to help you because I'm falling in love with you."

"You don't know what that means." Her eyes were only inches from his, but she didn't flinch. "Love doesn't mean taking over somebody else's life. That's what Dewey tried to do, and I let him. I let him because I believed it was love.

172   *ONE PERFECT ROSE*

But now I know what real love is. Love means trusting another person to do what's right for them, and what's right for you. And I'll tell you, Jase, letting you bail me out of my troubles isn't right for either of us. You'll go on thinking forever that that's the way things should always be between us. Making things right. Making more things right. Never believing that I could make them right without you. Never letting me make anything right for you."

"That's not true!"

"No? You don't trust me. You don't believe I can make a life for myself without your help. You don't believe I can get the girls without your money or your fancy lawyers. You've been thinking about hiring a lawyer ever since you met Alice and Bill, haven't you?"

"So?"

"So it won't come to that. They'll let me have the girls when I'm ready. I know them. The girls are more important to them than getting back at me. But you don't trust me to know that, do you?" She slid out from under his arm and went to the back seat to get her suitcase.

In the seconds it took, he realized what he had done. He had not bided his time; he had not waited for the right moment to approach Becca. His timing had been off by a century. He watched her carry her suitcase toward the cottage. All his anger knotted inside him. "I just want to help you," he said loudly enough for her to hear.

"Then forget about this weekend. It was a mistake!" She hefted the suitcase a little higher, determined not to let him see her drag it.

"If love is trust, then where's your trust in me?"

She turned. "I never said I loved you."

"No, you never did."

"I don't have room in my life for love. And neither do you." She started back up the sidewalk.

He watched her lift the suitcase higher, as if trying to prove she could manage it alone. But he didn't go after her to help. Before she reached the cottage he was inside the house, and the door was locked behind him.

Chapter Eleven

The door slammed against the wall of Jase's office, and he didn't even bother to look up. "So you think there's some merit in the idea?" he said into the receiver. "A resort seems feasible to you?"

The ear not glued to the telephone picked up the rustle of a skirt. His eyes flickered to Pamela, who was settling herself across the desk from him. "I'm sorry, I missed that," he said.

He listened attentively, nodding at the words of the man on the other end of the line. "Okay. I'll expect all the facts and figures by the end of the week. Sounds like you've done the homework we need." He cradled the receiver and made a few notes before he gave Pamela his attention.

"Resorts, Jase? Heady stuff."

"Just an idea I'm working on."

"Tell me about it."

He picked up his pen, the same one Pamela had said was worth more than half the furniture in The Greenhouse, and tapped out an impatient rhythm. "Since when have you been interested in my business?"

"I'm always interested in everything about you."

"In changing everything about me."

"Not everything. You have a nice smile. I wish I could see it more often these days. What is it? The weather? July's hot as—"

"I know how hot July is. Everybody in town knows it."

"Is it the move? Isn't the house coming along fast enough?"

He pictured the house. *House Beautiful* wanted to picture it in an article on America's Tudor architecture. The grounds alone were a picturebook masterpiece, thanks to Becca. At least, he assumed it was thanks to Becca. He hadn't gotten more than a glimpse of her in three long weeks, but he hadn't sought her out, either. He was a businessman who knew how to cut his losses.

Only it had never hurt before.

"The house is fine. Great, in fact. Everything will be finished by mid-August. I couldn't be happier."

"Oh, I think you probably could," she said dryly. "I mean, if this is happy, you'll have to do unhappy for me sometime, so I can see the subtle differences."

"What's the point of this?"

"So tell me about the resort?"

Jase had grown up with Pamela. He knew mercurial shifts of subject came naturally to her. "Don't mention this to Becca."

"Uh-oh."

"No uh-oh. I just don't want to tell her until I'm sure I want to go through with it. You know she comes from a place called Blackwater in Kentucky."

"She's told me a little."

"It's a hole, only it's a hole surrounded by some of God's finest scenery. There's nothing else there, but the

scenery grabs and shakes you." He stood restlessly and
went to the window.

A view from the window.

He turned away quickly. "Anyway, when I was there, I
started thinking how much they needed some industry to
move in and give people jobs. There's nothing now, even
the mines are closed. No one's had much training, so it
would have to be something that unskilled people could do.
The only assets they have are scenery and cheap, cheap
land, a lot of which is for sale."

"I think I can see what's coming."

"There's nothing quite like what I'm planning in the
area. There are plenty of parks, and there are resorts not
too far away. But nothing really exclusive. I want to build
a private club and capitalize on the scenery and the isola-
tion. Something better than first class, something only the
richest could afford. Lots of acreage between houses, lots
of prestige. We could draw from cities all around, Lexington, Louisville, Cincinnati, even as far as Pittsburgh and
Cleveland.

"How is this going to benefit anyone in Blackwater?"

He examined her face to see if she was joking. "How
could it not benefit them? There would be service jobs ga-
lore. There would be a market for any crafts they wanted to
sell. There would be patrons for the few stores that are already there and a wide open field for anyone who wanted
to build more. Anyone who wanted to raise a garden could
sell vegetables. Anyone who wanted to keep a few hives of
bees could sell honey. The potential is limitless."

"*You* think so."

"Anyone will think so. It's only a risk to me. I'll have to
sink a lot of money into the project." He smiled cynically
as he remembered something he had said to Becca. "But
I'm always looking for ways to spend money."

She frowned. "What do you mean?"

"I won't come out of this with much, but I won't take a loss, either. It's something I want to do for Blackwater."

"You want to do it for them."

"That's right."

"What happens if they don't want you to?"

The question seemed so absurd that he couldn't even think of an answer.

"You haven't thought about that, have you?"

"Of course they'll want me to. Their standard of living will skyrocket."

Pamela sighed. "You still don't understand people, do you? Not everyone has your enthusiasm for change."

"You're trying to tell me the poor want to stay that way?"

"I'm trying to tell you the poor have a right to decide how they're going to live their lives."

"I know what I'm doing."

She unfolded her legs and stood, coming around the desk to kiss him on the cheek. "That's your fatal flaw. You always know what you're doing."

"I didn't hear this lecture when I came to you with my idea for turning the factory into apartments."

"That's because you weren't taking anything away from anybody. And, by the way, that's what I came to talk to you about." She stared past him at the window. "You know, I don't know how you stand this view day in and day out. I feel like a fish in an aquarium. The whole world's out there, and I can't touch it."

"I don't want to talk about the view."

She turned, obviously surprised by the intensity in his voice. "Sorry. Did I hit a nerve?"

"What did you want to talk about?"

"I just thought you'd want to hear that everything's going better than we expected for Friday night. We finally got the band to donate their time and talent in exchange for the publicity they'll get. And two more restaurants have kicked in donations. One's even going to send a chef to make crepes to order. That was Mother's idea. You should see her manipulate people, Jase. It gives me chills, but it's effective."

"So Mother has her assets?"

"The first time we sat down to plan, she told the board in no uncertain terms that they were a bunch of cowards. She demanded they shoot for three times the goal they'd set or she wasn't going to lift a finger to help."

"Our mother?"

"Ours. The one whose fingers look like they've never been lifted in her life. Then she proceeded to tear into everybody, ripping them open to see what they could do best. By the time she was finished, people were agreeing to do things they'd never thought about before. It was amazing."

"Will you meet the goal?"

"Truly?" She shrugged. "I don't know. Instead of pricey tickets, Mother insisted we solicit contributions at the party, so who knows? We made up the guest list backward. Mother publicized it in the *right* places. Then people had to call us and ask to come before they got an invitation. A lot of people have invited themselves."

"Well, that's unique."

"Everything's unique. Having the party at the factory is unique. There's not even any air-conditioning."

"It fits the theme."

"'A Night in the Tropics' isn't exactly my idea of a good time in July. I'd be more inclined to attend 'A Night in the Arctic.'"

"Why are you here, Pamela?"

She perched on the edge of his desk. "That's pretty good, Jase. We talked for what, a minute, two, before you asked me to get to the point? You're slipping."

"I have ten hours of work to cram into three."

"That sounds like an improvement, too. Anyway, I want you to invite Becca to the party. I already have, and she's refusing to come. She's worked as hard or harder than anyone else to make it happen. She's—"

"She's what?"

"She's working two jobs, but she still finds time to make telephone calls, assemble packets of information, anything she can do from the cottage, since her car isn't running anymore."

"She had the car towed away before I could do anything about it." He wasn't oblivious to the symbolism of that act. The day after they had gotten back from Blackwater, he'd come home from the office to find that Becca's car was gone. One of the electricians had told him that a wrecker had taken it away for scrap. And that afternoon, Becca, as she had every Monday, left fifteen dollars for the first round of car repairs in his mailbox.

"She deserves to come to the party," Pamela said, "but she says she has too much to do. We need her there. She's the best example I know why the apartments are so important."

"You want to show her off like a trained monkey!"

Her eyes widened. "I beg your pardon?"

He jammed his hands into his pockets. "She's a lot more than a good example of a homeless woman. She's a person. With feelings. Maybe she doesn't want to share her life story with a bunch of people who can't tell that party from the one they attended last week for the symphony or the zoo or the art museum!"

"Boy, you've got it bad, don't you? Excuse me while I pull my jaw off the floor."

"Time to leave, Pamela."

"I'm about to. But let me clue you in on something first. Becca has some other reason for not coming. It's not me. I have never, never, embarrassed the women I work with. I have nothing but respect for them. And I more than respect Becca. What you don't see is that she respects herself. She's not ashamed of anything about her life.'' She got up to search for her purse. "Maybe you can't say the same.''

As she walked out the door he wondered who was left for him to alienate. "Pamela?''

She turned. "I'm ready and waiting.''

"I'm sorry. I really am. I know better.''

"That's right. You do. So will you invite her or not?''

He was trapped. If he said no, he had to explain. "I'll talk to her.''

"Good. I'm counting on you.''

He wanted to tell her that this time he had no assurance the famous Millington determination was going to get results. But that was much too hard to admit. Especially after an apology. "I'll do my best,'' he said.

"We'll both be at the factory this evening working on decorations.''

"I'll be there.''

The worst job in preparation for the party had been to shovel truckload after truckload of trash and debris out of the factory building. One of Jase's work crews had seen to that, along with ridding the building of all four-, six- and eight-legged occupants and tacking wire mesh over all the windows that weren't boarded over. The theme might be "A Night in the Tropics,'' but nobody wanted to carry it to extremes.

Once the building was clean, volunteers had swarmed in. Mrs. Millington had insisted the decorations be concentrated in certain areas so that the rest of the building would be uncluttered for guests to examine.

There was to be a display near the entrance showing the plans for the building's renovation and a model of a proposed apartment. There would be information about The Greenhouse and the increasing problem of homelessness and abuse of women. More frivolous areas would be set up throughout the first floor. One entire corner was supposed to evoke a rain forest, another a tropical island with a volcano. Tables with food donated by some of Cleveland's finest restaurants were to be scattered throughout, and liquor was to flow freely. A reggae band was scheduled for the night, and Mrs. Millington had insisted on a limbo contest.

The frivolity was incidental to the real theme, and no one would leave without realizing it. A dozen guides had been trained to lead tours through the building and answer questions about the renovations and the reasons for them. Pledge cards would be given out at the end of the tour, and anyone who pledged five thousand dollars or more would have their name on an ornamental plaque commissioned to be hung in the entryway when the renovations were completed.

When Jase arrived, the rain forest was under construction. Two hundred square feet were slowly being turned into the Amazon basin. The trees and plants, supplied by local nurseries and florists, would arrive on Friday, but in the meantime, the rest of the area was being readied. He found Pamela cutting thin strips of iridescent plastic to hang from the high ceiling. He had vetoed the use of an industrial humidifier spewing mist into the air because of possible damage to the floors. The plastic—much to his mother's chagrin—was going to have to simulate rain.

"Remind you of your high school prom?" he asked.

Pamela looked up, a waif incarnate with her hair plastered to her head from the heat and old jeans cut off at the tops of her thighs. "The Eleanor Rexford Academy was too snooty to have a prom. We had a spring formal, and it was held at a country club. Decorations were considered tacky."

"Maybe that's why these fund-raisers have appeal. Everybody who attends was deprived of the public school experience."

"You're welcome to help me make rain."

"Thanks, but I'm here to see Becca."

"She's over in the forest. Probably on a ladder. She's the only volunteer who's not afraid of heights."

"She's spent a fair amount of time on my roof learning to patch slate."

"Go get her, tiger."

"I don't do miracles."

"No? Have you admitted that before?"

Becca was easy to spot. Jase skirted the men setting up a stage for the band and a crew of half a dozen women covering chicken wire with papier-mâché to resemble a volcano. Becca stood out, since she was the only person balancing on one leg twelve feet above everybody else attaching strips of artificial rain.

He didn't like the looks of her ladder. And he particularly didn't like the way she was ignoring the principles of physics.

"Becca." He didn't shout, but doubtlessly his voice carried to the rafters beyond.

She didn't answer.

"Becca? Would you come down for a minute?"

"When I've finished what I'm doing."

He winced as she leaned farther out. "If you come down, I can move the ladder so that will be easier."

"Don't you think I know how to move a ladder?"

He noticed that the papier-mâché crew had stopped their chatter to listen. "Nobody moves one better. I just needed something to do."

"Why? Isn't there anybody here you can boss around? We should all do what we do best."

He ignored a gasp from the direction of the volcano. "Shall I come up there?"

"Suit yourself."

He eyed the ladder and decided there was no assurance it would hold them both. "Where did this thing come from, anyway?"

"I believe it belongs to Jason Millington the Whatever. So don't worry, it must be perfect."

He was on rung three before he realized she had goaded him into this. "You're being unreasonable."

"Now that's not how we'd say it in the hills of Kentucky. We'd say something like—"

"Never mind how you'd say it." He climbed to rung six. His face was level with her heels. He climbed until it was level with her backside. One part of him admired the curves three inches from his nose. The other part wanted to turn those curves over his knee. "Are you happy now? I've humiliated myself and put us both in danger just to give you what you wanted."

"I never said I wanted you up here."

His face was level with her shoulders now. Becca could feel the warmth of his breath against the bare skin of her back. "Don't you?" he asked.

"Go away."

"Not until you've talked to me."

"You picked a funny time to have a talk. I live one hundred yards from your house, but you haven't been inclined to talk to me there in weeks."

"I haven't seen you!"

"You don't see if you don't look."

"Why would I look for you? You as much as told me to get out of your life."

"Well, apparently you didn't listen too well."

"Will you get off this damn thing and come outside with me for a little while?" His lips were inches from the sweetest curve of silk smooth skin along her spine. "If you don't, I'm going to kiss every vertebrae in reach and give these virtuous ladies something to talk about for the next twenty years."

"It's your reputation, not mine. I have no reputation."

"Becca."

She could fight everything except the warmth mushrooming inside her at the way he said her name, the warmth and the tiny, betraying shudders that had started as soon as he was close enough to touch her. "Back on down. I need a break, anyway. But just for a little while."

"Have you eaten?"

"You're taking care of me again."

"No, I'm taking care of myself. I'm starving."

"Fine. We can grab something cheap, and you can talk with your mouth full."

"Kathryn always said that was a good idea. She was highly in favor of doing two things at once, as long as both things were fun."

"Don't expect this to be fun."

He started down. "I don't know why not. Some of the most pleasurable moments of my life have been spent with you."

"Don't start that, Jase, or I'm not going anywhere."

He waited for her at the bottom of the ladder. She took her time backing down. He glanced in the direction of the volcano. "Ladies, your papier-mâché is drying out."

The volcano crew returned to work with renewed and guilty vigor.

Becca joined him on the floor. "I meant what I said about cheap. I'm dressed to work."

"I know a place you'll like. We can walk. It's on the edge of the Flats."

He waited until Becca had washed her face and hands, then walked with her down the street. The Flats was rich with Cleveland history. There on the banks of the Cuyahoga River, in 1796, Moses Cleaveland had first set foot on the land that would someday bear his name—or a reasonable facsimile thereof. Shipping and industry had made their mark over the centuries, leaving behind imposing bridges and impressive old buildings. In recent years the Flats had become a fashionable playground, and bars and restaurants cluttered the winding streets.

Jase and Becca walked under bridges and across parking lots. "So how's Constantine's?" he asked when Becca still hadn't said a word.

"You ate there the day before yesterday. You should know."

"How do you know I ate there?"

"Mama told me."

He had specifically asked Mama not to mention him. Now he knew where Mama's loyalties lay. "What else did she say?"

"She said you were asking about me."

"Did she phone you while I was there, or did she at least wait until I'd left?"

"I don't like you checking up on me."

He had been so glad to see Becca again that he had swallowed all irritation at her sarcasm in the factory. Now irritation rose in his throat. "Look, I wasn't checking up on you. Not the way you mean. I care about you. I wanted to be sure things were going all right. You vanished from my life like a magician's assistant. How am I supposed to get my information if I don't see you? If you won't talk to me? I needed reassurance."

They walked another half a block before she answered. "I guess I can see that."

"So how is Constantine's going?"

"Fine."

"Great."

She heard the angry way he clipped his "t." As long as she hadn't come face-to-face with him in the last weeks, she had managed to convince herself that she had every right to be upset at Jase's interference. He had no rights over her just because they had made love. He'd had no right to tell her what she should do with her future or how to do it. And he'd had no right to suggest, even in a roundabout way, that she was doing less for her children than she could.

Now she realized that she had never once let herself consider Jase's feelings. She had been afraid to consider him. She was afraid, period, and she wasn't even sure of what. All she knew was that she was afraid, and walking beside him magnified that fear. Knowing she had hurt him enough to make him angry made it even worse.

"I don't make a lot at Constantine's," she said, "but it's better than minimum wage. And the more the regular customers get to know me, the better they'll tip."

He relaxed a little. "Is the work hard?"

"My feet are tired by the end of a shift, but I'm holding up well. I know you don't believe this, but I'm strong. I can handle a lot now that I'm well again."

"You look good."

She resisted the urge to pat her hair. "That should increase my tips."

"You look great. You look like somebody I've been wanting to see for three weeks."

"Then why haven't you?"

"Because you told me to get out of your life."

She didn't know what to say to that. And in a second she didn't have a chance, anyway. They walked up an incline toward a sign advertising Shorty's, an unprepossessing building set off from the rest of the bars and restaurants.

Once they were inside they were back in the fifties. The decor was glass block and shiny silver sheet metal. The booths were vision-shattering turquoise, and each featured a coin-operated jukebox. Jerry Lee Lewis was just finishing "Great Balls of Fire."

Despite her stated preference, she had expected Jase to take her someplace deathly quiet with hovering waiters. The waitresses here, dressed in white uniforms, black aprons and saddle shoes, didn't hover. They ran, and as she watched, one dropped into a booth to chat and calculate the bill with her customers.

"Bring back memories?" Jase asked.

"I wasn't alive in the fifties. I can see I should have been." She smiled at him.

The smile was a brilliant stab in the gut. He realized he was addicted to her smile. And three weeks without one had left him shaken.

They were early enough that there was no line to get in, although that wasn't often the case. They were led to a booth and sat across from each other as Jan and Dean crooned "Little Old Lady from Pasadena."

The menu was diner food. Becca ordered an egg salad sandwich, and Jase got the Blue Plate Special, a patty melt and fries.

"So, why did you come looking for me this evening?" she asked when the waitress had gone. "If you thought I'd told you to get out of my life."

"Didn't you?"

"I told you that you had to learn to trust me."

"There's nobody I trust more."

"Are you listening to yourself? That's not the same as saying you trust me completely. So maybe I'm tops on the list, right along with Pamela and whoever else you've let yourself be close to—if there is anybody else. But the only person you really trust is yourself. You think you're the only one in the world who can make the right decision, whether it's for you or for somebody else."

"If I didn't trust myself completely, I wouldn't have gotten where I am today."

"And if you don't start trusting somebody else, you're going to stay exactly where you are today and never move another inch."

He was staring into eyes so dark they should have been impenetrable. But they weren't. He saw pain, right along with courage. "How'd you get so wise?" he asked at last.

"The Commonwealth of Kentucky gave me a lot of time to think."

"I'm going to back off. Your life is your life. I'm sorry."

She could only guess how hard it was for Jase to apologize. And her guess was that this was one of the few he had ever uttered. She reached for his hand, and a rush of gratitude filled her. She had missed him more than she could ever have told him. Now he had paved the way for their being together again.

She threaded her fingers through his, and the image of their bodies entwined danced before her eyes. She looked up at him and saw that the images lived for him, too. "Thank you for understanding," she said.

"I'm trying."

She brought his hand to her cheek. "Is that what you wanted to tell me?"

"No. I wanted to interfere in your life again."

"There's a sign on the wall over there that you should read."

He turned and his eyes followed her pointing finger. The sign read We Do Not Serve Bullies.

"I'm not going to bully you. Pamela asked me to talk to you about going to the fund-raiser. She wants you there. I want you there, as my date. But if you don't want to come, don't."

"Good for you."

"I really would like you to come with me."

"I'd be pleased to come, Jase. I just couldn't imagine being there when you and I were still angry at each other. I didn't want to..."

He squeezed her hand. "Didn't want to what?"

"I didn't want to watch you with another woman."

He realized they had never talked about that aspect of his life. She had told him about Dewey, but she had never asked him for reassurance that she wasn't just one of many women he hopped in and out of bed with. She had trusted him.

"I wouldn't have been with another woman. There is no other woman, hasn't really been one since I met you." He thought of Cara and the new man she was dating. He hadn't done it consciously, but since he'd found Becca, he had cut everyone else out of his life. He had made a commitment without knowing it.

"Why?"

He smiled. "Now who needs reassurance?"

"We're so different, Jase. How can anything come of this?"

"Do you remember the story you told me about your grandmother and her search every summer morning for one perfect rose?"

"Sure."

"Well, I guess I've been searching, too. But I discovered something your grandmother never did. Wild roses with lots of blooms and thorns, the kind that scramble to survive in the worst soil, are as close to perfect as roses ever get. I guess I'll take a wild rose over a pampered hybrid any day."

She smiled at him. "Just don't try to train this wild rose to any trellis. She has to grow in her own place and her own way."

"I'll try to remember."

"I've missed you."

"We wouldn't have a chance if you hadn't."

"A lot."

They only dropped hands when the waitress brought their dinner.

Chapter Twelve

"So what in heaven's name are tropical play clothes?" Becca looked at a copy of the invitation to the fund-raiser that Pamela had brought with her to the cottage. "Play clothes are what I buy my girls, and I don't think I'd feel too playful in corduroy overalls."

"Play clothes are my mother's idea of communicating what her rich and oh-so-cutesy friends should wear. Nothing formal enough to be ruined by the heat or doing the limbo, but nothing as low class as casual."

"As my great, great, great, great-uncle Daniel Boone must have said and often, I'm still lost."

"I'm going to dress like I'm going on safari. Shorts with enough pockets to store food for a week's camping trip and a jungle-print shirt. Some people will come in serviceable rhinestones."

"I'm fresh out of both."

"Why don't you go Hawaiian?"

"I don't—"

"I do. Stand up." Becca complied. Pamela looked her over with a practiced eye. "I know just the thing. I have a bikini top—now don't get excited, it's a very conservative bikini—and there's a short wrap skirt to go with it. It doesn't fit me anymore, but it will be perfect for you. It's a bright tropical print."

"You're talking about a bare stomach."

"Exactly. You'll appreciate it in the heat. You could wear silk flowers around your neck. Much classier than rhinestones."

"Real flowers."

"Even better. And sandals. Do you have any? They're on sale everywhere this month, or we can look at The Greenhouse."

Becca liked the way Pamela just took her financial status for granted. She didn't make outrageously generous offers, and she didn't pretend Becca could afford anything expensive. She accepted Becca's lack of money just as she accepted her brown eyes and Kentucky accent.

"You don't think I'll look silly?"

"Silly?" Pamela stepped back a little. "Becca, you're really lovely. Don't you know that? There will be women there who spend four hours a day on their faces and bodies, and every one of them will wish she looked just like you."

Becca could feel her cheeks heat. "I don't want to embarrass your brother."

Pamela's face grew serious. "Look, this is none of my business, but is there something going on that you want to talk about?"

"Would you like some iced tea?"

"Please."

Pamela followed Becca into the kitchen. She had made her offer to listen, now she waited.

Becca got the ice out of the freezer. She didn't look at Pamela. "Your brother and I are as different as two people can be. I know what I am, Pamela. I'm a nobody from the Kentucky hills. Worse than a nobody. I've spent time in jail. I'm not ashamed of that, but I know it puts me on the other side of the world from Jase."

"And Jase has told you that? He's made a point of it?"

"No."

"I don't think I understand."

"He's never made a point of it. But I have eyes. Jase likes to fix things. He can't stop himself. I have a life that needs fixing, so he steps in and tries to do it himself. I don't know if I'm real to him. If I didn't have so many problems, would he even look twice at me?"

Pamela watched her put ice in two glasses, add mint leaves and sun tea from a jug on the windowsill. "Let me be sure I've got this. You're afraid my brother is falling in love with you simply because he thought somebody needed to fall in love with you to improve your life?"

"I didn't say anything about love."

"Well, I did." Pamela held out her hand for the tea and took a sip. It was just strong enough, just sweet enough. "I've been watching you two fall in love, and I've got to say, it's been hard to see. I've never seen two such bullheaded people in my life. You're both trying so hard to make sure everything's perfect. I don't know which of you is the worst perfectionist."

Becca took the time she needed to let that sink in. "How can I be a perfectionist? Look at my life."

"You're a fixer. Look at this yard and the garden at The Greenhouse. Look at Jase's house. Look at this tea! And from what you've told me about your past, you worked so hard to fix things for your husband and his family that you ended up in jail because you didn't know when to stop."

"Because I tried to fix things?" Becca had never thought about herself quite that way.

Pamela nodded. "Just like my brother. But let's be clear about one thing here. I don't know if Jase has ever risked himself to fix anyone's life before—no one's but mine, anyway. He grew up trying to make life bearable for me, stepping between me and my parents so I wouldn't get hurt, sending me funny cards and letters when I was away at school, sneaking me in and out of the house so I could do things normal kids did. He got used to fixing things early, and he went on to fixing his part of the world as soon as he could. But along the way he never let himself get too close to anyone but me. Not until you came along."

"But maybe that's because no one else needed him as much as he thinks I do."

"Or maybe it's because he never needed anyone as much as he needs you."

"Tell me why. Why would Jase need me?"

"Because he can't fix things twenty-four hours a day, Becca. He's got to have a refuge. You look at yourself and see a life that's still a mess. He looks at you, I look at you, and we see a woman who'll never be beaten. That's what he needs, and somewhere deep inside he knows it. He needs someone with the same strengths that he has. Someone strong enough for him to lean on from time to time."

Becca finished her tea before she spoke. "I'm in love with him, Pamela. I was only in love once before, and that time was a terrible mistake."

"This time won't be."

"I hope you're right." She stood to clear away the glasses. "When can I borrow the bikini?"

Pamela stood, too. "I'll bring it over tonight. Roll up your T-shirt and work on a tan while you're pulling weeds."

"Thanks. Thanks a lot."

Pamela touched her shoulder. "No. Thank you. You're the best thing in Jase's life. And he's always going to be one of the best things in mine."

On Friday a late afternoon rain cooled the air and raised the humidity. Becca picked roses and marigolds, zinnias and daisies, before the storm, preserving them in the refrigerator along with the ferns and vines she planned to use on her Ohio leis. She had found a book at the library with instructions, and she left herself part of the afternoon to make two, one for herself and one for Jase. They were his flowers, after all.

By seven the leis were finished, and she was nearly ready. If the bikini top was conservative, she was a terrible prude. It covered the essentials, but only just. She had made her lei extra thick and long to compensate—she wasn't sure it did anything except draw attention to all the bare skin above and below it. The skirt was shorter than some of the shorts she owned, and when she moved, it bared one leg outrageously.

She was tucking roses into her hair when she heard Jase's knock. She stepped back from the mirror for one more look. She was tanned from all her hours in the sun, and that same sun had lightened her hair until it was unmistakably blond. The turquoise and lavender print at the top and skirt set off the warm glow of her skin. She liked what she saw. She just hoped that Jase did, too.

He did. Unmistakably. He stared at her as if she were a vision from another place and time. "I guess I did okay," she said.

"A masterful piece of understatement."

"I made you a lei, too." He was wearing an aloha shirt— she imagined he'd had more than one occasion to buy one on Waikiki. "It will look perfect."

He slipped off her lei and set it on a table by the door. Then he hauled her close and kissed her. She shut her eyes and tasted the full range of flavors and emotions his kisses always inspired. His hands stroked her bare back as he kissed her. Thoughts of the party disappeared.

He was the first to pull away. "Enough of that, or we'll never get there."

"Wouldn't that be a shame?"

"Don't tempt me."

"Then maybe I'd better go put on something else to wear."

"No, you can tempt me a little. More than a little." He picked up the lei and slipped it back over her head. It was laced with wild roses, and the light sweet fragrance went right to his gut. He kissed her again. Lightly. "Part of the tradition."

She crossed the room to get his, then returned the favor.

They were almost to the factory when she brought up something that had been bothering her. "You know, I haven't met your mother yet. I was never decorating while she was there."

He heard all her unspoken questions. What was his mother going to think of her? Was he going to introduce them? Was he going to tell his mother the truth about Becca's life?

He tried to put her mind at rest. "I'm not close to my parents. I've never told them about you because we don't discuss anything important. But I want you to meet them. I love them, even if I don't understand anything about them."

"What are they going to think about me?"

"Honestly? I don't have any idea. I don't think I know them well enough to guess."

"Go ahead and try."

"They'll think you're not good enough for me, just the way they think nobody is good enough for any Millington. They see themselves as aristocracy, even though the first Millingtons on this continent came over from England straight out of debtors' prison."

"You're just saying that."

"The next generation wasn't much better. One deserted during the Revolution and had to leave the colonies to escape being hanged. The rest of the family kept moving west to get away from their problems, and finally my great-

great-grandfather hit it big in Ohio, although there's plenty of evidence that he stole and gambled his way to prosperity. I heard all the stories from Kathryn, who thrived on family history. My parents refuse to discuss it.''

She laughed. Out loud, from somewhere deep inside her. ''Thank you.''

''I thought maybe a little perspective wouldn't hurt.''

''It didn't hurt a bit.''

They left Jase's car with a valet at the factory's front door. Becca lifted her chin and steeled herself to get through the rest of the evening.

On the first floor, lighting, a forest of plants and weeks' worth of decorating had transformed the old factory into a tropical paradise. She had been there that morning to help oversee the arrival of the forest, but she had not been able to visualize the finished project. ''It's perfect,'' she said, taking Jase's arm. ''Perfect!''

''It's hard to believe.'' He put his hand over hers when she started to pull it away. ''Come on, let me introduce you to some people.''

''I thought I'd just go see if anyone I knew—''

''You're staying with me. For a while.'' He looked down at her and smiled. ''Please?''

''Because you asked.''

Immediately he was the center of attention. The idea was his, the factory was his, and the lovely young stranger with the figure his mother's ladies-who-lunch crowd would kill for appeared to be his, too. He introduced her to couple after couple. He had no way of telling her who they were, what giant corporations they represented or what portion of Cleveland they owned, and he was just as glad. He introduced her as Becca. The guests exchanged five or six words with her and wanted to know if she was acquainted with the Reynolds or Jacksons or Hennesseys of Louisville. Lovely state, Kentucky. Such beautiful horses and acres of bluegrass, such fine mint juleps and Southern hospitality.

She smiled and chatted as if she were perfectly at ease. Jase listened to her and relaxed. He had worried that she would be too uncomfortable to enjoy the party. He realized he should have known better.

"Jason, I don't think I've had the pleasure of meeting your friend."

Jase turned and found his mother at his elbow. "I'll introduce you in a minute, as soon as Becca gets a break." He kissed his mother's cheek. She was dressed in a khaki silk jumpsuit that had probably cost more than some of the donations they would receive tonight. "You've done wonders, Mother. The party's already a success."

"Do you think so?" She asked the question as if there could be no doubt.

"You've never done anything more worthwhile. This will make a difference to a lot of people."

"You're beginning to sound like Pamela."

"Worse things could happen."

"The two of you always did gang up on me."

"You needed ganging up on."

He wondered why he had never told his mother what he really thought about anything. He had detached himself so early from his parents that in a way he had never given them a chance. "This cause is Pamela's heart, Mother. And it's becoming mine, too. You've endeared yourself to both of us by working so hard for something we believe in. Relax and be proud, and when Pamela thanks you, give her a hug, not a lecture, and tell her she's welcome."

Surprisingly tears sprang to her eyes. "I don't know what you mean."

"Jase, you haven't introduced me yet."

He turned and found Becca at his side, obviously concerned that something was wrong. He made the introduction.

Becca extended her hand. "Mrs. Millington, this is a wonderful party. You can't have any idea how much it will mean."

Jase's mother took her hand. She had quickly gotten herself under control. "So I've been told."

"I've never seen anyone who could have organized something like this and made it work. Now I know where Jase gets his talents."

"You're not saying they come from me?"

"Sure I am. That's exactly what I'm saying." Becca smiled warmly. "It's a very big compliment."

"The party wasn't so difficult."

"Oh, I've been watching it happen. I know how much work it was. I'm one of the people who took orders for the last weeks."

"You've been helping?" Dorothea cocked her head. "How did you get involved? Through my son?"

"I used to live at The Greenhouse."

"Oh, you're on staff."

"No, I was a resident. I was homeless and sick and badly in need of help. I got it there, and then your son gave me a job overseeing the landscaping and renovations on his house."

Dorothea looked stunned. "You lived at The Greenhouse?"

"I sure did." Becca refused to look penitent. "And if I hadn't lived there, I might not be alive to be having this conversation. So, you see, I know what you've done firsthand. And I know what this place will mean to women just like me when it's finished."

Dorothea stared at her. Jase was just about to step into the humiliating gap in the conversation when she exploded. "How on earth could something like this have happened?"

"Mother . . ." he warned.

She pushed away the hand meant to restrain her. "How could somebody like *you* be without a home?" she asked Becca. "What kind of world is this, anyway?"

"A middling unfair one."

"Will you tell me how this came about? I don't want to pry, but I want to understand."

"I'd be happy to."

Jase watched his mother spirit Becca off into an undecorated corner. He was still standing there staring after them when Pamela found him. "Where's Becca?"

"She's off being quizzed by our mother."

"And you let that happen?" Pamela asked angrily. "Mother has no right!"

"She knows that. She as much as told Becca the same thing." He gripped Pamela's arm when she started off to find them. "Don't you dare butt in."

"Somebody's got to—"

"Get off the white horse, Pamela. Mother's about to need a mount herself."

"What on earth do you mean?"

"I mean that all those years we were so sure we didn't have anything in common with her, the seeds of who we are were there in Mother all along."

"You're not making any sense."

"That's because you're listening through twenty-eight years of hurt. Dorothea Millington didn't know how to be a mother, and sometimes she wasn't even sure how to be much of a person. But there's been a decent woman hidden in there all along. And right now she's fighting like hell to come out. With Becca's help you and I are going to sit back and watch her emerge."

Becca stood on the sidelines with Jase's arm around her waist as speeches were made. The evening had been a remarkable success. The pledges had begun to come in, and there was excitement in the air that the goal would be reached. She and Dorothea had discussed the final push that would be needed to make it happen. She hadn't discussed it with the man beside her.

She wasn't sure she exactly liked Jase's mother. Becca looked at Dorothea Millington and she thought about the day she had seen somebody drowning in Blackwater River. The swimmer, a young man, had been so sure of himself, so certain he was strong enough to get across. Halfway out, he had begun to flounder. She still remembered the horror of watching him go under once, then again. She had been a child, hardly old enough to dog paddle, but she had wanted more than anything to save him.

She remembered his hand, waving, waving, as he sank for the third time. Then another hand had grabbed his, and somebody had pulled him to shore. His rescuer hadn't been nearly as big as him, and hadn't seemed nearly as strong. But he had rescued him anyway.

And somehow, for some silly reason, when she looked at Mrs. Millington, she thought of the young man who had been so sure he could make it and almost hadn't.

She didn't know why.

Now she watched Mrs. Millington come back into the center of the circle of party-goers. Shareen had just spoken. She looked like an African goddess tonight, and her speech had been just about that powerful. Becca saw the dawning of understanding on the faces of some of those gathered to listen.

"There's someone else who I've asked to speak tonight," Mrs. Millington said. "Someone who has opened my eyes a little as to why we're really having this party. There's probably no way that anybody who's here just to have a good time and give a little money can really understand what it's like to be alone, without resources and hope. I guess I don't understand it myself and never will. But Becca Hanks does, and she's going to say a few words about that. I listened a little while ago. I hope you'll listen now." She smiled at Becca. "Ready?"

. Becca felt Jase's reaction. He stiffened, and his arm tightened around her. She drew away from him before it tightened enough to keep her from moving. Then she was in the center of the circle. She could see people whispering to each other, and for a moment she wished she hadn't agreed to this.

She threw her head back, and she caught a woman's gaze and held it. "I look like you, don't I?" she asked. "I look like I belong here, and I don't know how many times tonight I've been asked if I come from Louisville, or if my folks have had a horse in the Derby. Well, when I was growing up, I didn't know what the Derby was, because we didn't have a television set, and the only horse I'd ever seen pulled a plow on a rocky acre of land down the holler a ways."

She took a deep breath. "I come from coal mining country. Only there're no mines there anymore, no jobs to speak of at all. There's a lot of poverty, though. More than you can imagine. Just about as much as you've got here in Cleveland, though not nearly as many rich folks to go with it. When I was seventeen and my parents were both gone, I thought maybe I'd settle for that, and I married a man who didn't know what it meant to work or dream. I ended up in prison because of a crime he committed, and I lost custody of my twin daughters."

She could see the shock on the faces surrounding her, but she had their attention. There wasn't a sound in the room. "When I got out, I knew I had to change my life. Only there wasn't a way to do it where I came from. So I worked everywhere I could, and I followed a trail of jobs to Cleveland. I sent most of my money home to my children, and there wasn't enough for a place to stay. So I stayed in my car. I'd tell you to try that sometime, but don't really want you to, because it's hell. And I wouldn't wish hell on anybody else.

"You can't find a job or keep a job if you don't have an address. Pretty soon you can't find an address because you don't have a job. You start going hungry, and in the winter you're not sure you're going to make it through the next cold night. You still want to work, to make a life for yourself, only you can't, because you're sinking too fast. That happened to me. Then one day I woke up in a place I didn't know. I saw a woman in white bending over me, and I thought I'd finally died and gone to heaven. But it was a hospital. Those ladies in white just barely saved my life."

She smiled a little, because she was trying not to cry. "There wasn't much left to save, but there were some folks who didn't let that stop them. The Greenhouse took me in, and they took care of me when I was able to leave the hospital."

She swallowed and looked around the room. The guests seemed transfixed, as if she were someone from another planet giving a lecture. "Jase Millington gave me a job I could do and be good at. The Greenhouse, Jase, they gave me respect for myself again. Now I'm working two jobs and saving money so my little girls can come to Cleveland and live with me. But that wouldn't have happened if somebody hadn't reached out a hand. I didn't want a hand, folks. I wanted to do it alone. But that's the thing I had to learn. Sometimes everybody has to have help. All of us need help sometimes. And a little help can make the difference between a life wasted and a life saved."

She looked straight at Jase. "I'm not telling you this because I like to talk about what I went through. I'm not telling you this so you'll feel sorry for me. There's no reason to feel sorry for me now. I'm on my way. But there are a lot of women like me who aren't. Not yet. But they will be if you dig deep inside your pockets tonight and give what you can.

"This may look like a big old factory to you, but when Jase and The Greenhouse board are through with it, it's going to look like home to a lot of people. And there's nothing that looks better. I can tell you. There is nothing that looks any better than home."

She nodded. "Thanks for listening." Then she started toward Pamela, who was wiping her eyes. In a moment she was being hugged hard by both Pamela and Shareen. She could hear Mrs. Millington in the circle behind her.

"Now you know what this is really about," Mrs. Millington said. "Think about that when you write your checks. I thought about it when I wrote mine. I'll be thinking about it for quite some time." She signaled to the band, and they began to play.

Becca felt her knees grow weak and tears well in her eyes. She didn't like either sensation, but when she felt strong arms circle her and turn her against a broad, masculine shoulder, she gave in to both. She sobbed, and she shook, and she let Jase hold her.

"Becca." He smoothed her hair. "You were wonderful." He put his lips against her ear. "So brave. Too brave."

"Somebody had to tell them."

"It didn't have to be you."

"I'm glad it was." His arms tightened. "But now everybody knows about me, Jase."

"So? What do they know? They know you're full of spit and courage."

"You don't have to hold me."

"Yes, I do. Try and stop me."

She pushed him away a little and gazed into his eyes. "You're holding an ex-con. And now everybody knows it."

"I'm holding the woman I love."

She didn't even have time to react. She felt a hand on her shoulder, and she turned. A man she hadn't met was standing there. He was elderly and rotund, with half a ring of feathery white hair, almost like a halo, just above his ears. "That was quite a speech, young lady."

She managed a smile. "Thank you."

"My name is Juno McIntire." He thrust his hand into his coat pocket. He was the only man in the room wearing a suit and tie. "Here's my card. I want you to come and see me tomorrow. At one?"

She frowned. "About a donation?"

"In a manner of speaking."

"All right."

"I'll send a car for you."

"I can take the transit."

"No, a car will be faster. Just give me your address."

She looked at Jase. He nodded slightly. She borrowed his pen and scribbled the address of the cottage on the back of Juno's card.

"She's quite something," Juno told Jase. "You have better taste than some of your projects downtown have indicated."

"It's good to see you here, Juno. I didn't expect you."

"I like to go where I'm least expected."

Becca handed back his card. "I'll see you at one."

"I'll look forward to it." He made his way toward the door.

"Odd," Jase said.

"Did you say I was the woman you loved?" Becca asked, Juno forgotten.

He smiled down at her. His eyes gleamed suspiciously. "That was a long time ago."

"Did you?"

"I'll tell you when we get home."

"I'd like to leave now."

"Pamela's getting my car for us."

"I want to fly."

He thought about what awaited them. At home, in his bed. Together. "I'm planning on it."

"I love you, Jase."

He held her close and smothered her words against him to keep them warm and safe. "Tell me that in an hour. Over and over again."

"I promise."

As always, her word was good.

Chapter Thirteen

Jase had one leg between Becca's, an arm thrown over her back and his cheek snuggled against her neck. She awoke to the sensation that her life had changed. Thoroughly. No longer was she alone. She could protest. She could demand her independence—and would—but Jase was in her life to stay. Now she knew what love for a man really was. And she knew what it meant to be loved.

She felt his hand glide over her naked back. She wasn't surprised that they had awakened together. Jase was sensitive to every movement, every sound, she made. He had been sensitive to changes in her from the moment they had met.

"Can't sleep?" he asked against her shoulder.

"It's late. Do you know how late?"

"I don't care."

"Don't you have places to go and people to see?"

"You're the people I want to see. This is the place I want to go."

"It's almost eleven."

"What?" His head came up. "You're kidding."

"About something as serious as wasting time?"

His eyes were heavy-lidded, his smile slow and worth waiting for. "Did we waste time?"

"Sleeping's always a waste of time."

"What about the rest of the time?"

"I can't seem to remember anything else."

"You might need a refresher course."

She stretched, moving against him as she did. "Do you think so?"

He grasped her hand and moved it to the place where their bodies entwined. "Part of me thinks so."

She pretended surprise. "My memory's slow coming back."

His hand slid up her side and rested against her breast. "Is anything clearer now?"

"You might want to try that again."

His thumb began a slow rotation. "I'll try something better."

"Umm . . ." Her leg curved over his in possession. "I remember two people on a bed. Together. Just like we are now."

"Are they sleeping?"

"Definitely not."

"You're doing fine." His lips sought the curve of her neck, the line of her collarbone, the luscious swell of her breast.

"Oh, Jase." Her arms tightened around him.

"Do you remember someone saying that last night?"

"Definitely."

"Was it you?"

"Definitely."

"Are you repeating yourself?"

"Definitely."

He lifted his head to see her expression for the next question. "Shall we stop now that your memory's returned?"

"Definitely not."

Juno McIntire's office was on the top floor of a downtown skyscraper. Becca tried not to be impressed, or rather, she tried not to let how impressed she was show. She was still in shock from the limo ride. She hadn't realized what Mr. McIntire had meant when he'd said he would send a car. Now she wondered how she could have been so silly. Had she thought he was going to operate a two-door compact by remote from downtown? Had she really expected the car to show up without a driver?

The truth was that she hadn't thought at all. Limos and skyscrapers were so far out of her experience that they were objects from fairy tales. Six months ago she had entered this same building hoping to get a job cleaning. The maintenance manager hadn't even looked twice at her when he'd found she was an ex-con. She hadn't been good enough to scrub the sinks and toilets, yet here she was on an elevator heading straight for the penthouse.

She tried to remember what Jase had told her about Mr. McIntire. Eccentric millionaire, he'd said. One of Cleveland's richest men. Other things Jase had said this morning were much more memorable. She had been too enchanted with them to ask many questions about Juno McIntire.

Eccentric and rich and respected. She knew about the respected part because when the lobby guard had learned her destination he had practically bowed and scraped. She didn't understand why people got so fired up about other people with money. Money was important only because it could buy the things a person needed to survive. After a certain point, it didn't matter anymore. Jase—who should know firsthand—had said he had so much money he didn't know how to spend it all. There was something wrong with that.

Since it was Saturday, the building was largely deserted. The limo driver was accompanying her to the top floor, though she wasn't sure why. What were they all afraid of? Did they think she could get lost in an elevator? When the elevator stopped, the driver stepped in front of the doors to keep them from closing on her. She wanted to tell him she had never been squashed between elevator doors before, but she suspected he knew her acquaintance with elevators was limited. The only elevators in Blackwater had led straight down into the center of the earth.

"Mr. McIntire told me to take you right to his office," the man said.

"I suppose you're not going to just point me in the right direction?"

The man smiled for the first time. "I'm going to personally escort you there."

She walked beside him. She'd already learned that if she tried something as simple as following him, he stopped, as if that was the height of bad manners.

He stopped at the end of the hall and knocked on a shiny wood door with a brass nameplate. "What kind of name is Juno?" she asked.

"One that makes men in corporate boardrooms shiver with fear."

"I didn't see anything to shiver about last night."

"May it always be so."

He opened the door at a barked order from the other side. "Good luck."

She shook her head, perplexed that he thought she would need luck. "Thanks."

Inside she saw Mr. McIntire far across the room. His office reminded her of a storybook she often read her daughters about a sultan and genies and magic carpets. The Oriental carpets on Mr. McIntire's floor weren't magic, but no one who could afford them would need magic, anyway. The wood lining the walls was unfamiliar but exquisite, exotic grain matching exotic grain.

"Well, what a pretty place to work," she said, approaching his desk.

He stood. "You like it?"

"It's big enough for a family."

"How do you like my view?"

She walked past him to the windows and looked down. "Can't grow things in the air. It's pretty, but I think I'd rather be able to walk outside and see something I'd planted."

"You've got your feet firmly on the ground."

"I guess." She turned back to him and smiled. "Do you work every day, Mr. McIntire? You're the only one in the building besides me, your driver and the guard."

"No. I'm just here because of you."

She was intrigued. "I could have come on Monday."

"I wanted this settled. I never wait. That's how I came to have an office like this one."

"Well, if I ever aspire to an office like this, I'll remember that."

"I've been doing some checking on you."

"Have you?"

He came around his desk and gestured to a cluster of chairs and a table in the corner. "Let's make ourselves comfortable."

She crossed the room and seated herself, sinking deeply into plush blue upholstery. He joined her. "Damn silly world," he said, "when a man can find out anything he wants in a few hours. There's a trail of paper following each one of us around everywhere we go. You've got one, too."

She wasn't surprised. Some of it would have the official seal of the Commonwealth of Kentucky on it. "And what does my paper say?"

"That you're a good woman who got caught in a bad situation. Did you learn anything from it?"

For some reason she wasn't offended. She liked Juno McIntire, although for the life of her she wasn't sure why. "I did. I learned that I have to do what I know is right, no matter what anybody else thinks. And I learned that I have to take care of myself, no matter what anyone else wants to do. And I guess I learned that sometimes that means accepting a little help now and then. But only if you're willing to pay it back."

"And you've found ways to pay back The Greenhouse. I know that."

"Little ways. Nothing could really pay them back. They gave me my life."

"If you had a lot of money, Becca, and you were going to give it away, would you give it to The Greenhouse?"

She smiled. She had hoped this was the reason for his invitation today. He was considering a large donation. She just hoped she could convince him. "I sure would. See, there're things you look for when you're giving money away. Not that I've ever had any to give. But still, I think I know a few things about it."

"Let's hear them."

"First, you have to be sure the organization you're giving money to has the right idea. It's not right just to throw money at people. The right thing to do is help people learn to take care of themselves. I mean, some people can't, and that's a fact. But most people want a chance to try. They want jobs or training so they can find a job. They can't work or go to school, though, if they're sick or hungry or homeless. So people's needs have to be put in order. You know what I mean? You've got to handle the basics first, but always with the idea of moving people away from needing help, not getting them hooked on it."

She paused for breath. "I didn't say that very well."

"You did fine."

"What if there was a flood somewhere? The first thing you'd have to do is find new places for people to live, right? Make sure they had food and medicine, too. But later, when the waters went down, you wouldn't want to keep giving them food and medicine and shelter. You'd want to build dams or levees, so there was never another flood. Then they wouldn't need help again. That's what The Greenhouse tries to do in its own way."

"I see that."

She smiled. "Do you? I'm glad."

"And I see that you've got some excellent ideas. I thought maybe you might have."

"It's nice you think so, but—"

"In fact, your ideas are exactly mine."

"Are they?"

"So exactly mine that I have a job for you right here working with me."

"A job?" For a moment she didn't understand. Then she was touched that he wanted to help her. "Oh, you must have thought I was talking about myself when I talked about people needing jobs. But I wasn't. I've got two jobs right now. You don't have to make up one for me."

"Oh, I'm not making up a job, Becca. I've had an opening for six months, but no one I've interviewed has fit the slot. You fit it perfectly." He held up his hand to stop her response. "I know you'll be done with the landscaping at Jase Millington's soon. And I'm willing to wait until you are. But hear me out now. Because I think you'll like what I'm going to say. And I know I'll like having you work for me."

Jase lounged in the doorway of Constantine's and watched Becca bustle around the room taking care of the last of the evening's customers. She poured coffee and cleared tables as if they were the most important jobs in the world. Constantine and Mama had made a good decision when they'd hired Becca. She was worth two of almost anyone else.

She bustled by with someone's check and saw Jase standing in the doorway. She flashed him her knock 'em dead smile. "What are you doing here?"

"Waiting for you."

"You didn't have to do that. I take the bus."

"I know. I wanted you home faster."

This time her smile was different. It almost sizzled. *He* sizzled just witnessing it. "Let me get you some coffee while you're waiting," she said.

"Don't bother."

He chatted with Constantine, who sang Becca's praises until she was finally finished for the night.

Outside in the fresh air she took his arm. "It's been such a day!"

He knew it had been such a morning, such a perfect morning waking up with her in his arms and keeping her there an hour longer. He didn't know anything about the rest of her day, but his had felt strangely empty, even though he had been busy. He had wanted her with him to share what he'd learned about the possibilities of a Blackwater resort. He had wanted to see her surprise, then her pleasure, when he told her that he was going to help make profound changes in the way people lived in the town of her birth.

"How did your appointment with Juno go?" he asked.

"I'll tell you when we get home. I want to see your face."

He unlocked her door, but he pulled her close before she could get in and reminded himself of the pleasures of kissing her. He couldn't remember ever feeling as if he didn't want to let go of a woman, but he didn't want to let go of Becca. He was beginning to believe he was never going to let her go.

They were home before either of them spoke again. "My place or yours?" Jase asked.

"They're both yours. You choose."

He led her toward the cottage. The house reminded him of work that still needed to be done, and he was in no mood for that. At the point where the path forked, she pulled him right. "There's a full moon. Let's look at the roses."

He let her take him there. Moonlight silvered the garden, but it was the roses that gleamed and preened themselves under its caressing rays. Becca had wrought a miracle here. He thought how pleased Kathryn would have been.

He put his arm around her waist. The night was perfumed with the roses' fragrance. "I'm almost through here," she said. "There isn't much more I can do. Everything's been cleared and trimmed and given a chance to grow again. I've done what I could to make it easy for a yard service to come in and weed and mulch and fertilize a couple of times every year. By the end of the week I'll be finished."

"I'll still need somebody here to supervise the renovations."

"I'll stay till the end of the summer. I can keep up with the yard, too, but I won't take any more money. My rent will be enough for what I'll be doing."

"Don't be crazy. What are you going to live on? You don't get paid enough at Constantine's to support yourself and send money back to Blackwater, too."

"I'm not being crazy."

"You'll earn every cent I pay you."

"No cents."

"No sense."

"Jase, let's not fight. Besides, you don't know everything yet." She slipped her arm through his. "There's more to tell."

He felt something unfamiliar creep through him. A moment passed before he realized it was fear. He could almost feel her slipping away from him. He had just found her, and now she was slipping away. "Go ahead and tell me," he said.

"Let's go inside."

Inside the cottage she busied herself flicking on the lights. The little house had become so much hers that Jase knew he would never enter it again without seeing her here. Now it was warm with the glow of lamplight and polished wood. Vases with summer flowers were tucked into corners. Mementoes of Kathryn's that he hadn't wanted had found their way here. Watercolors hung on the walls; old straw hats decorated with faded silk ribbons hung from the arms of a wooden coatrack.

"I'll make coffee."

"It's late." He held up his hand. "I know, you'll make tea."

"Mint tea. From the garden. I'll have to show you where everything grows, Jase. So you can pick it for yourself when I'm gone."

"You don't have to go."

"I think I do."

She busied herself with the tea and teapot. He thought of the night she had told him about her past, thought of perfectly brewed tea neither of them had wanted and a plate of gingersnaps that had remained untouched. Tonight was different. She fluttered, but not from fear or shame. She was bursting with excitement. He admired the self-control it took not to share it, even as he battled his own growing apprehension.

She didn't speak until the pot was on the table between them. Black-eyed Susans sat in a vase beside it, mixed with tall blue ageratum. The tablecloth was beautifully mended linen and lace. He had the strangest feeling that in this nearly perfect setting, she was going to tell him that she wanted him out of her life.

"I told you I'd tell you what happened at Juno's."

He noted that she was calling his old adversary by h first name. He had the utmost respect for Juno McIntir although they had never agreed on anything and never bee on the same side of any dispute. Juno had his ideas abou the direction Cleveland should go in, and Jase had his. An right now Jase had his first taste of real dislike for the old man. "I'm assuming he gave money for the renovation the factory."

"I think he will. But that's not what we talked about."

He heard alarm bells that weren't really ringing. "Wha did you talk about?"

"Me."

"By far a more interesting subject."

"He must have thought so." She sat forward so that sh could see his face. "He offered me a job."

"Did he?"

"A wonderful job. He's the chairman of a charitabl foundation, funded mostly with his money, I guess. Any way, he fired his director at the beginning of the year. H said she didn't have any horse sense. She had an educa tion, and that was all. She kept trying to fund projects research ways to help people, instead of just helping them So Juno's been looking for someone to take her place. H wants somebody who knows what it's really like to be poo Jase. He wants somebody like me. He wants me!"

Her enthusiasm and pride were almost blinding. "Wha did you tell him?"

"Well, I listened first. I had to be sure he wasn't jus making this up. But he showed me volumes of record about what the McIntire Foundation has done in the pas He's not inventing anything. He has a job, and he needs m to do it. He even showed me payroll records so I'd see wha the last director was paid. He wants to pay me the same. H says I'll be doing the same work, only doing it right, so should get the same money. It's more than I ever dreame I could make! Enough to rent an apartment, pay child ca expenses, take care of the girls and even save some so I can go on to college. There's a company car that goes with it, too. And I can set my own hours. If one of the girls is sick, I can stay home and work, or just make up the time later. It's a job made in heaven!''

He couldn't think of better news. Yet if that were true, why did he feel as if someone had just punched him in the gut? ''Juno's not an easy man to get along with.''

''I like him. I don't know why anybody's scared of him. He's really a pussycat.''

''Pussycat? Juno McIntire?''

''Well, if I'm not scared of you, why should I be scared of him?''

''So you're leaving here. Just like that.''

She cocked her head and watched him. There was something going on that she didn't understand. ''Not just like that. I told you, I'll finish what needs to be done in the yard. And I'll stay on to watch over the renovations. That way I can save enough for a deposit on an apartment. Juno says I can ease into the job there whenever it's not a problem for me to be gone here. I'll have to quit work at Constantine's, but not right away. I'll give them time to find and train somebody else.''

He didn't care about the renovations or the yard. She could leave tomorrow and he would still have gotten a bargain. She was going to let Juno McIntire solve problems she wouldn't let Jase solve.

She frowned. ''Aren't you happy for me, Jase?''

''Of course I am. It's wonderful.''

The frown eased a little. ''I could hardly wait to tell you.''

He knew he should let her bask in her good fortune a little longer, but he felt isolated, as if it had nothing to do with him. He wanted to be part of the excitement on her face, the sparkle in her eyes. ''I have something to tell you, too.''

"Good news? I don't know if I can stand any more good news, but I'm sure willing to try."

"I think it's good news. Great news. I've been doing some research. It's an idea I had when I went down to Blackwater with you."

"Blackwater?"

"It's about Blackwater and something that could make a big difference there. It's probably hard for anybody who's lived there to see, but Blackwater's got enormous potential. Maybe not under the earth anymore, but above it. It's got some of the prettiest scenery I've ever come across. And there're always people looking for scenery. I want to build a resort. There's plenty of cheap land to do it on, and there's land by the river for sale right now, near the waterfall where we took the girls."

Her frown had returned. "A resort?"

"A big, expensive resort. Summer homes for people in nearby cities. People who want mountain air and views. People who want clear lakes for sailing—"

"There aren't any lakes in that area."

"But there could be with a little manipulation of the river and some of the creeks. It would be a gold mine for Blackwater. There would be jobs for anyone who wanted them, markets for things people wanted to sell—"

"Dam up the river? That river's been running through those mountains for centuries. And houses mean cutting down trees, bulldozing roads through the mountains, tearing up more of the land."

"Nobody's going to destroy anything that doesn't need it. We're not a bunch of strip-miners. The whole area would look better than it does now. It would have to. Blackwater would get a face-lift."

She stared at him, horrified. "It wouldn't be Blackwater anymore. It would be some fancy resort town with shops full of designer clothes and cute little ice cream parlors."

"And those shops would be run by people from Blackwater."

"No, they wouldn't. Maybe Blackwater folks would get to work in them sometimes, and maybe they wouldn't. You have to have money to build or lease a shop like that. Who has it? Strangers, that's who. And who'd want a bunch of hillbillies selling designer clothes? The only jobs the local folks would get would be the dirty ones. And maybe they wouldn't even want those. Blackwater wouldn't be their town anymore. Why would they want to stay there?"

"Are you listening to yourself?" Jase slammed his fist on the table. "Don't you see that's what's wrong with places like Blackwater, Becca? Nobody there has any vision of what needs to change."

"Maybe they're too busy trying to survive to have visions. Maybe visions are a rich man's luxury!"

"Well, I've taken the luxury of having visions for them, then. I thought you'd be excited. I thought you'd be glad that somebody cared enough to want things to change for those people."

"Nothing would change! Don't you see that? You'd be as bad as the mining companies. You'd come in and tear up the land, give folks little, piddling jobs that don't amount to nothing. Somebody'd benefit, all right, but it wouldn't be the folks who live there!"

"They could help make decisions."

"What kinds of decisions? Whether they want this creek or that creek dammed up? Whether this house or that house gets torn down to the ground? Whether this mountain or that one gets blasted away so some rich folks can have a nice flat place to put their million dollar summer cottages?"

"You're not thinking straight."

"My thinking is as straight as the line between this cottage and your house!" She leaped to her feet. "And I'd like you to walk that line right now!"

He stood and grabbed her arm. "What's wrong? Do you hate it so much when I try to make a difference in your life? I was doing this for you!"

"No. You were doing it because you can't leave anything alone! I'm nothing but a project to you! Something you can change, just like you have to change everything to suit yourself. I thought maybe you loved me, that maybe it was really me, *me,* you loved. But it's not, is it? You look at me and you still see something that needs changing. You've tried to change me often enough. Now you're trying to change a whole town, a whole way of life you don't even understand. Why, Jase? Can't you just accept me and love me the way I am? Can't you be proud and happy for me when I make changes myself?"

"I am proud. I am happy!"

"No you're not. You don't want me to take this job of Juno's because you didn't think of it first! I knew something was wrong, but I couldn't see what. Now I do. You want to be my Prince Charming. You want to be the one to change my life, stick the old glass slipper on my foot and make me live happily ever after. You can't stand the thought that I've found my own way. You can't love me for that. So you go off and try to change where I come from!"

His hand dropped to his side. "I've had enough of this." He turned to leave.

"Oh, no, you haven't. Not yet. You've got to hear one more thing. I love you. And I want you to love me, not love what you can do for me. You're not comfortable unless you're meddling. You've got to learn to be comfortable before I'll have you back, Jase. I don't want to be something you do. I want to be what I am. A woman who can take care of herself. A woman who can take care of you when you need her. A woman whose roots are what they are! A woman who's just plain all right like she is!"

He didn't turn. "I'm going back to Blackwater! And I'm going to see what the people there think of my idea."

"You mean you haven't talked to them already? Didn't it occur to you before this that they might want to have their say?"

"They'll have their chance."

"Are we going to have ours?"

He heard something like a sob in her voice, but he still didn't turn. "Apparently not. You want me to take you just the way you are, but you don't want me the way I am. This is me, Becca. I don't sit still. I move. I change things, and I'm not sorry I do."

"You can change *things*. You can't change people. You can't change me. I'll do that myself. All I need you to do is watch and be proud."

"If you just need an audience, you're looking for it in the wrong place. I thought you needed a lover, somebody who cared enough about you to want to make things better if they needed to be better. I guess I was wrong."

She didn't answer, and he didn't wait. He left the cottage, and with each step he took, he knew he was leaving her life.

He could not make himself turn around.

Chapter Fourteen

Blackwater was dingier, sadder, than Jase had even remembered. There were no historic or interesting buildings to renovate or restore. Becca had been right about one thing. Most of what was here would have to be torn down or changed so completely that it would no longer be a shadow of itself.

He saw nothing wrong with that.

Anger had carried him the necessary miles to Blackwater. He hadn't wasted his time driving. On Sunday, the day after his fight with Becca, he had flown to Lexington and rented a car. Charlie Dodd, the man who had done his initial research and feasibility groundwork, had met him at the airport.

Charlie was all business, a middle-aged, climb-the-ladder-of-success kind of guy who had little appreciation for the scenic beauty around him. He had talked dollars and cents all the way to Blackwater.

They drove to the site and walked every inch together. Charlie waved his arms and paced off sections. He pulled figures out of the air as if they were dangling there for his convenience.

"You aren't going to make a bundle," he said as they drove back to Baldwin, where they both had rooms for the night. "No one else is going to do this if you don't. Hardly anybody could afford to invest so much money to get so little. I still don't understand why you want to do it."

"Because it needs to be done."

Charlie made a noise to indicate that Jase's logic was beyond him. "These people don't want anything to change. They're happy being poor."

Jase answered that in one compound word that his work crew wouldn't have dared to use around Becca.

"Why are they poor, then?" Charlie demanded. "This is a free country. Nobody has to be poor."

"They're poor because they haven't had a chance to be rich."

"And you're going to give them one? This deal isn't like you at all, Millington. Don't fool yourself. This project's not going to make anybody rich, not even you."

Jase dropped Charlie at the motel but turned down his invitation to dine there. He'd had enough of Charlie and conversation about the resort. He had hoped Charlie and his facts and figures would help him keep his mind off of Becca. Instead he'd heard her voice loud and clear over Charlies' incessant chatter. He couldn't turn it off, just as he couldn't block out his visions of her. He didn't know how he was going to sleep in the same motel where they'd made love so passionately.

He wondered what Blackwater's residents did for fun on an evening like this one. At least once the resort was built there would be more entertainment available. The fancy ice cream parlors that Becca had taunted him about were just one improvement that would follow in the resort's wake.

Stores and movies and fine restaurants would open. Black-water's residents would have choices of things to do.

He pictured Matty and Syl and their kids mixing with Louisville and Cincinnati's well-to-do. The picture was in-congruous. Not because Matty and Syl weren't good enough for anybody, but because they wouldn't have the cash for that kind of entertainment. Not even if Matty got a job—and what kind of job would Matty get?—and Syl was able to work in town instead of fifty mountain miles away.

He realized where his thoughts and his car were leading him. He was halfway back to Blackwater before he pulled off the road at Better'n Home. There were roughly the same number of cars and trucks in the dirt lot that had been there before. He hoped his joyriding buddy was available for a little heart to heart.

Inside, the blond-haired waitress greeted him as if he was an old friend. He felt like an imposter, since his ticket to friendship, his relationship with one Becca Hanks, had been summarily canceled. But he wasn't going to announce that to the world. He imagined Better'n Home, with its huge contingent of Becca's admirers, would never be an appro-priate place for that announcement.

He sat in the same booth where he had eaten ham and red-eye gravy. He remembered that the biscuits at Better'n Home had melted in his mouth, and he wondered if the cook would take a job at the resort or struggle to keep this place going instead. He couldn't imagine Lexington's fin-est eating regularly at Better'n Home.

The night's special was chicken and dumplings, enough for two men his size. He was on the second man's portion when three members of Becca's fan club walked in and came over to his table, including the joyrider who had taken him on the wild trip through the mountains.

He greeted them and gestured to the empty seats. They sat and ordered pie.

Jase waited until everybody was happily occupied with chocolate meringue or coconut cream before he mentioned the resort. He eased his way into it.

"What would you think if somebody wanted to open a resort just outside of town, a place where city people would buy houses and come, mostly in the summertime?"

"What kind of resort and where?" The joyrider seemed to have been informally appointed spokesman. He was a large man, bearded and pot-bellied.

Jase explained. He wanted honesty, so he was honest about his intentions. Becca had been right about more than how much of Blackwater would have to be torn down. She had been right when she questioned why he hadn't consulted anyone living there. He never wanted her to make the same accusation again.

There was silence for a while after he'd finished. The men seemed to be digesting his words along with their pie.

"Smells bad," one of the men said at last. "Smells real bad."

Jase was genuinely surprised. "What does?"

"Comin' in here. Changin' things."

"Don't things need to be changed? How many of you are working? Don't you need jobs?"

"Doin' what? Carryin' some rich man's golf clubs? Diggin' his swimming pool where I used to go swimmin' in the creek? I work west of Baldwin. I'll drive the distance and come back here, but not if it's changed."

Jase wondered if he was the only sane person left in two states. "I guess I don't understand."

"Blackwater needs changes," the joyrider said. "Don't think we don't know it. But not changes from outside. Not from somebody who doesn't know who we are."

Jase didn't flinch. After all, he'd heard the same line, or something close to it, before. "Who the hell are you, then?" he asked wearily. "I guess I really *don't* know."

"We're like these mountains. We can take a lot of swipes, even take it when our guts are ripped open to make money for somebody that's already got it. But we stand tall, and we're still here when those folks are gone. Things change in Blackwater, though maybe not so's a stranger could tell. But nobody gave us a medical clinic. We got that for ourselves 'cause we got sick and tired of watching our friends die. And we got ourselves a library 'cause we got sick and tired of our kids not learnin' to read good enough. We've got a rec center because we made it happen. Every year that goes by, we do something good for Blackwater. The best thing you can do is leave us alone."

Jase wondered how many times he had to hear a message these days to finally listen. "There's got to be something I can do. There's always something."

"Not if it means you want us to change. We'll change when we're ready, and then maybe not the way you think we should. But this is our piece of God's earth, and we'll keep it the way we found it. You try a resort, we'll fight you every step of the way."

Jase looked at the three stern faces and knew he'd been bested. They weren't three lone men. They were part of something he still didn't completely understand. But he was understanding it better. He *was* understanding it better.

He was still working on a cup of coffee when the men left. Their parting words had been friendly, but the threat was implicit now. No one was going to thank him if he tried to make Blackwater into what he thought it should be. And if he thought city government was a pain in the neck to work around, he really ought to give a bunch of ex-coal miners a try.

He was on his way back to Baldwin when a familiar curve in the road caught his attention. He slowed and pulled to a stop in front of Syl and Matty's house. The kids were in the front yard chasing each other in circles, and Matty was sit-

ting out on the porch watching them run. He guessed that
Syl wasn't home from work.

He got out of his car and walked up the rise to see Matty.
He ruffled the oldest boy's hair and called greetings to the
others before he got to the porch. His arrival barely called
a halt to the frantic game of tag.

Matty stood and waited for him. She looked tired, the
way anyone looked after a long, satisfying day. He wondered what Matty had to be satisfied about.

"You didn't bring Becca," she said.

"She's back in Cleveland." He wasn't about to tell her
that he would probably never bring Becca anywhere again.

"Sit a spell," she said. "It's so pretty this time of
evenin'."

He sat because it was better than lying in a motel room
wishing he was anywhere else.

"You want to tell me about it?" she asked.

"I'm that transparent?"

"Just about."

"I don't understand your cousin."

"And you thought maybe I could help?"

He hadn't realized it, but that was why he was sitting
here. He was sitting here waiting for somebody to help him,
because for once he couldn't help himself.

"There's nuthin' much to understand about Becca. She
wants somebody to love her, somebody who sees what she
has to give. She hasn't had much luck that way. First man
she loved used her like a doormat. Second one kept trying
to convince her she wasn't good enough for him."

"Second one?"

"You."

He stopped rocking. He hadn't even realized he'd started.
"Good enough for me? Of course she's good enough for
me."

"Just the same way Blackwater's good enough for you? With a change here, a change there. Changes you think it needs."

"How do you know all this?"

"Think we don't have phones here? It's Blackwater, not Backwater. We've got phones and TV, and some of our men and women've even been to college."

In the yard, fireflies flickered as the children laughed and shouted. The mountain air smelled of roses and honey-suckle. Laughter and fireflies and roses. Simple pleasures he had never taken time to enjoy. Right beside simple truths he had never taken time to know.

"The two of you are from different places," Matty said. "Can't get much more different, and that's a fact. But the way you can get along is to respect those differences. You can't change each other. Nuthin' you can ever do will make Becca just like you, not even if you burn Blackwater down and build Disneyworld where it used to be. Blackwater's Blackwater. You're you. Becca's Becca. There's room for everything and everybody."

He thought about the woman he knew so well now. Did he really want to turn Becca into Cara or a woman like his mother? Hadn't it been Becca's uniqueness, her pride, her damned stubborn pride, that had charmed him in the first place?

"I wanted to make her life easier," he said.

"Ain't nobody's right to make life easy. It's not sup-posed to be easy. Dewey wanted life easy, and look where it got him and her. Seems to me you just want to make your own life harder. You just keep pushin' and pushin' when you don't have to."

"What do I do now?"

"You look at yourself, and you see if you've got what it takes to love a woman like Becca. Then you let her lead the way."

Even the idea made him uneasy. But the truth was that Becca had been leading him from the first day he'd met her. While he'd been trying to change her, she had been changing him. If she hadn't, he wouldn't be sitting on Matty's porch having this conversation.

"I'll call off the resort," he said. "It was a bad idea."

"Terrible. But leastwise you see it now."

"I love her," he said, and he knew it was really true. He loved Becca enough to want her to be who she was. And what greater gift could she ever give him?

"Are you going to go back and tell her?"

He thought about all the ways he could do that and wondered if she would believe any of them. Over and over again he had shown her that he didn't trust her to make it on her own. What reason would she have to believe an apology?

He rocked and considered. "Matty," he said at last, "I need help."

"Be glad to."

"Good. Because you're the only one who can."

He described what he needed, and she nodded. "Easy enough. Come back early in the morning."

Jase knew she was right when she said this would be the easy part. The hard part was yet to come. But he'd always liked challenges. He just hoped that this time his good luck held out, because he was going to need every bit of it.

It took three transfers to get from Shaker Heights to The Greenhouse. What would have taken twenty minutes by car took Becca more than two hours by bus. Usually when she took the bus she brought a book to read. Today she stared out the window. Soon she wouldn't be riding the bus at all, but the joy of that, the thrill of having her life on the right track, hardly touched her.

Jase had left early that morning, for Blackwater, she supposed. He hadn't said goodbye, of course, but she had heard his tires screech as he backed out of the driveway. She imagined he was there now, plotting and scheming to make Blackwater his next success story.

She could hardly bear the thought that he'd left so angry. She'd been too angry at first to feel anything else. Then, little by little, other feelings had crept in. Hurt, then love, a rush of it, swifter than the river after a flood.

He'd been wrong to think he could just walk in and make Blackwater over to suit himself, but he had done it because he loved her. In his own bullheaded, ornery way he had been asking over and over again to be part of her life. She had shut him out, shut him out and slammed the door. Sure, she'd had her reasons, most of them good ones. But she hadn't once thought about him or what he needed.

For too long she'd had to think only about herself and the girls. She hadn't left room in her life for Jase or any man. He'd tried to make room, and all she had done was get angry at him.

She got off the bus three blocks from The Greenhouse and took her time getting there. The block was looking better. One change spurred another. Little by little the neighborhood was coming back from a long, slow decline. That was how it had been for her, too.

She stopped in front of The Greenhouse and saw the changes that had been made here. The fence was perfect now. No pickets were missing, and it glistened with fresh paint. Someone had continued her work in the flower beds. Striped petunias and bronze marigolds stretched toward the sunlight. The gingerbread trim on the house itself was no longer flapping in the breeze. New trim had been integrated with the old. She imagined Jase was responsible. He had never mentioned it to her, but that was like him. He never asked for credit for what he did. He liked to make a difference. Usually that was reward enough—unless it was her he was trying to help.

She saw a flash of skirts in the side yard at the swing set. There were new children at the house, girls the age of her own. She felt such gratitude that now she would finally be able to bring her babies to live with her. They would be the family they had never been able to be before. But they would be a family without Jase as her partner, without Jase as their father. Her eyes widened. She realized where her thoughts had led her, where they had probably been leading for weeks.

"You look shocked about something."

Becca looked up to see Pamela in the doorway. "I—I guess I was just admiring the new trim."

"Nice, isn't it?"

Becca started up the sidewalk to the house. "Real nice."

"What brings you here?"

"I came to talk to Shareen. I didn't know you'd be here."

"Dorey's having a birthday party, so I'm filling in for Shareen this morning. Will I do?"

Becca didn't think Pamela would do at all. She was too close to Jase to be objective about Becca's decision. But there was a two-hour bus ride, two hours each way, that made it impractical to come back tomorrow when Shareen would be in. If she wanted to settle things, she had to do it now with Pamela.

"Come on into the parlor and I'll get us some tea," Pamela said. "Did you take the bus?" She watched Becca nod. "I'm leaving in half an hour. I'll drop you at home if you're ready to leave. I've got some errands to do in that direction."

"Thank you. I have to go to work this afternoon." Becca followed Pamela inside and went to the parlor to wait. When she had lived at The Greenhouse she had loved this room. Now it reminded her of Jase's house. For a long time to come, everything was going to remind of her Jase.

She was rearranging a basket of dried flowers when Pamela came in with two glasses of iced tea.

"You can't sit still for a minute, can you?" Pamela asked. "Just like my brother." She thrust out a glass. "It's too strong and probably not sweet enough. I should have let you make it."

"I want to come back here." Becca took the glass but didn't even raise it to her lips. She set it on an end table, and she spoke fast. "Not for long. Just for a little while, until I can get an apartment. I've saved most everything I've earned, except what I've sent back to Blackwater for the girls. And I'm starting a new job next week where I'll be making good money, so I can save faster."

"There's room for you."

Becca sighed, and all her defenses drained away. She sat. "Is there?"

Pamela flopped into a chair. "Did you want me to say there wasn't?"

"No. I've made up my mind."

"And I know what that means."

"I'll work while I'm here. There's more gardening I can—"

"Cut it out, would you?" Pamela stretched her feet in front of her and wiggled her sandaled toes. "You're welcome. Isn't that good enough?"

Becca felt tears fill her eyes. "Welcome?"

"Welcome. And if you need to stay longer than our limit, you can come to my place. You'll always be welcome there."

Becca had expected a lecture, or at least a discussion. She hadn't expected to be so readily embraced. Pamela trusted her feelings in a way Jase did not. "I don't know what to say."

"Don't say anything, then."

"Don't you care why? I mean, it doesn't matter to you?"

"I assume you and Jase had a fight. But it's not my business, is it? The two of you have to work out your own relationship. And if you can't do it by talking about your differences, if you have to do it by running away, then maybe that's what you have to do."

"I'm not running away."

"Did Jase ask you to leave?"

"Of course not!"

Pamela cocked one brow. "You didn't run away, and he didn't ask you to leave. Maybe the cottage burned down."

"I made an awful scene. Well, helped make it, but a lot of it was me."

"Did you ever fight with Dewey, Becca?"

For a moment Becca was confused by what seemed like a change of subject. "Sometimes I'd try to reason with him. He hit me pretty often, hard enough to knock me to the ground one time."

"And I guess that was a good reason not to fight with him if you could help it. Would Jase hit you?"

"No!"

"So what's the worst thing that can happen if you fight?"

Becca put her head in her hands and rubbed her forehead. Pamela was clever. Kind and clever. With just a few sympathetic questions she had gotten right to the heart of the matter. "I could hurt him."

"I'm sure you could."

"I did hurt him, Pamela. No matter how hard I try, I keep hurting the people I love." She thought of Matty, of Dewey and the twins, even of the Hanks. And all the people in Blackwater she had let down when she'd gone to jail. All the people who had believed in her.

"Well, you're no different than anyone else. We all end up hurting the people we love," Pamela said.

"I try so hard to make everything right, but it never really is! I keep making mistakes. I don't want to make any more. I don't want to hurt Jase anymore!" Tears fought their way free. In a moment Becca was sobbing.

Pamela sat across the room from her and let her cry. She was afraid to offer comfort, because she knew how badly Becca needed to cry this out. When it looked as if the flood was abating, she crossed the room for a box of tissues. She brought them to Becca and knelt in front of her. Becca took a handful.

"You're always going to make mistakes," Pamela said. "And sometimes you're going to hurt people. But most people are just about as tough as you. They can survive your mistakes. Jase certainly can. The two of you have just got to stop trying to make everything perfect. Nothing's ever going to be perfect."

Becca wiped her eyes. "I told myself on the way over that I wouldn't let myself get talked out of moving."

"You're still welcome here."

"But I was just being bullheaded. I make up my mind and that's that. I don't really want to leave the cottage."

"I know."

"I love Jase. I think I've just been afraid that if I loved him too much, it would be like it was with Dewey. I guess there's still a part of me that thinks I'm to blame for what Dewey was."

"And there's a much bigger part that knows better."

"There is." Becca gave her a watery smile. "But when I'm scared, the other part comes creeping out."

"And Jase scares you."

"What I feel for him scares me." She blinked away the rest of her tears. "Outside I was thinking that now he would never be a father to my girls. I'm thinking about marriage! That scares me to death."

"Lord, it would scare me, too."

"We haven't even talked about it."

"That doesn't surprise me. You've both been too busy trying to change each other."

"I don't know how to say I'm sorry. I said it so many times to Dewey that I promised myself in prison I'd never say it to another man again."

"You know the line that goes, 'Love is never having to say you're sorry'? It's baloney. If you're sorry, you're sorry. What you promised yourself in prison is that you'd never say it unless you really meant it."

"He's going to be sorry, too. I know him."

"Then you can apologize together."

Becca managed a smile. "We must look like a couple of crazy people to you."

"Crazy in love."

"You're right about us trying too hard, and about me being scared to death to make mistakes."

"Actually, you're the one who pointed that out. You just needed to tell somebody and try it on for size."

"I paid for my mistakes."

"No. You paid for everybody else's. For Dewey's. For a society that doesn't care enough about vulnerable people. Heck, you've earned so much credit paying for other people's mistakes you can afford to make as many as you want."

Becca hugged her. Then she stood. "I'm going to go check on the garden, see if the carrots are ready to pull."

"You do that."

"I'll be ready to go when you are."

"And you won't be coming back?"

"I won't be coming back. I guess I knew that all along."

"Good. Because we can always use the bed for somebody who needs us. You don't need us anymore."

Becca gazed at her for a moment. "I guess I needed a friend."

"You've got one. For life."

"Someday maybe I can do something for you."

"Maybe so. It seems to me with all this love in the air, I might just fall victim myself someday."

Becca smiled. This time it felt real. "I can hardly wait to watch."

Chapter Fifteen

Jase pulled up in front of the Hanks' house and parked his rental car. "I'll be back in a few minutes," he told Charlie. "We'll get to Lexington in plenty of time for both our flights out."

Charlie made a noise that could have been interpreted any way. Last night, while Jase had been at the Better'n Home café and Matty's house, Charlie had gone out to survey the local Baldwin nightlife. Charlie was five drinks and four hundred dollars in the hole this morning, and his opinion about the intelligence and cunning of mountain people, particularly crap-shooting, poker-playing mountain people, had risen to a new high. His opinion of himself was at an all-time low.

"I'll just die here," he mumbled. "Slowly."

Jase didn't tell Charlie that that couldn't happen soon enough to suit him. He just slammed the car door after he got out. As hard as he could.

He took two little packages out of his suitcoat pocket on his way up the walk. He didn't know what had possessed him to buy Amanda and Faith presents. He had almost missed his plane because the line in the airport gift shop had been so long. But now he was glad he had made the effort. He wanted to see the girls, not only to report on them to Becca—she would have to let him talk to her if he was talking about her children—but just for his own satisfaction. He knew Becca was right in believing the girls were well cared for here. But he didn't like either Bill or Alice Hanks, and he wanted to reassure himself that they weren't passing on their sour view of life to Becca's children.

Alice answered the door, and surprise wiped away her perpetual frown. "Didn't know you were coming."

"I'm on my way out of town. But I brought the girls presents. Could I see them for a few minutes?"

"Becca's not with you?"

"She's working this weekend."

"Seems to me she'd take off and come see her babies."

"Seems to me she's killing herself so she can *get* her babies. And it seems to me you'd understand how hard she has to work to send you money and take care of herself, too. When she remembers to take care of herself!" He thrust the packages toward her. "Never mind. Please give these to the girls and tell them I was here." He turned without another word and started down the walk.

"You can see them if you like."

He counted to three before he turned. "Good."

She stood aside and let him pass through the doorway, but her frown was firmly fixed in place again. She led him through the house, into the backyard where the twins, in green and blue rompers, were digging in a sandbox. There was no sign of her husband.

He immediately knew which girl was which. And he knew more. The two little girls looked like the woman he loved. He hadn't brought them gifts because he wanted to check on them. He had brought them gifts because he wanted to see them. They made him feel close to Becca. They always would.

He went to the sandbox and sat on the edge. Both little girls looked up at him, then back down at the sand.

"I have a sister," he said. "When she was little, she always wanted to play in the sand with my cars. Do you have cars?"

Faith looked up again and favored him with her mother's smile. "No."

He held out the package. The clerk at the gift shop had wrapped it in tissue paper and stuck on a bow. Faith made short work of it. "Cars!"

He didn't know what had gotten into him. He wondered if the Hanks would approve of such whimsical presents for little girls. Faith approved. Wholeheartedly. She squealed, and in a moment the five tiny metal cars were in a heap in her pile of sand.

"Me, too?" Amanda asked.

He handed her the other package. Her squeal was more ladylike, but just as delighted.

Faith got up to plop her little sandy bottom in his lap. She put her arms around his neck and laid her blond head against his shoulder. "Where's Mommy?"

He prided himself on honesty and integrity, but now he thought seriously about kidnapping the children and taking them back to Ohio. Seriously enough to be quiet for most of a minute. Then he realized that he couldn't. All he could do was wait for Becca to settle her life. To trust her to settle it. Her own way. And with Juno's help, it wasn't going to take long. He said a silent prayer of thanks to old Juno, something he would never have guessed he would do.

"She's back in Ohio," he said. "Thinking about you both. She sends all her love."

"Her's coming soon?"

"Soon as she can."

Faith snuggled against him, and he held her tight. But Amanda got up and went over to a tree where a heap of toys lay. She searched through the pile, as if she was looking for something special. Then she came back, clutching something to her chest.

"What have you got, Amanda?" He held out his hand.

She shoved a doll toward him. It was blond, like her, a young child with pigtails. From the beautiful craftsmanship he recognized it as one of the kin dolls that Becca had told him about at the waterfall.

He took the doll and examined her. The doll looked remarkably like both girls. He suspected that wasn't a coincidence. "Did your grandmother make this?" he asked. "At her church?"

Amanda put one finger in her mouth, but she nodded.

"She looks like you."

"Give her to Mommy."

For a moment he didn't understand. Then something inside him broke in two. "You want me to take it with me and give it to your mommy?"

Amanda nodded again. Faith reached for the doll and kissed and hugged it; then she handed it back to Amanda, who did the same. Solemnly Amanda held it out to him again.

She frowned when he didn't take it right away. She moved a little closer and stared up at him. "You're crying?" she asked.

He held out his free arm, and she went to him to give him comfort.

Jase followed Mrs. Hanks to the front door, the kin doll tucked against his chest. He had left the girls out back, making roads and tunnels in the sand for their new cars. Just from watching he was already certain that Faith was going to follow in his footsteps at M.I.T.

"I appreciate you letting me see them," Jase said.

"I been thinking about what you said."

That surprised him, although he doubted her thoughts had been productive ones. "I don't want to see Becca hurt any more. She's been hurt enough by this family to last her a good long while," he said.

"We're taking care of her children. That's not good enough for you and her?"

"You're taking care of your son's children. If they were just Becca's children, they'd be out in the streets." He exhaled slowly. "But I don't have any rights here. And you're doing a good job with Amanda and Faith. I can thank you for that much."

"What are you to Becca?"

"I'm the man who's going to marry her. As soon as she's willing."

"The girls need a father."

His expression didn't change. "And a mother."

"Don't you think I know that?"

"You want the truth? No, I don't. I think you're going to make it hell for her to get them back. She doesn't think so, but I do."

"She's right. You're not."

He waited.

She turned toward the door. "My son was everything to me. When he died, I wanted to kill somebody myself. You know what that's like?"

"No."

"I hope you never do. I couldn't kill nobody, couldn't do it if somebody'd put a loaded gun in my hands and pointed it for me. But I could hate. I found out what it was like to hate. I been hating for a good long time now, turning most of it toward Becca. But the way Dewey turned out wasn't Becca's fault. He was all Bill and me had, and we spoiled him till he thought he could do anything he wanted. I liked hating better'n knowing that. But now I know it, and I can't hate Becca anymore. We could have helped her stay out of jail, wrote letters about her, mortgaged the house so's she could have a real lawyer, but we didn't. So we got to give her something back. When she's ready to take care of the girls, we won't fight her.''

Jase didn't really know Alice Hanks, but he guessed that was probably the longest and most emotional speech she had ever made. Once again Becca had been right, and he had been dead wrong. He wanted to comfort Alice, but he knew there was no comfort to offer.

"What about your husband?" he asked. "Will he fight it?"

"No. Bill's too sick to take a fight. Truth be told, I think he wants the girls out of here so he can get more rest. Just as long as we can see them from time to time. Watch them grow up."

"They'll always be your grandchildren."

"You'll tell Becca what I said? I won't tell her myself."

"Maybe you'll be able to someday."

She shook her head, and he knew she meant it. She had come as far as she was going to.

"I'll tell her, then. She'll want to have the girls soon."

"I'll have them ready when she does."

Charlie was asleep in the car when Jase got in. He slept all the way to Lexington, and Jase had plenty of time to think. He had time to think in the airport and on the late flight back, too. He didn't know if a man could change much in a couple of days, but he wasn't the same person he had been when he'd left Cleveland for Blackwater. He was humbled—probably as much as he would ever be—and for once he was unsure of his future.

Nothing had ever been hard for him. Now the hardest moments of his life lay ahead. Somehow he had to convince Becca that he loved her the way she deserved to be loved. As a whole person, a person he trusted completely, a person who could run her life her own way. He wasn't sure where compromise came in anymore, or when he had a right to state his opinion. Giving up control, giving up power, was so new to him that it was uncharted territory. But he knew he could get through it with Becca at his side.

If she was willing to stay by his side.

He had a special package, a cardboard box wrapped in plastic bags, that he'd carried on the plane, along with the kin doll the girls had given him to bring back to Becca. When he finally got to Cleveland he carried both to his car, along with his garment bag, and stored them carefully in the back seat. Then he started for home.

Becca couldn't sleep, even though she was exhausted from a busy afternoon and evening at the restaurant. She'd had no reason to expect Jase to come back tonight, but somehow she had. She didn't want another moment to pass with anger between them, but it looked as if at least another day was going to go by. The problems between them were crazy ones. They were too much alike in some ways and a million miles apart in others. But the problems could be solved if they both wanted them to be.

She didn't know if that was what Jase wanted or not.

By midnight she gave up pretending she was even going to shut her eyes. The moon was still almost full, although the night was cloudy. She remembered the evening just a few nights before when she had stood beside the moonlit rose garden and told Jase that soon she would be able to leave him. She had been so full of herself, so proud of her new independence. But in her rush to show him that she could make something of herself, she hadn't shown him or told him that she still wanted to be part of his life. She had wanted to prove she could make it alone before they made it together. Only she had forgotten to add the last part.

How could she have forgotten?

She slipped on a summer dress and the sandals she had bought to wear to the fund-raiser. She couldn't stay inside another moment. She wanted to visit the roses again, in-

hale their sweet fragrance and think about how to talk to
Jase when he came back home. The old roses seemed a tie
to both her past and her present. She needed their comfort.

Outside she breathed the sweetly scented night air. The
smell of rain was in the air, too, a sharp clean smell that
blended with the fragrance of flowers.

The yard was as lush, as perfectly cultivated, as a city
park. She felt a thrill of pride that she had done this herself. As the yard had changed and thrived again, so had she.
She could make things grow, make things blossom and bear
fruit. She wandered toward the roses, caressing leaves and
picking flowers. She would teach her daughters to garden
so that someday they would know the same triumph.

She had almost reached the roses when she saw a shadow
moving among them. She stepped behind a tree and
watched, her heart beating in her throat. There was crime
in Shaker, just as there was anywhere, but she had always
felt safe in Jase's yard, even at night.

The shadow stood, and she saw it was a man. The
shadow moved with purpose and economy, and she saw it
was Jase.

She almost called out to him, but she stopped herself and
watched instead. He walked to the side of the garden and
bent low, then lifted something from the ground and carried it back to the row where he had been working. He knelt
there, as prayerfully as she had often knelt in the same
place.

"Jase?" She stepped out from behind the tree. "What
on earth are you doing?"

He turned his head and gazed through the darkness.
"Becca?"

She moved toward him. Slowly, half afraid she was
dreaming this. "What are you doing? I thought you were
a burglar, though I guess a burglar wouldn't be too interested in the roses."

"Stop. Be careful where you step."

She looked down and saw that just ahead of her, laid out in a neat row, were half a dozen small clumps wrapped carefully in newspaper and tied with twine. "Mercy. What on earth?"

"Roses."

She bent and examined them. "Roses?"

"From your home place. Matty helped me dig them up. She said the old roses send out shoots all the time to make new plants. We tried to get one of every kind for you. They might not all make it, but if they don't, Matty says there're more where they came from. There's a good-sized pillow rose. We forgot to get it when we were there before."

She touched one of the clumps in wonder. "You saw Matty?"

"Yesterday, and early this morning. We dug them together, before I left Blackwater, so they wouldn't dry out. But I was afraid they might not last the night, so I'm heeling them in until you decide where each one should go. We might have to enlarge the bed."

"Who taught you about heeling them in?"

"Matty did. Matty taught me a lot." He stood and started toward her.

"Roses, Jase? For me?"

He reached her, but he didn't touch her. He wiped his hands on his pants. "A piece of your life here, Becca, with a piece of mine. Pieces of both our hearts."

She stood. "They'll thrive here. But you're right. We'll need to dig a bigger bed."

"I'll help."

They stared at each other, and then they were in each other's arms. She wrapped herself around him so tightly that she wasn't sure anything would be able to part them. "I thought I'd lost you," she said. "I'm so sorry. So, so sorry."

"For what? For being strong enough to survive without me? That's what I love about you, but I couldn't see it before."

"No, for not telling you that I want you to be part of my life. I was just so busy being proud of myself."

"You had every right to be proud!"

"And I am, but not so proud that I don't want to be with you. I just needed to know I could make it, Jase. But I never wanted to make it so far you wouldn't be there with me."

He kissed her forehead, her nose, her cheeks, her lips. He held her so tightly that he wasn't sure she could breathe. But he couldn't seem to let her go.

Slowly they sank to the thick, dewed grass bordering the roses. They were surrounded by roses, sheltered from prying eyes. Even the moon seemed to look away, its silver glow dimmed by gathering clouds. Becca wasn't sure who undressed whom, who fumbled with buttons and zippers and belt buckles, but in moments they were undressed and exploring each other as if to be certain nothing had changed—although everything had.

His skin was sleek and warm, the shape and angles of his body familiar. She buried her face against his chest, seeking, knowing with her lips, all the places she had kissed before.

His hands found her breasts, her hips, the secret, most vulnerable part of her, and she gasped with pleasure. Their legs tangled; their arms embraced; their bodies caressed, until there was nothing, no part of either of them, that was hidden from sensation.

She lifted herself to Jase as he sank into her. There was nothing tender or gentle about their reunion. She demanded and he possessed. He demanded and she took everything from him. She gave, then took more, until there was nothing else to take except pleasure so shattering she wasn't sure either of them could survive it.

They did. She lay in his arms for a long time afterward, breathing in the scent of roses and their lovemaking.

"I can't believe we did that," she said at last. "Here, in front of the roses."

"They approved." He helped her up and found her dress. The clouds had thickened, and he felt the first drop of rain. "Put this on, then help me get the roses into the ground. The rain will take care of the rest."

She giggled, a carefree, joyous sound he had never heard from her before. In the immediate aftermath of their lovemaking he had wondered if they would ever reach such heights again. Now her laughter stirred more than his heart. He wanted her again, and soon.

"You, a gardener," she said as he pulled on his clothes.

"And what's wrong with that?" He swung her around, over and over because he couldn't let her go, and kissed her once more. Then, as the rain began to fall, they set the rest of the roses in the trench he had dug and buried their roots in the rich loam of the garden.

They were soaked by the time they raced for the house, chosen instead of the cottage because it was closer. Inside he saw that she'd been busy while he had been in Blackwater. Vases of flowers filled the rooms.

Becca saw that he had noticed. "It was all I could think of to do," she said. "I wanted you to know you were on my mind while you were gone."

There were flowers in his bathroom, too. Bouquets on the sink and the wide ledge of the whirlpool bath. He ran the water, then undressed her again so that they could enjoy the tub and the flowers together.

It was only afterward, when they were cuddled together under his sheets, that he found the concentration and the courage to talk to her. She lay half sprawled across him, a position as perfect as any he could think of. But he slipped out from under her caressing leg and left the room for a moment.

Becca watched him go. She knew that they still had things to talk about, but she didn't know if she was ready to say anything more. Everything was so perfect. For just a little longer she wanted to hold on to the feeling of being loved without reservation.

Jase came back into the room. She savored the breadth of his chest, the muscled length of his legs. She couldn't imagine ever looking at his gloriously naked body without her breath catching a little.

"I brought you a present." He sat beside her and held out the kin doll.

She took it and without a thought clasped it to her chest. "Where did it come from?"

"Amanda gave it to me to bring for you."

Tears filled her eyes. She blinked them back. "I won't need one before long."

"No, you won't." He touched her leg. "When you're ready, Alice and Bill will give you the girls. Alice told me so today."

"She did?" She looked at him from under wet lashes. "You didn't . . ."

"Pressure her? Threaten her? No, I didn't. Not that I didn't want to. But I wouldn't have, even if she'd told me she was going to fight for custody. What you do, and the way you do it, is up to you. I realize that now."

She covered his hand. "What did she say?"

"In her own way she said she was sorry. She knows that the trouble in your marriage was Dewey's fault, not yours, and she knows she owes you something. She says she and Bill will give up the girls without a fight as long as they can still see them."

She rested her cheek against the doll's yellow pigtails and said a silent prayer of thanksgiving.

He watched her holding the doll and knew that soon it would be one daughter or both in her arms. "Alice will never be able to tell you that herself."

"It doesn't matter."

"There's something I have to tell you, too, but there's nobody to carry my message. So I guess I'll have to do this myself." He felt her hand tighten on his, and he smiled at her. "I don't feel very courageous."

"You don't know what it means to be afraid."

"I do now. I was afraid I'd lost you."

"I was afraid you wouldn't want me anymore."

He bent forward so that he could look into her eyes. "I was wrong about Blackwater, Becca. I wanted to change it because you wouldn't let me change anything else in your life. I wanted to help, even if nobody else wanted me to. I'm too used to changing things and taking charge."

"You wouldn't have felt that way if I'd let you into my life. But I didn't know how to, not without giving up my pride." She touched his hair. "But I want you in my life, Jase Millington the Whatever. I want whatever you have to give me."

"Nobody I talked to in Blackwater wants a resort. You were right. It would destroy what's there, but it took a lot of pounding for me to see that. Change has to come from the people who live there, the kinds of changes they need and want."

"So you're giving up?"

He smiled a little. "I tried to. I really did."

"And?"

"I have an idea. But I won't do a thing about it if you don't like it. It's up to you and the people of Blackwater to decide if it's a good idea or not."

She realized she wasn't even nervous about what he had come up with this time. She believed him when he said he wouldn't push. They had both learned a lot. Jase would never change completely. He would always be full of ideas, most of them superb. But she knew he was going to struggle not to force others to accept what they knew wasn't good for them. Just as she was going to learn to accept what she needed and not let her stubborn pride shut him out of her life.

"Let's hear it."

He took the kin doll. "This is Blackwater's wealth. Family. Roots. Tradition. You said it yourself by the waterfall. I didn't pay much attention, because I was too busy bulldozing mountains in my mind. But the kin dolls could go a long way toward solving some of the town's immediate problems."

She was fascinated. "How?"

"By making and marketing them out of Kentucky. You were right. Families live all over now. Children grow up without roots and ties. There are a lot of people who need kin dolls and what they represent. I have a friend who's marketing manager of an upscale catalogue. I know she'll be interested. Handmade dolls would sell for a lot. Eventually they might even be mass produced. The people who make them can form a cooperative. I can help them get started, or someone more informed about it could help. The point is that the people can decide how they want to go about setting up a business. All I'd have to do is give a little nudge."

"Nudge?" She smiled. Gloriously. "Nudge, Jase?"

"Just a little one."

She threw her arms around his neck. "It's a wonderful idea! Perfect. This comes from them, not you. It's just that you're the only one who's seen the potential!"

He relaxed and held her. He had really been afraid she would be angry. "Help me tell the difference from now on, okay?"

"Always."

"Always?"

She released him. "We've never talked about always, have we?"

"I think always is another wonderful idea. Let me know if I'm wrong."

"I come with a family."

"I want the girls. I want you, too, if you'll have me. When you're ready."

She knew she was going to be ready sooner than he suspected. But she was too busy kissing him to discuss a timetable.

There would be plenty of time to make plans. All the time in two lifetimes.

* * * * *

COMING NEXT MONTH

Summer romance has never been so hot!